# TALKING
# TO STRANGERS

# Short story collections available from The Alchemy Press

*Rumours of the Marvellous* by Peter Atkins

*Evocations* by James Brogden

*Give Me These Moments Back* by Mike Chinn

*The Paladin Mandates* by Mike Chinn

*Nick Nightmare Investigates* by Adrian Cole

*Leinster Gardens and Other Subtleties* by Jan Edwards

*Merry-Go-Round and Other Words* by Bryn Forty

*Compromising the Truth* by Bryn Fortey

*Tell No Lies* by John Grant

*Monsters* by Paul Kane

*Where the Bodies are Buried* by Kim Newman

*Music From the Fifth Planet* by Anne Nicholls

*Music in the Bone* by Marion Pitman

*Talking to Strangers and Other Warnings* by Tina Rath

*The Complete Weird Epistles of Penelope Pettiweather, Ghost Hunter* by Jessica Amanda Salmonson

*Dead Water and Other Weird Tales* by David A Sutton

# TALKING TO STRANGERS
## AND OTHER WARNINGS

Tina Rath

THE ALCHEMY PRESS

Published by
The Alchemy Press, Staffordshire, UK
www.alchemypress.co.uk

# CONTENTS

# INTRODUCTION

## Gail-Nina Anderson

A few years ago (maybe even *several*) *Marie Claire* magazine ran an article on "Women with alter egos" which featured photographs of Tina under the memorable heading "I am a part-time vampire." The piece went on to quote Dr Rath as saying, "I am liberating the child in me who wants to show off and be the centre of attention. As a vampire I am larger than life."

Well, no one who knows her is going to quarrel with that. Sometime actress, librarian, debt-collector, poet in residence to the Dracula Society, professional Queen Victoria impersonator, and now moving into folk singing, Tina can fill a room with her personae and her personality. She also writes stories.

We first met, if memory serves, back in the first flourishing of Gothdom, when even ladies already nicely mature and never willowy, grabbed at the excuse to wear satin corsets and yards of black lace in public places ("...it's amazing what you can find at Marks and Spencer"). Our favourite excuse went something like "trust me, I'm an academic" as Tina (way ahead of the current scholarly trend) was working on a PhD thesis about vampires in popular fiction, following on from her MA dissertation on the vampire in the theatre.

In those heady days the late lamented Vampyre Society brought us together in Whitby for Dracula-themed quizzes, dinners and mad midnight dips in the freezing cold North Sea. Or perhaps we first met via the Dracula Society, which back then still offered a rather more restrained bookish chance for camaraderie, travel and, of course, visits to Whitby for Dracula-themed quizzes, dinners and the occasional mad midnight dip.

Or maybe we met at a British Fantasy Society convention; or a Fortean Times Unconvention; or...

You get the picture: it wasn't exactly difficult to find common ground with someone who not only enjoyed the same sort of supernatural-themed literature and folklore that I loved, but who knew so much about it. Tina's reading, always voracious, ranges across styles, literary forms and periods to inform her own literary output, not only with those favourite themes on which we love to play endless variations, but also with an unusual sense of *craft*. Like her poems, Tina's tales invariably exhibit an innate sense of structure which allows for a satisfying conclusion – and often a sting in the tail. I've always thought that, unlike many modern authors, she would have flourished in the late 19th/early 20th century culture of popular literary magazines, where a well-turned slice of fiction was always in demand and a surprising number of weird themes made their appearance among the high adventure and domestic romance.

This is not to suggest that her writing is rooted in the past, except in the sense that she has read all the classic ghost stories, plus their sources and descendants. While a lively appreciation of historical modes and manners may inform a tale such as "It's White and it Follows Me", elsewhere she takes a mischievous delight in the fine details of a distinctly modern, mundane daily world as preparation to opening up the scene to reveal the veins of the uncanny running through it. A packet of biscuits disappointingly empty, a dating site that caters for chubby-chasers, or an incomprehensively comfortable pair of high-heeled shoes – these pin down moments of instant recognition, just before it all starts to get strange. Similarly, her narratives signal petty jealousies, bad judgements, tense households and horrible families, circumstances all too familiar, but also the dramatic framework from which hang the classical myths, folk tales, witch hunts and fairy stories that inform her (and our) supernatural universe. Transformative magic isn't an external intruder here but functions quite naturally as part of the environment, requiring only a slight tweak in the reader's point of view to become apparent.

Above all, these unashamedly entertaining stories display an unusual deftness of touch, inviting us to enjoy the words on the page. They don't outstay their welcome or labour their points because they don't need to – Dr Tina Rath knows how a story works. And perhaps most surprising within the genre of the weird, quite a few of them have happy endings – this is, after all, a world of fantasy.

What else does the reader need to know? Tina is married to a musician, likes spectacular costume jewellery, is a practising Roman Catholic, and boasts a wonderfully quirky collection of ceramic rabbits and owls. She has appeared on *Mastermind*, in panto, and on *Woman's Hour*; she is an avid cat lover and can speak with great authority on London's phantom bear traditions.

New readers start here…

# TALKING TO STRANGERS
## IN FINSBURY PARK

The flying saucer landed in Finsbury Park at about half-past seven on a rainy autumn evening. No one noticed. It had touched down in the back garden of the small terraced house which the Smiths were currently buying from their building society and none of the family happened to be looking out of the kitchen window at the time. Mr Smith was lying on the sofa, waiting for the football to come on, half-dozing and half-watching a programme in which a famous television expert was proving, very much to his own satisfaction, that it was impossible to communicate with creatures from outer space, always supposing that there were any, because: "There's just no common ground. Even if we could understand the words," he insisted, flailing his arms to emphasise his point. "We just couldn't understand the concepts."

Mrs Smith was doing some ironing while she waited for Mr Smith to drop off completely so that she could switch over and watch a miniseries called *Sinners Wear Scarlet*. Jason Smith was in his bedroom supposedly doing his homework, but in fact miming enthusiastically in front of his wardrobe mirror to the greatest hits of the Saber Toothed Ferrets, and Samantha Smith, his small sister, was playing schools under the dining table with a class made up of three Little Ponies, two teddy bears and a singing mermaid, currently silenced for lack of batteries.

This peaceful domestic scene was shattered by a knock at the back door. Mr Smith, who was half-expecting his brother-in-law to call round to borrow a tenner, stayed firmly where he was, closing his eyes to simulate deep sleep, and Mrs Smith went to the door. On opening it she saw, standing on the garden path and glowing faintly purple in the orange light that London reflected into the night sky, a figure out of nightmare.

It was six feet tall and skeletally thin. It had no face to speak of, only a lipless mouth and fiery eyes. Mrs Smith, assuming, naturally enough, that this was an emissary from the television programme *You've Been Had*, which she particularly disliked, was just about to shut the door firmly when she saw the huge, dully metallic looking saucer parked on her back lawn. Huddled disconsolately beside it were a medium-sized version of the figure in front of her (wife? she wondered wildly) and two smaller ones (the kiddies?). Mrs Smith recognised a family in need of help when she saw one and she looked more kindly at her caller.

The creature was holding up a small glowing capsule and for one ghastly moment she thought he was asking her to swallow it. Then she understood why he was tapping the side of his head, and realised that he meant her to put it into her ear. With a vague feeling that it might be a good idea to humour him she did so. At once there was a burst of high-pitched crackling and a curiously mechanical voice in her ear said, "This is a two-way translation facility, programmed by the Acme Pan-Galactica Translation Service for your convenience. Speak normally and it will translate your vocal efforts..." Then a more normal voice, clearly that of her visitor, cut in.

"Gracious Brood-Lady," it said, "can I desiderate the shelter of your jolly cavern for self and brood the while I holloa for a mechanic for my defunct vehicle?"

She gulped. But they did look miserable, standing there in the rain, and she was a good-hearted lady. She stood aside and let them in.

"Bit early for Halloween, isn't it?" said Mr Smith on seeing their visitors, but Mrs Smith shushed him hastily.

"Have you got one of these for my husband?" she asked in the high careful voice she used for foreigners, tapping her capsule vigorously. Their visitor fumbled enthusiastically at his waist and produced a handful of capsules (from a belt? pocket? or could it be a pouch? she wondered).

"For the whole brood!" said the voice in her ear.

Jason and Samantha had drifted in and were staring at the alien visitors.

"Are we going to be abducted?" Jason asked hopefully, seeing the all-time cast iron excuse for not doing his homework about to be handed to him on a saucer.

"Now Jason don't be silly," said Mrs Smith, distributing translation capsules. "Mr and Mrs – er…"

"Vreel" said her capsule.

"Mr and Mrs Vreel have had a breakdown and they're going to wait here, out of the rain, until a man comes to fix their – er – saucer. Now why don't you take–" she indicated one of the smaller figures who, by managing somehow to look oddly scruffy, even in that shiny metal skin, suggested that he must be a small boy "–er–"

"Vreel," said her capsule.

"Ah – why don't you take Vreel upstairs and show him your computer."

"Okay," said Jason. "Come on then." He shambled up the stairs followed by the small silvery figure.

"And perhaps – er—" she waved a hand at the other small one…

"Vreel," said her capsule.

"Oh. Perhaps Vreel would like to see your dollies, Samantha."

(Surely they couldn't all be called Vreel! But then all her family was called Smith … and perhaps there was some kind of variation that the capsule was not conveying. There was certainly something to be desired in the Acme Translation Services grasp of idiomatic English.)

"Now, I'll get us all a nice cup of tea. Would you like to see the kitchen, Mrs Vreel? I bet it's a bit different from what you're used to…"

She led the silent Mrs Vreel off to make some tea. Mrs Vreel seemed rather subdued, as well she might, Mrs Smith thought, landed on a strange planet with two children, and no chance of getting them home before their bedtime, probably because that husband of hers hadn't had the saucer properly serviced. Mrs Smith began to get out her good china, and reached for a packet of biscuits – or rather, as it turned out, just a packet. The biscuits had been eaten and the empty shell left on the shelf. She crumpled it up, crossly.

Mrs Vreel glanced up. "Does your brood-mate do that too?" she asked. "Vreel is always leaving the empty grockets in the storage unit."

"Does he leave the tops off jars as well?"

Mrs Vreel nodded grimly. "And he always opens a fresh jar of Vrillni before the last one's finished."

In less than two minutes they had moved on to gynaecology.

In the sitting-room Mr Vreel was showing Mr Smith the workings of the Acme Galactophone on which he had called the mechanic. Soon they were discussing hyper-wharp drives...

Under the table, Samantha and Vreel sat examining Samantha's class of 2002.

"Here," said Samantha generously handing over the silent mermaid. "Would you like to hold her? She's supposed to sing, but Father Christmas forgot to bring the batteries."

Vreel shyly took the doll and ran a thin curiously jointed finger along its tail, which turned a sort of rosy silver under her touch. The doll squirmed between her hands and began to comb her hair with her fingers, and to sing in a small eerily sweet voice. It had become, to all appearances, a living, though miniature, mermaid.

"That's clever," said Samantha. "How do you do that?"

The fair head and the metallic silver one bent towards each other. Soon three tiny ponies in unusual colours were trotting about under the table.

Upstairs Jason and Vreel sat on the floor.

"What's your planet like?" said Jason.

"Boring," said Vreel. "Yours?"

"I bet ours is more boring than yours."

"Bet it's not."

"Want to hear some really wicked sounds?"

"All right."

The cries of the Saber Toothed Ferrets scythed through the night air.

"Do your brood-parents ever let you turn the sound right up, properly?" said Vreel.

"No way," said Jason. "Yours?"

"Nah. But..." He pointed at the CD player. A tiny simulacrum of the Ferrets manifested on top of it, and proceeded to enact their latest video.

They watched and listened.

When the doorbell rang it was Mr Vreel who answered it. "Behold the mechanic!" he exclaimed, flinging the door open.

Mrs Smith, coming from the kitchen with a belated tray of tea almost screamed at the sight of the mechanic. It was hard to tell if there was a living creature inside the small space cruiser or if the cruiser *was* the mechanic. Whatever it was, it was huge and covered with flashing lights. It had altogether too many arms, most of which ended in some kind of tool. Apparently it had already examined the saucer and both Vreels and Smiths waited for his verdict.

The mechanic gave a sharp intake of breath. "I suppose you know your big-end's gone," it said. "You know you're going to have problems with this, Squire. You just can't get the parts for these old models..."

However, it seemed he could offer the Vreels a tow.

They hurried back to their saucer with sincere expressions of gratitude, promises not to forget their hosts, and pleas to look them up if they ever found themselves in the neighbourhood of Alpha Centauri...

The saucer closed, the mechanic positioned itself (himself?

Mrs Smith wondered) on top and the whole thing ascended into the sky with a bright flash of light and a faint whooshing sound.

Jason Smith returned to his radically improved cd player. Samantha retired beneath the table to teach her ponies to jump over tiny hurdles constructed from pencils. Mr Smith lay down on the sofa. Mrs Smith picked up her iron.

"What a nice couple," she said.

"Yes. Real pleasure to talk to, that chap," Mr Smith agreed drowsily. "Oh, turn the TV over if you like, love. I'll never stay awake for the match."

Mrs Smith searched for the remote control. As she did so the television expert said, "So, interspecies communication is quite impossible. I mean, what would you say to your goldfish, always supposing it could understand your words…"

Mrs Smith turned on her miniseries.

# THIS IS HOW IT HAPPENED...

Well, okay, this is how it happened.

I am in the kitchen microwaving a pizza because mum has taken the Twins of Evil to a dance display in a church hall in Leyton where, they tell me, there will be Producers and Agents, no doubt slavering to sign them up; I am about to spend the evening eating and netsurfing, although Mum did hint, pretty broadly, that I might use my time to clean the kitchen. She pretty well gave up on me for the entertainment business when it became obvious that I was going to top five foot nine. Little and Cute is the only thing that means "employable" in her book. The Twins thought I might have a career if they ever revived the carney freak show, and even designed a poster with the slogan COME AND SEE THE FAT UGLY GIANT LADY done in various colours of glittery pen, but I retaliated by calling them Piggy and Porky and that lasted longer than the poster...

Anyway, the point is, I am alone in the house so when I hear a voice say, "You shall go to the ball," I freak and drop the pizza, but while I am on my knees trying to gather up the greasy fragments I see, out of the corner of my eye, a pair of feet in high-heeled buckled shoes floating some six inches above the floor, and they are attached to a smallish lady in a black dress and cloak, carrying a shopping bag emblazoned with "A present from Whitby" and a vampire bat.

So I say, "What ball?"

And she says, rather snappishly, "The charity ball at the Hotel de Posh in London's Mayfair and you're going to dance with the Prince."

It doesn't take too much thought to guess which prince so I say, "I would not dance with Prince Froggy if we were the last couple left after the zombie apocalypse."

And she says, sniffly, "Well perhaps he does look a bit – amphibious – but it's in the family," and as I am struggling to my feet she does a sort of flourish with her free hand and the kitchen is immaculate and smelling of lavender, and I am wearing a frocky-horror show of a dress, but, and this is spooky, I can feel pizza grease under my feet and I know I am still really wearing my manky top and leggings and it is all delusion.

So I say, "I assume you're my Fairy Goth-Mother. Why don't you do something useful like letting me win *Britain's Got Talent*?"

And she sniffs again and says, "Can you sing?"

As it happens, I can, so I loose "Vissi d'arte, vissi d'amore" on her and while she is still shaking her head to get the ringing out of her ears I add, "I have worked out a strictly pre-watershed pole dancing routine to go with it. I end hanging from the pole by my crossed ankles singing the last four bars upside down."

"Hah," she says, "you could sing the whole aria standing on your head, juggling flaming torches with your feet, but that kind of voice would never be allowed to win. Anyway, you dozy little… My dear little Goth child, you won't need any flaky talent competition once your picture is all over the papers as the mysterious beauty who danced all night with the Prince, you can write your own contracts, so come on…"

I am starting to see she could be right, but I say, "I wouldn't go outside in this dress if the house was on fire. I look like one of those dolls they used to cover bog rolls with."

Which is by no means an exaggeration because it is made up of layers of pink and blue frilling, and features bits of glitter in random places. It also seems to have been crocheted.

So she says, "What d'you want to wear then?" and I show her the picture on my phone from the file Too Vulgar for the Kardashians, and she narrows her eyes and nods.

But before she can do the flourish I say, "Let me take my top and leggings off," and she makes an unnecessary business of turning her back while I strip off, because I decide to take everything off. You really can't wear the kind of dress I have in mind over the kind of bra and pants I am currently in, but then she does the hand thing and I am wearing a second skin of silver sequins with practically no back and a plunging front saved from indecency by a necklace like a frozen waterfall of what can only be diamonds.

She rummages in her shopping bag, muttering, "Some things can't be done with glamour," and hands me a pair of stripper's sandals, half-transparent, half-silver, with stratospheric heels, also smothered in diamonds, and when I slip my feet into them they are as comfortable as a pair of velvet bags filled with oiled feathers, which is when I really begin to believe in magic. She hurries me downstairs where a huge car is waiting, driven by a chauffeur who leaps out to open the back door for us revealing, incidentally, that he has a long grey tail … and off we go.

On the way she pins my hair into a fashionable messy-up do, and barely has the last pin gone in when we are there, and I am walking up the steps surrounded by paparazzi shouting, "Smile Kim, this way Kim!" and into the ball room which is full of people not having a good time and we are just in time to see Prince Froggy try to jolly up the proceedings by demonstrating how to whip the table cloth off one of the little tables surrounding the dance floor without disturbing the glasses, the plates and the crystal vase full of white roses.

I've seen it go spectacularly wrong before but breaking the little gilt table as well is definitely a first and he looks so crestfallen. I go up and say, "Let's dance." And we do. And I see why I was picked for this because I can dance – not professional standard, not as well as I can sing, but beyond competent. And so can Prince Froggy. I suppose they teach them at Sandhurst or something. Anyway, he's good, and dances like he enjoys it. Also he is almost freakishly tall (I suppose it is the long froggy legs…) so we are well matched.

And people move away so we are doing a sort of exhibition

tango which would get us a good seven on *Strictly* unless someone wanted to be bitchy. I see one of the Ruperts who was watching the table debacle, who is obviously a friend of Froggy's, go up to the band and say something and they play a selection of ball room dances, and we give it our all, which is a lot, and all is going well until I hear a clock strike twelve in a rather doomy way ... and my clothes vanish. Everything but those sandals, which do not help.

And Froggy turns around and grabs a tablecloth and this time it works; he whips it away cleanly and hands it to me with a bow. So I tie it in a sort of sarong just above the bust and we finish the dance to great applause, at which point I realise my Goth Mother is just behind me suggesting that if I don't want to take the night Tube home we'd better be moving, and we dash down to the car. It doesn't change into a pumpkin but into a crystal and gold pumpkin shaped coach, driven by a giant rat, which is a bit gaudy but it gets us home where mum is already watching YouTube footage of the whole thing, which guests and staff have been putting up all evening, and the Twins are in Super Sulk mode.

And the rest is history. Or will be someday. No, Froggy and I do not marry. He casts off the constraints of royalty and opens a dance studio called Glitter Balls, which soon becomes a chain of dance studios (it was one of my first investments and my accountant says it should guarantee me a comfortable old age) and I have my pick of contracts, turning down a film provisionally entitled *Cinderella Lost Her Drawers* for starters in favour something a bit classier. In fact I have gone back to my singing lessons, and I might go in for opera, seriously. Who knows?

And Piggy and Porky? They had already signed their contract to play the Babes in *The Babes in the Wood* panto in Slough with a disgraced footballer playing Robin Hood and a past-it Page Three Girl as Marion. She got top billing. The Twins came after the footballer. Nice.

# A VISIT TO BLASTINGS MANOR

The visitors to Blastings Manor already looked harassed although their tour had hardly begun. Their guide, in contrast, looked very cool and efficient. She only allowed them to pause for breath on the second landing of the Great Staircase where, she informed them:

"The third Duke's twin sons killed each other when Cromwell's Ironsides attacked the Manor, led by the elder twin. The younger commanded the defenders. They met just here and stabbed each to death while their father watched helplessly. When he saw them die, his hair, which had been 'of a most bewtiful chestnut hew' turned snow-white, and he never smiled again. He commissioned the great stained-glass window above us as a memorial of the tragedy. It depicts Cain killing his brother Abel."

They looked up at the window. It was remarkably, even horrifically, realistic. The more sensitive, glimpsing the distorted face and bloody head of the dying Abel, looked quickly away. Fortunately their guide was already hurrying them on. By the time they reached the Long Gallery the ladies, especially, were glancing wistfully at the sofas. But these, like the rest of the furniture at Blastings, were firmly cordoned off.

The Duke had insisted upon this. When his agent suggested opening the Manor to the public, to pay his massive debts, his Grace proved unexpectedly amenable. However, he made certain stipulations. He had no objections, he said, to the Unwashed scuffling their feet along his floors and breathing over his family portraits, if they paid for the privilege, but he was damned if they were going to put their bottoms on his chairs. (It is hardly necessary to say that "damned" and "bottoms" were not exactly the words employed by his Grace.)

So visitors to Blastings were not precisely made welcome. The grounds were patrolled by armed keepers, with orders to shoot anyone straying from the rather restricted routes allocated to visitors. School parties were actually accompanied by the head-keeper, his shotgun carried suggestively over his shoulder. And there was definitely nowhere to sit down.

"The Long Gallery," announced the guide, "is haunted by the first Duke, who was killed here in a duel. The trail of bloodspots on the floor was left by the dying man as he dragged himself towards his wife's bedchamber."

Those ladies who found themselves actually standing on a blood stain leaped away with muted cries of revulsion.

"These spots," the guide lowered her voice dramatically, "cannot be erased." Then briskly, in more normal tones: "The Duchess, who was slightly deaf, did not hear his agonised moans but when she opened her door next morning and discovered his hacked corpse she instantly ran mad, rushed shrieking down the Great Staircase and drowned herself in the fishpond. Some say she haunts Blastings Park in the shape of a White Lady with flowing hair, but others insist that this is the ghost of a beautiful young nun who vanished after being abducted from her Convent by the first Duke's grandfather."

She threw open a massive oak door and lead them into a small dark room. "Here, in the Blue Room, the fourth Duke diced with his dissolute cronies for the possession of his lovely young wife, on their wedding night. The evil old Marquis of Braintree won, but she stabbed him to death in defence of her honour and was hanged at Tyburn for his murder. The judge sobbed as he pronounced her death sentence and three jurymen committed suicide not long afterwards. After dark, the click of dice, drunken laughter, and the terrified sobs of a woman, can be heard from within."

They backed out as rapidly as dignity would allow.

"In the Red Room," she continued, herding them into an even

smaller darker bedchamber, "the third Duke imprisoned his orphaned niece in an attempt to force her to marry his younger son, to keep her fortune in the family. She died suddenly with neither clergyman nor doctor in attendance, and the Duke gave out that she had killed herself 'in a fitte of the melancholike dumpes'. However, it was widely believed that he had starved her to death. Guests sleeping in the Red Room (it is never used by the family) have spoken of seeing a strange young girl who asks them for food. She appears to be a living person, but looks 'terribly thin'. Those who meet the 'thin ghost', as she has come to be called, die within the year of a particularly nasty form of anorexia nervosa."

This time they fled the room with no regard for dignity at all. It was really something of a stampede and one lady was almost knocked over in the rush. The guide remained calm.

"We now move to the Great Hall, down the Little Staircase, which has hardly been used by the family since the beautiful and virtuous Lady Marjorie was dragged down the stairs to be burned. Her stepmother, who had falsely accused her of witchcraft, afterwards died of remorse, confessing everything on her deathbed. She haunts Blastings churchyard in shape of a huge black hound with fiery eyes, whose breath causes plague, murrain, and severe attacks of impetigo.

"Lady Margaret's ashes were buried under the bottom stair and a sickening smell of burning is said to fill the stairway occasionally."

Several people began to cough, and one lady was forced to press her handkerchief over her mouth and nose. They moved on. Very quickly.

"Before we reach the Great Hall we visit the Chapel," the guide announced, patting her shining red hair and brushing her immaculate blazer. "The mural on the north wall was painted by order of the fifth Duke. He was blackballed by the Hellfire Club for excessive depravity, and retired to his estate with a mute servant 'who was never out of his company'. The Duke could never say where he came from, only repeating 'he is used to a hotter clime than ours'." She paused to let them draw the obvious conclusion.

"While the Duke lived at Blastings there were rumours of midnight gatherings in the Chapel. Six village girls disappeared at yearly intervals. Seven years to the day after his arrival here the Duke was found dead under the mural. Some say his throat was cut, others that his head was turned back on his shoulders, breaking his neck, but all agree on the look of agonised horror which disfigured his features. The strange servant had vanished. After the Duke's death the superstition arose that if anyone gazes fixedly at the mural for the time it takes to count thirteen, he will see the Devil."

The Chapel was evacuated even more rapidly than the Red Room had been. Even the lady who had been staring absentmindedly at the mural all through the commentary waited until she got outside to have hysterics.

The double doors of the Great Hall stood open. Beyond them, safety and sanity beckoned. The visitors made for them at a gallop. Fragments of the guide's commentary reached them as they ran. Strange discoveries: "…the bones of a number of babies … uncovered during restoration work … perhaps a foundation sacrifice … but none were earlier than the beginning of the *nineteenth* century…"

The fate of a certain Lady Barbara: "…fragments of human skin are said to be still clinging to the doorposts…"

The peculiar tastes of the second Duke: "…found arm and leg bones … split, perhaps to obtain the marrow…"

But they would not listen. Gaining the open air at last they ran for their coach, a reassuring scarlet splash at the end of the drive.

Dusk was falling. A white figure flitted eerily through the trees, but they did not wait to see if it was a night-gowned Duchess or a white-robed nun. Among the gravestones in the nearby Blastings churchyard they glimpsed a black shape with fiery eyes. Strange chanting came from the Chapel, mingling weirdly with the sounds of drunken revelry from the Blue Room, while the one lady who was brave enough to look back, insisted that she saw a hand with very thin fingers beckoning through the bars of the Red Room's window.

A much-shaken party fell panting into their coach.

"Ready for off, then?" said the driver. They chorused weakly that they were indeed. Until one bold spirit protested: "We never tipped the guide!"

There was a pause. They looked back at Blastings Manor. It seemed quite different when viewed from the safety of the coach. The white shape fluttering in the trees was undeniably a truant sheep. The black one, slinking through the churchyard was a homely sheepdog. The house itself lay peaceful, even beautiful, in the setting sun. Several ladies, rather ashamed of their earlier panic, were about to volunteer to go back with some money when the driver said, in a horrified half-whisper, "Guide? There's been no guide at Blastings since that awful tragedy—"

"Well, we had a guide," the bold spirit persisted. "Most knowledgeable. Rather attractive. She wore a very smart blazer—"

"Red hair?" breathed the driver.

"Well, yes…"

The driver crashed his coach into gear and drove off as if all the demons in Blastings were after him.

And no one dared to ask what the guide's tragedy had been.

# BAREFOOT WITHOUTEN SHOON

*Lyarde is an old horse and cannot well draw;*
*He shall be put into the park holly for to gnaw.*
*Barefoot withouten shoon there shall he go,*
*For he is an old horse and cannot more do.*
*While that Lyarde could draw, the while was he loved;*
*They put him to provender, and therewith he throve.*
*Now he cannot do his deed as he did beforn,*
*They lay before him peas-straw, and bear away the corn.*
*They lead him to the smithy to pull off his shoon*
*And put him to greenwood, there for to gone.*
*Whoso cannot do his deed, he shall to park,*
*Barefoot withouten shoon, and go with Lyarde.*

– John Lydgate

The Man was standing outside, looking at Bayard.

Gwen caught a glimpse of them through the open kitchen door, and though she rarely seemed see anything that went on around her she saw that. She saw, too, a look on the Man's face that troubled her. Nothing in this alien place was very important to her apart from Bayard. Perhaps she loved him because he had been bought at around the same time as she had, and from the same dealer in exotic curiosities, a man who knew his market and trotted out first the white horse and later the pale girl before the Man, knowing he would make a sale. Perhaps he had found them in the same place, though where such a place could be, he would not, Bayard could not, and Gwen did not say then, and she had forgotten long ago.

Gwen wandered out, unnoticed, for who cared what she did now? She joined the little group clustered round the Man staring at Bayard with such disdain. It did not strike her as strange that she knew the horse's name, but not the Man's, though she had lived alongside them both for the same long time. After all she did not know her own real name. Somewhere, someone had called her Gwen because of the white-gold hair and silk-white skin which had once made her valuable. So valuable that the Man had hand-fasted her to him with a ring that the smith had made for him from iron and silver. He explained that the ring made her his in a special way, even more his possession than the purchase price that he had paid over to her last master. But the other girls had told her that it meant that if she went with another man while she wore that ring the Black One would come and drag her off to the wildwoods. She was scared of the wildwoods, and they knew it. Even in the long-ago, when she did sometimes leave the farm she would never go with them when they went nutting or gathering brambles at the very edge of the woodland. The wildwoods were dangerous, full of wolves and bears and savage men all covered with hair … the Man had told her about them, when he still spoke to her. When she was valuable. Never as valuable as Bayard of course, because he had been given a noble name, the name of a magic horse in a story, and she was just Gwen. Sometimes the Man gave her other names, names for the night – honey-love, and treasure, poppet and pigsnie – but she had hated them and was glad when they stopped. He had always sounded so gluttonous and Gwen had been really afraid that some night he might swallow her whole…

"Ah, she's a dear maid to me," he would say when he talked about the price he had given for her, which grew steadily over the years. But she was not dear to anyone now. The marvellous hair had thinned and lost its gold, and the skin dried and withered. Now she kept what remained of that hair twisted up under an old rag, and the smith's ring hung loose on her finger, under her swollen knuckle. The Man only gave her food and shelter because she was still useful in the kitchen and the dairy. She worked hard there, almost frightening the young maids with the strength that remained in those seemingly frail arms and hands. She did the milking and churning and made butter and cheese for the prettier ones to carry to market to chaffer and laugh with the customers.

"Butter as gold as your hair, milk as white as your pretty duckies," the men would say, "it takes the touch of a pretty girl's hand to make the butter sweet," and the girls would toss their heads and preen their breasts, and never think of old Gwen, left at home in the kitchen, whose withered hands had done the work. Or of Bayard who had once been the Man's riding horse and now dragged them and their wares to market – until yesterday when they hitched him to the shafts but he could not pull the cart, and the girls had to walk to market carrying their baskets, and cursing. That day their wares had sold poorly because they were late and in no mind to smile at customers or laugh with the men, when they thought of the long trudge home, and the Man realised he could get neither work nor money out of Bayard anymore.

"He's no use," the Man pronounced, running a hand over the horse's ribs.

The Bayard in the story, Gwen remembered, had fallen into the hands of a wicked king who had tied a stone around his neck and thrown him into a lake. Would the Man tie a stone round Bayard's neck and drown him too? And could she stop him? But the old Bayard had saved himself, smashing the stone with his hooves and running off to live wild in the woods…

The Man spat on the cobbles. "We wouldn't get a penny piece for him, not even for hound meat. He's not worth the coin Jan Butcher would charge us to put him down. Take him to the smith and tell him to pull his shoes off, then we'll turn him loose." He stood back, shaking his head. "I paid a long price for him, too. More fool me. 'The more they are fair, the worse they do wear,' and that's a true saying," and Gwen knew that he was thinking not just of Bayard but of her.

She watched them lead the horse away. His head hung down

as if he were weary, or ashamed, and she felt a movement inside her breast as if a hand had reached inside to squeeze her heart. Not really knowing what she did, she trailed after them, out of the farmstead, down the lane, and up the village street to the smithy. It was so long since she had been seen outside the farm that people stopped to stare at her as she drifted past, as if she were a noonday ghost. Some of the men laughed, thinking of how the Man had once boasted of his bargain, but the women shook their heads, wondering what he could have done to her to wear and waste her away like that.

By the time she came to the smithy, Bayard was standing patiently while the smith took his front hoof in his hands and pulled out the nails that had held his iron shoe in place for so long. She wanted to cry out, to beg him to stop, but she could say nothing. Bayard's shoes were soon gone and he stood, as if bewildered, until the Man took off his belt and lashed him across the hindquarters and shouted at him to take himself off. He reared then, like a war-horse that had been trained to fight, and screamed. A horse's scream is a terrible sound and the idle crowd round the smithy who had been laughing a little fell back from him as if they were suddenly afraid of those naked hooves. Gwen wanted him to dash amongst them, trampling and slashing at them, smashing skulls and breaking bodies, but he did not. Instead he turned and jumped the hedge and ran across the fields towards the wildwoods. And then she did cry out, trying to warn him, trying to turn him back. But she could not form the right words and maybe he would not have stopped for her...

"Whoso cannot do his deed, he shall to the park
Barefoot withouten shoon, and go with Bayarde," the Man was saying complacently, just as if he had made the verse himself instead of just changing the horse's name from Lyarde to Bayard. He looked round at his men and then, with some surprise, at Gwen. "Barefoot withouten shoon," he repeated, moving his head from side to side like a bull baited by dogs,

making up his mind which to attack.

Gwen looked down at her feet. Unlike the farm girls she did have shoes, a pair that the Man had given her years ago to keep her feet from the mud of the farmyard. They were strong shoes, with iron tips, the soles well clouted with iron nails, and they had worn better than she had. Perhaps, now, the Man would take them away from her.

Instead he shook his head again and shouted, "Get back to your work." And everyone drifted away.

Gwen went back to the farmstead but not to her work. Instead she sat down in the hearth and wept for Bayard while the farm girls gathered round and laughed. Some made jokes about her and what she would most miss about the horse, jokes that she did not understand because her time with the Man had not taught her that either man or woman could take pleasure in such things, but she knew they were intended to be cruel so she wept the more. And then one of the girls, who was little and venomous, was excited by Gwen's tears and said they must pull off her shoes so that she could follow Bayard to the woods. The others hung back at first but she seized the shoes herself, and crammed them on her own feet and then they grew braver and pulled and tousled Gwen. When she made no resistance, but only held her hands before her face and cried, the girl caught the glint of the Man's ring on her finger and tried to snatch that from her too. But loose as it was it could not be drawn off past the first joint of her finger, and the girl slapped her and pulled at the thin hair that escaped from her head-cloth.

She might have gone on to do worse but the men began to come in for their meal, and one of the older ones, who remembered Gwen when she had been young and lovely, told the girls to leave off, for a pack of evil bitches. But he could not make the girl give back the shoes because she had a friend amongst the younger men, and she wound her arms round this young man's neck and said she must have shoes now she had to walk to market, and the older man was not sorry enough for

Gwen to want to fight him for her sake. So they sat down to their meal and Gwen went barefoot to her bed in the dairy where she slept, because it was chill enough in summer and bitter cold in winter and no one grudged her a place there. The Man had his own room, the girls slept in the kitchen, and the menfolk in the barn and the stables, and Gwen could lie alone and cry herself to sleep, for Bayard who must lie in the wildwoods with the wolves and bears, and the savage men.

But the next day she got up and worked as usual. The girl who had taken her shoes flaunted them, clattering boldly about the yard and the dairy, but Gwen paid her no heed and did not cry until she was alone in the dark. But on the third night after Bayard had gone, she thought she woke suddenly in the depths of the night. A cold bar of moonlight lay across her face, and at first it seemed as if it was the light which had woken her. Then she thought that someone had called her name. She slept in her ragged clothes so all she had to do was stand up and walk across the stone flags, moving silently on her bare feet. Hardly aware of what she was about she went light-foot through the kitchen, past the sleeping girls, and out into the moonlit yard. She took a measure of corn from the feed store, and slipped into the harness room to pick up the curry comb and dandy brush, hoof pick and the comb she had once used on Bayard's mane and tail. Holding everything carefully in her apron she walked through the orchard, adding some windfall apples to her plunder. In the field beyond the orchard she saw Bayard white as the moonlight waiting for her, as she had somehow known he would.

She combed him and brushed him and cleaned his hooves, then she laid her apron full of corn carefully in front of him and watched him while he ate. It seemed to her that he was looking sleeker than he had even three days ago, as if he had found good things to eat in the wildwoods, but she could not think how that could be. When he had finished and crunched his apples, he tossed his head and danced away from her, then turned back and tossed his head again as if he were beckoning her to follow him.

But when she saw he was going towards the wildwoods that lay so black under the moon she hung back, afraid. For a while he stood as if hoping she would change her mind, but when the cocks began to crow he seemed to take fright and galloped away. Gwen gathered up the combs and brushes and began to walk back to the farm. Sad as she was to see Bayard go, she found she was taking pleasure in the morning air, and the brush of dewy grass against her bare feet, and wondered why she had never felt this before. Or perhaps she had, but so long ago that she had forgotten. She repeated a line from the verse the Man had recited but now it sounded comforting, not threatening. "Barefoot withouten shoon, barefoot withouten shoon..." until she came to the farmyard when she fell silent and hurried to put everything back in the harness room before anyone should wake. Then it seemed to her that she fell back onto her bed of rags and slept so deeply that when she woke again she was quite sure that everything had been a dream.

But she sang the words to herself that day while she milked and churned and skimmed the pans of cream. And then, towards the end of the afternoon, with half her work still undone, she wandered out in the little patch of garden which the Man's mother had made, which had fallen into a kind of ruined sweetness. She sat down on the grass in the late sunshine, and sat watching the yellow leaves drifting down. The little birds fluttered round her and a squirrel came to chatter in the branches above her head, and she half-thought they were talking to her. "Barefoot withouten shoon, barefoot withouten shoon," they chattered and twittered, as if they were trying to tell her something she should know. Even when the girls called her to come and finish her work she sat still listening to the birds, and smiling, only moving when she heard the Man stamp into the yard, angry and tired after a day at the horse-fair where he had found nothing that suited both his fancy and his pocket.

The birds whirred away and the squirrel fled into the branches and she went back into the house. But the Man was already there shouting that he kept a crew of lazy sluts to do nothing but eat and sleep at his expense, for the fire was half out, and nothing was ready for his dinner. And when he saw Gwen hurrying to mend the fire he hit her a blow across the face that knocked her down amongst the ashes, and stamped out to the ale house. Gwen lay still on the hearth stone for a while, and the girls clustered round, half-scared, half-excited, thinking she might be dead. But when the Man's footsteps died away down the lane she stood up and set her ragged clothing to rights, and as she did so the rag she kept wound about her head slipped and the staring girls thought they caught the glitter of white-gold hair, but in a moment it was hidden and Gwen went about her work.

But the work was harder than it had been, somehow, and she was becoming as clumsy in the dairy as she had been when she was first sent to work there, when her beauty began to fade. And it was lucky for her that it was autumn and the yield from the cows was less, and there was not so much dairy work. One afternoon, when the Man was away, the girls even had time to go and gather nuts. Gwen watched them go from the doorway, and saw what she had not seen for a long time, for she had been afraid even to look towards the wildwoods, that they were not black now but red and gold and glorious, and she felt a stirring in her heart as painful as the one that had shaken her when they took Bayard to the blacksmith, but different… This pain felt like hope.

She went to her bed in the dairy and took off her head cloth and combed out her hair with her fingers. It was thick and full and the white gold it had once been. And when she held up her hands they were fine and soft, and the swollen fingers now as dainty as any lady's, and she trembled with fear because she did not understand what was happening to her. She had no mirror, but she went to the kitchen hearth and rubbed soot on her face in case that too was becoming as fair and beautiful as before and the Man might come to want her again.

The girls came back just as the sun was setting crimson behind the wildwoods so the leaves burned as if they were on fire. The girls were giggling and excited because they had met young men in the woods and though they brought few enough nuts, the one who had stolen Gwen's shoes had a necklace of bright berries and a wreath of ivy leaves on her head, for the young men had crowned her Queen of the Wood. And when she saw Gwen crouched by the fire, hands rolled in her apron to keep them out of sight, she cried out that she must have a ring as well as a necklace and a crown and pulled the apron away and snatched the iron ring from Gwen's finger, and never noticed how easily it came off this time. But when she tried to put it on it was too small for her plump hand, and she saw the places where the bright silver had worn through to the iron and she threw it into the fire, crying out that it was worthless.

Gwen felt that pain in her heart again and this time she felt she might die of it, as if everything inside her was wrenched and changed as the last link that bound her was burned away. For a moment the girls laughed, seeing her look so pale, the soot marks standing out on her skin like bruises, but she paid them no heed. She lifted her hands as if they had suddenly become light, as if she was going to dance. Instead she pulled the rag from her head and her hair tumbled down almost to her knees, glittering white gold in the fire light, and they fell back, afraid. She walked through them, and past them, and out of the door into the clear evening. The sun had vanished behind the wildwood but an autumn moon was rising, golden as good butter, and she walked into the moonlight out across the stubble fields before anyone thought to stop her.

The Man, coming back from yet another fruitless visit to a horse fair, saw her from the lane, his treasure, his honey-love, his poppet, restored to her beauty, and walking away. He ran after her but somehow, though she did not seem to move at anything above an easy walking pace, he could not catch up with her though he sweated and struggled. His eyes were fixed on her and he saw nothing else, until a cry from girls watching from the yard made him look up, and see what, see who, was coming from the wildwoods to meet Gwen.

A dark King on a white horse, the Lord of the Wildwoods came, riding upon Bayard to greet his Lady, with his courtiers around him, hairy woodwoses carrying clubs, pale tree women in gorgeous robes of red and yellow leaves, tree men armoured in bark and armed with sharp stakes, bears striding on their hind legs like men, and white wolves leaping and gambolling amongst them like hounds. Still the Man made a desperate effort and almost caught the ends of Gwen's hair, but he was just too late. The King held out his hand to her and she leapt up into the saddle before him, and they passed in a sudden blaze of moonlight and were gone.

And the Man lay helpless, moonstruck on the stubble, and was never right again, leaving his farm to decay, and he wandered on the edges of the wildwood for the rest of his time on earth, calling for Gwen, calling for Bayard, who had gone deep into the woods for ever, free and wild and barefoot.

# ILONA

Ilona wrung out her mop and began to dry off an area of floor. This did little for the tidemark of scum left by her first pass with the wet mop. Her grandmother had always said that the only proper way to clean a floor was to get down on your knees with hot water, hard soap, and a good stiff brush. She maintained that mops did nothing more than move the dirt about. Ilona would willingly have cleaned the floor using her grandmother's methods but that was not allowed. Nor was she permitted to change the water as often as she would have liked, or even to give the floor a good sweep before mopping it. But she had to be careful to do exactly what she was told. She needed this job. Even more, she needed to stay below the official radar. Don't draw attention to yourself. Don't make waves. Not when you're an illegal…

She was mopping hopelessly at the floor, trying to make some kind of visible difference, when she saw the Supervisor padding softly towards her, her white trainers making only a small squeaking sound on the vinyl floor. Ilona's hand flew to her throat, checking to make sure that her chain was tucked out of sight under her overall.

"Oh dear, did I startle you?" the woman asked. "You do seem terribly nervous, Ilenka. Have you got a guilty secret?" She laughed to show she was joking but both she and Ilona knew perfectly well that she was not. Ilona did have a secret. She was an illegal, and the Supervisor had given her a job because she was an illegal. It meant she had to accept a lower-than-minimum wage, while the Supervisor no doubt pocketed the difference. And she had to take the worst shifts. Which was why she often worked at night … which was why she forced the thought down.

"No secret," she muttered, pressing her hand to her chest as if the Supervisor could see through her clothes and guess her other secret, guess that she was still wearing her forbidden cross. The reasons why it was forbidden had been carefully explained to her, using words she did not really understand like Health and Safety and Diversity. But Lily Anne, the lady who was not an illegal because she came from somewhere called West India, and was the kindest person Ilona had met in this country, had told her that in this case the Supervisor had told her the truth. She had not picked on Ilona just to be nasty. Not this time anyway. No one was allowed to wear a cross. But Ilona's grandmother had given it to her, with her blessing, and told her never to take it off, and she had taken the risk, and wore it even though it meant that in summer, when the other ladies wore little vests and left their overalls unzipped, she was always covered to the neck.

As the Supervisor was moving away, Ilona said shyly, "Ilona."

"What dear?"

"Ilona. I am Ilona. Not Ilenka." It was important. No one must think she had two names, two identities. That would make them suspicious.

"Oh yes, dear. Of course. All these foreign names, they sound the same to me." She gave another braying laugh then glanced at her watch. "Well, I must be getting on. And so must you, dear. This corridor should have been finished by now."

Ilona hastily picked up her mop and bucket and manoeuvred them, along with her trolley loaded with all the impedimenta of cleaning – except hard soap and a good stiff brush – to a new patch of floor. But once the Supervisor was out of sight her movements slowed to almost nothing. She mopped languidly. She stopped to rest her back. And when the Supervisor reappeared towards the official end of her shift the long corridor was not even half finished.

"Oh, dear!" she exclaimed, with barely concealed pleasure.

"I'm afraid I'm going to have to ask you to finish this floor before you go off."

Any of the other ladies would have launched into a voluble account of the unpredictability of night buses, the danger of the night-time streets, the anxiety of her hubby if she wasn't home on the dot, finishing with a half-plea, half-threat relating to the union. But Ilona only bent her head and said meekly, "I finish it."

"I should think so!" The Supervisor baulked of half the pleasure of making the girl stay beyond her time by her failure to argue. But she made up for it by adding, "Really, Ivana, I'll have to have word with the Manager if this kind of thing goes on. It's looking like laziness to me…"

"I be quicker," Ilona said.

"Yes, quicker but without skimping. You must think of the patients," she snapped, looking at the grimy floor.

"Yes," Ilona said. "Tomorrow will shine."

The Supervisor sniffed. "Well. I shall certainly check first thing." She squeaked away.

As soon as she was out of sight Ilona sighed then straightened her back and picked up her bucket. She took it to one of the little sink-bays off the corridor, threw the filthy water away and refilled the bucket with a fresh scalding supply. Then she added the contents of a plastic bottle from her trolley and began, meticulously, to mop the rest of the corridor. She worked quickly and thoroughly and when she had finished the floor did indeed shine. Although mainly, she admitted to herself, because it was wet. It would dull soon enough. But meanwhile… She put her mop and bucket onto the trolley and steered it back towards the room she had been surreptitiously watching all the time she had been working. The walls of the rooms facing the corridor were made of frosted glass and the most you could see of what went on inside were shadows. But that was enough. She stopped outside the door for a moment summoning her strength. Then she pushed it open.

The old woman was lying on a bed. And the shadow was stooping over her. When Ilona snapped on the light the shadow reared up and became a nurse, a dull ordinary looking nurse – with blood running over her chin.

"What are you doing?" Ilona said. She had thought about it carefully and the English words came out clearly enough.

"What are you doing? How dare you come into this room with your filthy mop and bucket! Do you want to kill poor Mrs Patterson?"

"I think Mrs Patterson is dead already," Ilona said sadly.

"Your fault!" the nurse snapped. "You interrupted me when I was giving her artificial respiration."

"What that on her throat?"

"She scratched herself, poor woman, fighting for breath… Don't stand there questioning me…" The nurse stretched a hand towards the alarm button but Ilona stood her ground.

"You know button has been disabled. You did not want Mrs Patterson to call for help," she said stolidly. "No one surprised. No one like alarm buttons except patients, and what do they know?"

The nurse began to move towards the door and Ilona lifted her hand and pulled open the zip of her overall. The tiny gold cross glittered on her breast.

"Am I supposed to be impressed with that, you stupid superstitious peasant?" the woman snarled, thrusting her way past Ilona – but she avoided touching the cross. And when her foot touched the wet floor she stopped short with a high keening cry. "What have you done?"

"Washed floor, washed floor with holy water. So. Now I know what you are. I tell."

The nurse smiled, letting her white fangs show.

"Who – who will you tell? Do you think there is anyone who cares? They know all about us! Just as they know about you. They need you for cheap labour and they need us! Who do you think rids them of the bed-blockers, the old, the useless…? Why do you think they forbid you to wear the cross? If you say anything they will put you in prison and deport you. Or perhaps they will section you and you will be put in a closed ward at our mercy..." She looked at Ilona's stricken face. "But they would rather not have the trouble. Dry that floor and let me go. I will leave the hospital. What do I care where I go? Do, it, do it now, you stupid mare, and you can keep your job, go on sending a your few pence a week to your family..."

Ilona stiffened her shoulders. "No family now. Grandmother dead. Maybe one of you in the hospital where they take her. But you will move on, move on like dirt before the mop? I don't think so. I think you stop here."

She picked up her mop by its wooden handle and twisted off the head, revealing a sharp, fresh point.

# BEAUTIFUL BOY

Matron walked briskly along the corridor. Things had been ticking over nicely while she was away, but there were some small details that needed attention. That paintwork, for instance, could do with a good scrub, and she must see that it got one. And the windows, perhaps, were a little smeared... A word with the window cleaners might be in order. And Mrs Poole ... she must deal with Mrs Poole now. Mrs Poole was not her favourite resident. She had a soft but curiously penetrating voice honed by what must have been a lifetime of gentle but persistent complaint, with all the soft annoyance of a dripping tap, and she usually found plenty to complain about.

But this morning when Matron did her rounds Mrs Poole had hardly found anything at all. And that was worrying. Any break in routine was worrying. "No, there was really nothing wrong with breakfast," she had protested when Matron surveyed her untouched tray. It was just that she really didn't feel like eating. No, she was not in pain, just a little tired. No, she most certainly did not want to put off her "session" with the young man... And her voice had taken on such a high, querulous note that Matron had thought it better to leave her to calm down, making a mental note to check on her later.

The young man was part of the Living History project. It had been started while Matron was away, which was why she must be very, very careful not to breathe a word of criticism. And it was an excellent idea. Young people from neighbouring schools (all carefully vetted) were coming into the Home to record the memories of its residents. The whole thing, sympathetically edited – and supported with scans of any relevant photographs that could be found in old albums, or battered chocolate boxes, or whatever, and perhaps letters, if they weren't too private, postcards, the cover of an old ration book – would be put on a special website and used as a learning resource. And so far as she could judge, the whole thing was going beautifully. There had even been detectable improvements not just in levels of reported wellbeing, but odd things like a measurable drop in high blood pressure in several residents, and easing in the discomfort of varicose veins – benefits which even extended to the staff.

That, she had decided rather cynically, could be due to the hormone surges that one particular recorder seemed to be causing in the staff room. A beautiful boy was the general verdict, with even more beautiful manners. He always stood up, they'd told her, whenever a woman came into the room – every woman, including the cleaners – both when they came in and, courteously holding the door open for them, when they went out. Looking for a reason for those beautiful manners, in their staffroom discussions, they had decided he must be a foreigner but because he had no definable accent no one could quite make up her mind where he came from. Monica thought he could be Polish but Maureen had opted for Ireland…

So when Matron tapped on Mrs Poole's door and went in, she was not taken aback when the young man sitting beside her rose to his feet. She was a little surprised to see that he did not do it awkwardly but with an indefinable suggestion that her mere appearance would naturally bring men to their feet. And possibly cause them to throw roses…

Privately, now she had seen him, Matron thought that he must have been brought up by elderly people – perhaps by his grandparents – who had taught him old-world manners. There was something subtly old fashioned about his clothes too. Other young volunteers – boys and girls – wore baseball caps and trainers, t-shirts, sometimes with unsuitable slogans, and ripped jeans. This one was wearing dark trousers and a beautifully clean white shirt. But not a tie. A tie would perhaps have been a little creepy. Instead his shirt was open at the neck, giving him a look that the Matron, also the product of an old-fashioned education, identified as Byronic. Except that unlike his Lordship this boy was shiningly, angelically fair.

And she was much too old to be staring at blond boys, however beautiful, she told herself, looking away, reluctantly, from the boy to his companion.

"How are we getting on, Mrs Poole?" she asked.

(Very well, by the look of her. And she had seemed so ill and miserable this morning. It was wonderful how much the session seemed to have perked her up. The phrase "bright eyed and bushy tailed" occurred to Matron. But catch Mrs Poole admitting that...)

"I am a little tired, Matron," Mrs Poole said in flat contradiction to that bright-eyed look.

"Would you like to stop for today?" the boy asked. "I've got loads of material all ready, and I could start editing it..."

Mrs Poole shot upright. "Well, if you are bored with my, no doubt, rather drab reminiscences..." She flourished her hand in dismissal.

Oh poor young man... Matron was about to step in, expecting him to be horribly embarrassed, but to her surprise the boy simply laughed and patted the old liver-spotted hand.

"Marian," he said, "you are so naughty! You know you're my most interesting subject!"

It sounded too arch, too – what was the word? camp – to be genuine. Surely poor Marian would think he was sending her up. But she smiled, and bridled, and positively snuggled herself back into her chair.

"I'm sure I'm not!" she said, sounding quite kittenish. And quite sure that she was.

"Well, you're a naughty fibber then! If you're really feeling up to it I want to hear all about your wedding." He glanced quickly at Matron. "Do you mind if we carry on?"

"No, no, of course not. Now don't get up again." She backed

towards the door. The boy switched on his little recorder and Mrs Poole leaned forward and said in a voice suggesting she was revealing, at the very least, the true story behind the Abdication, "My mother had some rather grand friends and she managed to borrow a very nice wedding dress for me. Heavy cream satin, quite plain, but very elegant you know – nothing flouncy…"

How does he do it? Matron wondered. The professional part of her brain told her that she must warn him against touching the residents, not even a pat on the hand, even if they seemed happy with it – well, especially if they seemed happy with it. But then she must find out how he managed to mimic, so uncannily, the kind of man who would appeal so much to Marian Poole, the kind of arch flirty creature who surely didn't exist anymore.

She was expecting him to take the same tone with her when she waylaid him on his way out, to give her little warning: "But the old dears do so love it!"

Instead he responded just like the kind of earnest probationer she had once been herself. "I am so sorry, Matron," he had said – and was he actually blushing? – just a little surely. "I didn't think. I won't do it again."

She was just about to probe his background a little further when a scuffle at the far end of the corridor alerted her to a possible problem, which rapidly became an actual problem as a tear-stained teenage girl rushed past them. Distracted, she hurried after her and by the time she had shepherded the weeping Historian into her office, and asked an auxiliary to fetch a restorative mug of hot sweet tea, the boy was long gone.

"But what was she crying about?" Monica demanded. "I hope she didn't upset her lady."

"No. Well, I don't think she was upset. Surprised, yes," Matron said wearily. "Apparently the girl is upset about her grandmother."

"Oh, dear. Died recently, did she?"

"No," Matron said. "She's still alive. There's some sort of family situation…"

"Oh we all have family situations," Theresa said.

"Except for me," Matron thought. "Except for me…"

But the boy made up for any deficiencies in his colleagues. He listened to Mrs Lesley's stoic account of getting on that train as a six-year old, leaving behind on the platform the parents she would never see again; to Mrs Poole's story of her dull and "rather grand" wedding to the nice jolly looking boy in the photograph she showed him, looking, in his khaki uniform like a schoolboy who had put on fancy dress for the occasion, the nice jolly boy who never came back from France (did her complaining begin after that, Matron wondered remorsefully); to Mr Boyson's description of his war experiences which, rather unfortunately, seemed to have featured a great deal of illegal activity involving parachute silk ("lovely undies it made – many a bride walked down the aisle in a full parachute trousseau" – even Mrs Poole, Matron wondered) which he had enjoyed immensely; and Miss Fleming's story of her time as a land-girl, which startled everyone.

"'Backs to the land' was our motto," she had said, and judging by her stories she had certainly lived up to it.

"That's going to need some very sympathetic editing!" Monica said. "Whoever would have thought it? A little old spinster lady like that?" (But she wasn't old then, thought Matron and very probably she seemed bigger. Perhaps we all get smaller as we get older.)

And Mrs Cunningham's lyrical – almost poetic – description of her pleasure in moving into a council house in the fifties, with a garden and a beautiful bathroom and three bedrooms, that seemed so magnificent that her Donny, her youngest son expected, "for ever so long" that another family would be moving in to share it with them…

And to all of them the boy showed perfect understanding. Not sympathy. Anyone, Matron reflected, could show sympathy. And sympathy can be intrusive, even insulting – but what the boy offered was never that. And somehow he seemed to be able to pass it on to others.

As she made her rounds one late afternoon she found Mrs Lesley, jolly Mr Boyson, and the scandalous Miss Fleming sitting together while Mrs Lesley quietly recited a list of names. Remembering, Miss Fleming told her later, the people who had never managed to get on that train but boarded very different trains to a dreadful destination. It was important to remember, she said, and just not the good times... And Mrs Cunningham, who had brought up her children on a council estate, and owed her present comfort to the money-making talents of young Donny, sat in the recreation room with Mrs Poole, whose mother had had such grand friends, patiently teaching her to knit.

And most unexpectedly of all, Mrs Poole laid her hand on her wrist one day and said, "You look tired Matron. You must take more care of yourself. Whatever would we do without you?" The first time since she came here, Matron thought, that she has ever noticed that anyone else might be tired or ill.

"Thank you, Mrs Poole," she said formally. "Perhaps I will go and sit down for a while"

She went to her office. The days are getting shorter, she thought, as she switched on the bright overhead light which turned the blue autumn dusk outside to blackness. The recreation room was already decorated discreetly with garlands of autumn leaves made from paper in one of the craft sessions – pumpkins and black cats for Halloween (no skeletons, she had warned the young lady who led the sessions, no hags – and the girl had looked blank, then understanding...).

She sat down, pressing her clenched hand to her ribs, breathed hard for a moment, and then picked up the letter which had arrived that morning, the letter calling her back to the hospital for some more tests. She knew very well what those tests would find. Well, it would not matter so very much. In spite of Mrs Poole's words they would manage without her very well. She looked up from her letter and saw the boy standing on the other side of her desk. The room was reflected in the window behind him, the room, the desk, and her own tired face. But not the boy.

"I did wonder…" she said.

"Yes," he said quite matter of factly.

And, without moving it seemed, he was standing beside her.

"I take the pain away," he said. "Sometimes it's from the memories. Sometimes…"

"And sometimes," she said, "it's just pain."

He bent down until his lips touched her throat.

# THE MAN WHO LOVED HIS
# LUSCIOUS LADIES

Vernon Applethwaite finished his solitary supper, washed and dried the dishes, tidied his little kitchen, swept and mopped the floor, and made himself a cup of tea. Only then did he permit himself to sit down and switch on his computer. The little trill it played as it sprang into life never failed to give him a slight tremor of excitement, but, always a believer in delayed gratification, he first checked his emails and viewed various news items which had caught his attention. But then, oh then he ran his cursor down his list of favourite websites: Big, Bare and Beautiful, Bouncing Boobies, Fit and Fat... He visited every one of them and finished by calling up his favoured, most luscious ladies in all their glorious amplitude. But tonight it was only a courtesy call: he looked, he smiled, he murmured to the images of Kim, and Tracey, Maggie and Orianne – and passed on.

He passed on to a dating site for men wishing to meet larger ladies. His fingers trembled on the mouse. Would he be disappointed? Would he find, ever again, a lady with skin as wonderful as the roses and lilies of the gorgeous Maggie; or a figure like the cool blonde mountainous Orianne; anyone with the soft melting curves, the adorable massive glowing pinkness of Kim contrasting so delightfully with the warm chocolate of Tracey... Would it be better to remain in a world of memory? But no. It was time to try again, to look for a partner of flesh and blood.

Vernon would have been rather cross if anyone had described him as a chubby chaser. It sounded so ... undignified. He preferred to think of himself as a connoisseur, someone with a true appreciation of beauty, an artist even (think of Reubens –

think of those Victorian painters and their wonderfully pneumatic models) born out of his time perhaps or, he would have said, before his time because he was sure that soon everyone would come to admire large ladies as he did, but he did not chase anything – or anybody, come to that. He admired. He very nearly ... worshipped. Upon his desk, next to his keyboard, stood a reproduction of one of those primitive goddess figures that seem to be made up of rolls of clay. His Venus. His object of desire. But was a dating site the best place to find her? He had had his disappointments before. Although there had been his glorious successes too – and this site was one he had never tried.

He took a deep breath, squared his shoulders and opened the site. He sifted slowly through the photographs and profiles on offer. He was a little disappointed to recognise some of those pictures. He doubted, oh he really doubted, that the lovely Tamara from Fit and Fat was really exhibiting her truly startling figure and looking for "freindshipp, and who knows with a solvent mail gsh important because she likes a larf..." under the name of Sadie from Southend. And others, though he did not recognise the models, were clearly the work of professional photographers. In this context the trappings of glamour, which he had admired on other sites – the feather boas, the long strings of pearls gripped playfully between square white teeth, the wet-look basques in PVC were tawdry. They reeked of desperation.

He began to think he might be making a mistake. He would not find a soulmate here and he risked spoiling his vision of his luscious ladies by straying too far into these dubious byways... No! His mouse-finger twitched involuntarily, almost losing the picture which had caught his attention, but steadied, and pressed "Enlarge" instead of "Next". "Enlarge" indeed! This lady needed very little enlargement.

He studied her carefully. This was no professional photograph, just what had once been called "a snap", probably taken on a friend's phone. She was wearing a modest scoop-necked sweater, which permitted only a promise of cleavage, (but oh what a promise it was!) She was gazing out of the screen with the look traditionally associated with rabbits and headlights. Her dark hair was arranged in timid waves, possibly by the friend who took the photograph. It was probably the friend's hand too that had applied the pale pink lipstick and the chalky blue eye shadow. No, no ... this lady should have her hair drawn back into a simple knot – or perhaps plaited into a coronet. And her lips should be painted scarlet to blaze against that dusky-pale skin... Well, well, such things could be changed. Nervously he turned to her profile. "Doreen, late thirties" or more likely early forties, he thought, but none the worse for that, "likes to dance" – yesss! surely the tango, with those looks – "wltm single male for friendship/marriage. Looks not important but must be kind…"

Vernon sat back, nibbled at a hangnail on his thumb until a tiny bead of blood burst on his tongue, trying to compose the kind of email that would appeal to this timid – but so deliciously buxom – fawn. He imagined her scanning replies anxiously, probably with the friend who had persuaded her to put up her profile in the first place, rejecting this one as "too creepy", that one as "too old". For a brief, and he acknowledged to himself, unworthy moment, he wondered what the friend looked like. A threesome now ... but no. It was an insult to Doreen even to think of such a thing. And sadly, large ladies often had skinny friends. It was one of those laws of nature, like the one which in his youth had meant that the pretty girls always went to dances with plain friends, who wore glasses and couldn't be left on their own…

His email was brief and to the point. He described himself as a businessman, currently without a partner (he hesitated there, wondering if he should play the sympathy card and hint at a bereavement, and rejected it as an unnecessary complication) non-smoker, fond of dancing, a Londoner, a Londoner who happened to have been given tickets for a Tea Dance at the

Cremorna Hotel near Piccadilly. How delightful if Doreen could meet him there to dance and enjoy one of the Cremorna's famous cream teas.

(He had chosen his proposed meeting place and time with great care – a lady would feel more comfortable meeting in the afternoon, in the presence of quite a number of people. She would feel less awkward about not paying her way if she thought the tickets were a gift. And if things were going awry they could always dance with other people.)

He went on: no obligation on either side. If they enjoyed the afternoon they might exchange mobile numbers. Then again they might not … but even so he remained, hers truly, Vernon. He hesitated, wavered, almost decided against it. And then he pressed the "Send" button.

It was three days before her reply arrived. Her spelling was faultless, her grammar only a little rocky, she did not use text-speak and she gave him her personal email. And she said yes.

YES!

He hastened to purchase tickets for earliest possible date, and to email her details of when and where to meet, with a neat little map, showing routes from the nearest Tube stations. Then he prepared to wait, warning himself not to get too excited. There had been disappointments before when he met a lady in the flesh. Not quite the worst had been those occasions when she had patently used a photograph of her much younger self – or even of a more glamorous friend. Then he had simply vanished from the scene – he usually had a planned escape route, he was agile and still able, in an emergency, to scramble out of a window in the gentlemen's lavatories if it was absolutely necessary. It had been so much worse when she had lived up to her picture – physically – but her personality had proved sadly lacking – when she had been loud, blowsy, even not quite clean – he shuddered at the remembrance of the ring of grime he had detected round the otherwise delightful neck of Ruby from Portsmouth; or the way that Stella, so dainty at the beginning of their date, had become so quickly and loudly drunk. But he felt sure, somehow, that Doreen would not be one of these. She was much more likely to be too shy, to need too much wooing. Patient as Vernon was, there sometimes came a moment when he had to cut his losses and give up.

So it was with a nicely moderated excitement that he arrived in the lobby of the Cremorna Hotel to find that Doreen was already waiting for him. Mm... His first impression was not good. It is hard to decide what to wear for a tea-dance, but Doreen's dress was almost unforgivably wrong. It was a cheap stiff shiny tube of mauve satin that destroyed her curves completely. A large ribbon corsage in a subtly clashing shade of pink pinned to the shoulder did nothing – well, nothing good – for her complexion. But – but the mid-length skirt allowed the observer to see that she had the small feet and dainty ankles which can be the peculiar grace of the larger lady. And the delicate silk of her throat put that tacky satin to shame. He made his decision and stepped forward to introduce himself.

She appeared rather gratifyingly pleased to see him. He knew he was a reassuring sight – small, slight, whippet thin, wearing a nice if old fashioned suit, a clean shirt, and having all his own hair and teeth, both of them clean and well brushed – but he was by no means handsome. He was not expecting her shy but gratified response to his appearance and he was suddenly prepared to overlook the dress.

At first the afternoon went even better than he had expected. Doreen was a good dancer. Those neat little feet fairly twinkled round the floor. She did become a little breathless after a particularly strenuous quick-step, and while they were sitting down to allow her to recover she was approached by several would-be partners. But Doreen, as he was learning, was a lady. She did not desert the fellow she'd come in with...

Over tea he watched her eat jam and cream scones as daintily as she danced. And pour tea just as she should – correct use of strainer, and adding the milk last – even asking him if would prefer lemon! She was certainly shy but as she gradually thawed under the influence of the best scones in London he coaxed her life story from her. It was simple enough. She had been an only child. The last fifteen years of her life had been spent as a carer for her mother who had died a year ago. Reading between the lines he decided the mother had been the Witch Queen from Hell and it had taken Doreen twelve months to recover not so much from her bereavement as those years of caregiving. But now she was re-making her life. She had found a part-time job in a charity shop (Vernon wondered, and suppressed the thought instantly, if that was where she had also found that dreadful dress), and she had started to go out with old friends ... old girl friends she had emphasised shyly.

He confined his part in the conversation to nodding and murmuring encouragement, and discreetly signing to the waiter to bring another supply of scones. Meanwhile he amused himself by mentally re-dressing Doreen in something more becoming. Black lace? No. Too hard, too much – let's be frank – of a cliché. But lace would certainly display that superb skin to its best advantage – well, what he could see was superb. She might run to freckles or even wrinkles lower down... Still, assuming that she did not, then lace – cream? No, and not white either, but a pale silvery grey. With long sleeves and just the suggestion of a scoop neck, and perhaps just a subtle scatter of transparent sequins ... with a full taffeta skirt. And of course, a properly constructed corset, although there he might meet a problem. Ladies, even the most refined of them, tended to favour what he thought of as the burlesque look, which involved satin in violent colours, and black lace, while he cherished a nostalgic fondness for what he thought of as the real corset, sleek and all-encompassing, buttressed with large amounts of webbing, with broad shoulder straps, in a shade of pink he privately thought of as Elastoplast pink. He was just dwelling on the thought of the intriguing striations such a garment could leave on a lady's skin when Doreen dropped her little bombshell.

"…so then I suppose I began to comfort-eat," she said in her small apologetic voice.

Vernon very nearly dropped the half scone he had been nibbling.

"Never say that! Eating is not a comfort! It is an Art! It is an Experience…" He realised he had spoken too loudly. People were looking at them. Doreen was staring frozen, a piece of scone bleeding jam onto her plate. He lowered his voice deliberately and added a small rueful smile.

"I'm so sorry. It's just – well – there is only one phrase worse than comfort-eating, to my mind, and I was afraid you were about to use it." He dropped his voice still further and breathed, "I thought you might say you must start to diet. And you are perfect. Just. Perfect."

He was going too far and too fast. First he had embarrassed and now he had frightened her. He half-expected her to get up, to run away from the table and out of his life. Instead she looked across the scones at him, tears welling from those beautiful dark eyes.

"No one has ever said that to me before," she said. "And I could almost believe you mean it."

"I mean it," Vernon breathed. And he really, really did. To prove it he ordered a third plate of scones.

When the dance was over they walked through Green Park, hand in hand, and there was no need for any more elaborately arranged dates or anxious wooing. Vernon and Doreen slipped into the easiest relationship he had ever known. Doreen was far more adventurous than he had initially given her credit for. She squealed with delight when he outlined his suggestions for a re-vamp of her wardrobe, not even protesting at the corset (and it was all that he had hoped and more – especially those striations on Doreen's luminous flesh, which had not a wrinkle or a freckle upon it) and positively revelling in a game involving jam-filled doughnuts that even the peerless Kim had once vetoed as "messy".

But as is so often the case there was an unpleasant fly in the delicious ointment of their relationship. She had the improbable name of Krystal, and she was Doreen's best friend. She was indeed the one who had taken that photograph of Doreen, and urged her to join the dating site. Perhaps now she regretted it. Perhaps she was jealous of Doreen's luck. Perhaps she was genuinely concerned for her. Doreen, typically, as he was beginning to learn, blamed herself.

"It could be," she said unhappily, "that I told her too much. About us. I shocked her."

"Nonsense!" Vernon said. "Nothing shocks people these days." He hesitated. "Er – what did you tell her?"

Doreen, it appeared, had become rather lyrical about Vernon's ways with jam doughnuts. Vernon's private reaction was that Krystal had simply been jealous. Perhaps she would have liked to join in – but no. Even Doreen would draw the line there. So, very probably, would Krystal. Although she must have chosen that exotic name, and that suggested a certain breadth of mind… No, he must stop this. Doreen was quite enough for him. But even so, this could not go on.

He sighed and said, "I tell you what. We'll have a holiday. A short one. What they call a minibreak. No need to tell Krystal about it. Perhaps she'll have calmed down when we come back."

"But…"

"She's upsetting you," Vernon said firmly. "I don't like to see you upset."

"But…"

"It won't cost us anything. I can borrow a holiday cottage from a friend and I'll drive us down. We won't even need to go out to eat. We'll take a hamper full of finger food and…" he lowered his voice suggestively "…a whole heap of jam doughnuts."

Doreen giggled. She had, Vernon thought, quite the most attractive giggle he had ever heard.

"And," he added, seductively, "it's beside a lake. With a

private beach. No tourists about at this time of year. We could swim. Naked…"

Doreen squealed. Her squeal, Vernon had thought several times, was definitely less attractive than her giggle. "You're so naughty," she said, "but won't it be too cold?"

"We'll build a fire," he said. "And we'll dance on the sand by the light of the moon."

"Hand in hand," Doreen agreed, "like the Owl and the Pussy Cat… At their wedding," she added after a tiny pause.

"Indeed," Vernon said comfortably. "Just like a wedding. You'll be my little fluffy owl and I'll be your big pussy-cat." And he gave such a big pussy-cat growl that Doreen giggled again and forgot to say that she'd always thought that the owl was the bridegroom and the pussycat was the bride.

On the Friday evening they set off as arranged, with a big wicker hamper bursting with their favourite finger foods in the boot, and the minimum of luggage. Doreen found the cottage a delightful surprise. She had been expecting something rural, and, quite honestly, uncomfortable. She had thought of earwigs, and unpleasant sanitary arrangements. She was faced instead with a building constructed principally from glass and beautiful blond wood, a bathroom so modern that she wanted to pack it up and take it home with her, rooms with smooth slate floors and underfloor heating, which might have been – which indeed probably had been – constructed to provide a sympathetic environment for just the sort of indoor games that she and Vernon so enjoyed. There was, in particular, a central atrium which went up the full two floors to the glass roof, and opened out, through a sliding glass wall, onto a tiny lakeside beach which was both playroom and theatre for them.

On the Saturday evening Doreen was lying on the warm floor, propped against a huge shell-pink satin cushion. She was resting after some very enjoyable exertions and watching the whole room slowly transformed by a crimson sunset, which fired the soft steel of the lake and then blazed through the roof and the doors so that she was lying – as it were – in the heart of a fiery rose.

"What a goddess," Vernon breathed, raising his camera to record the extraordinary moment. But even as he pressed the button he heard Doreen give a faint shriek. He looked round – and saw what she had seen, the dark figure at the glass door, outlined momentarily against that beautiful bloody sky. Then the colour ebbed and Doreen seemed to shrink in on herself, no longer a goddess but a fat woman, naked but for a light veneer of jam and sugar, while the dark intruder became only too recognisable.

"Krystal," she moaned.

The glass doors rasped open as Krystal forced them apart, and she strode into the room. Vernon stood transfixed. He had been wrong. She was larger, curvier, and altogether more majestic even than Doreen. He shuddered with excitement and – yes! – desire!

He hardly heard Doreen whimper, "How did you find us?"

"I followed you," Krystal snarled triumphantly. "I've been watching his house for days. And I watched this one until I was sure... Doreen, I know what he is—"

But now Vernon most definitely was listening.

"He's what they call a Feeder," Krystal pursued venomously. "He wants you to eat and eat until you're the size of a – a walrus! Until—"

Vernon's expensive camera clattered to the floor and both women swung round startled. They stared at Vernon. And then they both began to scream and scream. Krystal turned and blundered through the glass doors, followed, as rapidly as was reasonably possible, by Doreen, still gripping her cushion as if it might provide some protection against— Against what Vernon had unmistakeably become.

Because Vernon, overcome by the sight of two such perfect specimens – and the approaching rise of the full moon – was now a wolf. And though he was a small man he made a very big wolf indeed. He loped easily after the two ladies, neither of whom was built for speed, especially not when running across a stony beach. Indeed, it almost appeared as if he was prolonging the chase for his own amusement. But after about ten minutes it came to its inevitable conclusion, and Vernon was enjoying the rare experience of having two splendid ladies at once. It was almost too much for him. But he managed. He was, just as Krystal had said, a Feeder – and now he fed, royally.

Next day he did the necessary tidying up. This included a bonfire (or, bone-fire, he thought, grinning to himself) on the beach, and steering Krystal's small car from a nearby promontory into a nice deep part of the lake. And a thorough flossing and high-strength mouthwash. It was attention to those small but essential details which had allowed Vernon to carry on for as long as he had.

He returned to his little flat and added Doreen's photograph to his collection of Special Ladies, with a momentary pang of regret that he did not have a similar memorial of Krystal. For a long while they would be enough for him … until hunger for a real flesh-and-blood woman stirred again.

And he smiled and licked his lips at his recollection of all that delicious flesh. And that hot, sweet blood.

# CHRISTMAS WITH THE FAMILY

Myrtle knew she had made a mistake as soon as she stepped off the train. For one thing it was atrociously cold, much, much colder than it had been in London when she set out that morning – or, it must have been, because if it had been like this, she would have worn a much warmer coat. Or decided not to go at all. A vicious wind loaded with salt and sand scythed across the platform, making her eyes sting and water. And the platform was empty. There was no one to meet her. Unless – of course, what a fool she was – Aunt Lily wouldn't be standing out here in this wind. She would have stayed in her cosy car and expected her niece to come and find her. Surely there must be a carpark. She dabbed at her painful eyes and looked round for one.

Apparently not. No carpark. No helpful signs directing traveller to a taxi rank or a bus station. Not even an indicator to tell her when the next train back to London might be expected.

"Pity," she muttered. "I might just have waited for it."

But this was a single-track railway. She had, following her aunt's instructions, boarded what had been quite wrongly described as "a lovely little chuffer train" for the last stage in her journey and it would presumably have to chuff its lovely little way along the same rail all the way back from whatever its ultimate destination might be before she could board it for London. And probably it wasn't coming back at all today – why hadn't she checked on the best way to get back before she set out? She usually had her escape route well planned, but now she would have to rely on Aunt Lily to take her to a likely station. Her heart sank even further at the thought.

She wandered along the platform. There was a ticket office but it looked closed. When she banged on the window nothing moved inside. Suddenly she was rather grateful that nothing had. For some reason a picture she must have seen somewhere, Death selling tickets to the *Lusitania* passengers came into her mind – and she moved sharply away.

There was nothing else. No one else. Just her, on a platform already darkening under the winter sky.

"'Boundless and bare, the lone and level sands stretched far away.'" Myrtle actually spoke Shelley's lines aloud. They were peculiarly apt. Only a little way beyond the station a strip of gritty sand was being pounded by a vicious sea. The beach – not surprisingly – was empty, and stretched away on each side to an empty horizon. She had a sudden fear that her aunt's elaborate, involved, but curiously imprecise directions for the journey had actually said "on no account get off at Sandy Bay" instead of "get off the train at Sandy Bay – remember those lovely picnics we used to have there". It was quite possible ... but no. Sandy Bay was the destination where her aunt assured her she would pick her up "in my trusty little car" and this horrible place was Sandy Bay. There was a large rusting sign which looked as if it had been used for target practice, to prove it. And no, she didn't remember any picnics. But if her family had been involved, she was reasonably sure they hadn't been lovely. She was probably repressing the memories. It was more worrying that she couldn't really remember getting up that morning, and why she was so unsuitably dressed for a cold winter's day.

Her aunt had had a whole series of "trusty" – sometimes "gallant" – little cars over the years. One of her cousins had once joked, rather unkindly, that the initial "t" could well have been omitted because the only thing they could all be trusted to do was to break down, or even fall to pieces, with monotonous regularity. Perhaps there had been another breakdown. Apparently her aunt still had no mobile phone – she had certainly not included a mobile number, but that might be because... A further rummage in her bag produced her own phone to confirm her cold suspicion that there was no signal at

Sandy Bay. She wondered why she had bothered to get out of bed. She really couldn't remember now why she had. It had been so warm. So comfortable and peaceful … she could almost feel herself sinking back into her pillow until she was jerked back to reality by the realisation that the bitter cold, in conjunction with those cups of coffee that she had drunk on the original train, out of sheer boredom, was beginning to make her bladder feel a little uneasy. A glance up and down the platform revealed that there were no lavatories. Anyway they would certainly have been locked. She was wondering if she was – or would shortly become – desperate enough to find a hedge or a bush to crouch behind, if such a thing could be found in this bleak landscape. She was even beginning to calculate how far the station wall would shield her from the road if she crouched down, when the swish of tyres warned her that this was no time to make the experiment,, and moments later the kind of horrible rattle-trap car that could only belong to Aunt Lily appeared over the hill.

Myrtle was surprised at the intensity of her relief. At how frightened she had really been when she thought she might have been abandoned. And then for one dreadful moment she thought the car was not going to stop. Desperately she ran along beside the wall, waving.

I don't care if it isn't Aunt Lily. It's a car. The driver can give me a lift to civilisation – somewhere I can get a train for London and never come back… In fact I think I'll be a lot happier if it isn't Aunt Lily.

But it was Lily. Myrtle knew that as soon as the car bumped to a halt and the driver scrambled out presenting Lily's unmistakeable silhouette against the grey skyline. Everything about her – even her teeth – seemed to have been designed for a larger woman and bought at a jumble sale. Lily was dividing her time between returning Myrtle's frantic waves and securing the flapping length of tweed that hung from her waist.

It must be a skirt, Myrtle thought. It just looks like a dog's blanket and I don't think she's even got a dog…

As she drew level with her aunt, Myrtle realised Lily was baying, "Hurry up, now, we're going to be late. We don't want to lose the reservation."

Myrtle opened her mouth to point out that she had been waiting for Lily, not the other way round, then closed it and looked helplessly round for a gate. "Where do I get out?" she asked.

"Get out..." Lily repeated incredulously, as if it was too ridiculously obvious. But then her voice trailed away. She and Myrtle both converged on the ticket office from either side of the wall to discover that it and the station entrance were firmly locked.

"I don't suppose they were expecting anyone to get off here today," Lily said.

Now, why would that be? Could it be that they thought people might be at home, in the warm, enjoying themselves? Myrtle asked herself, but aloud she said, "I suppose I'll have to climb over the wall then."

"Oh dear. Do hurry! I made the reservations for half-past three for a post-Christmas dinner. They were a bit ... difficult about it."

On a day like this, just after Christmas, I can't imagine the restaurant will be packed out. Especially any restaurant that Aunt Lily would choose for a family meal.

She remembered the succession of dreary venues over the years, chosen to cater for Uncle Eric's allergies. Oh, that terrible day when he had ordered nothing but a cup of hot water, using it to make herbal tea with the tea-bag he'd brought with him, and then arguing fiercely when 25p for hot water was added to the bill – and their grandmother's terror that her food – or even her plate or her cutlery might have been touched by a non-English person. Her grandmother was long dead and Uncle Eric must have succumbed to his allergies years ago, but no doubt the family had evolved some equally unpleasant and embarrassing replacements. Jane, one of that coven of female cousins, for instance, who would probably have progressed from drinking a little too much for comfort to being a completely embarrassing drunk by now. Or young Kathy who was noisily and painfully vegan.

Trying not to think of the ordeal ahead of her she balanced her handbag carefully on the wall and pulled herself up, scrabbling for purchase on the stones, grateful that she was wearing her old boots and it wouldn't matter how scuffed they got. They won't like the boots of course, but they never do like my clothes, she thought as she finally managed to sit on top of the wall, swing her legs over it and drop to the road below.

"At last!" Aunt Lily said, flinging out her arm in one of her uncoordinated gestures. Her hand caught Myrtle's handbag and sent it crashing down – on the wrong side of the wall.

Myrtle stood quite still for a moment, trying not to burst into tears, or punch her aunt very, very hard on the nose... Then she put her hands on the top of the wall and began to struggle over it again. It was harder this time, and the third time she did it, her bag slung firmly over her shoulder, was the hardest of all. She landed badly this time too, jarring her ankles, and realising that the need to find a lavatory was becoming urgent.

"Come along. Really, Myrtle you always were such a clumsy girl..."

But I'm not a girl. I'm very nearly an old woman and here I am, still dragging myself to these annual family get-togethers. Well, this will be the last one.

She fitted herself cautiously into the front seat. All the windows of the car were shut and there was a pervasive musty smell – perhaps Lily had acquired a dog after all. Myrtle reached for the handle to wind the window down, but she was stopped by Lily's shriek.

"Don't touch that! The window might fall out!"

"Oh."

The car moved forward with a teeth-rattling jerk. The seat belt tightened across her stomach and Myrtle exclaimed. "I really need to – to visit the ladies' room, Aunt Lily. Is there somewhere we could stop?"

"Nonsense," Lily cawed, glaring through the windscreen as if it were an enemy. "Surely you can wait until we get there. We're going to be so late – oh dear."

They had come to a crossroads and it was suddenly, horribly clear to Myrtle that Aunt Lily was lost. She came to a halt and looked wildly from left to right, and back over her shoulder. Then she scrabbled about and dredged a crumpled map from the floor. "You'd better take over the navigation," she said.

Myrtle heard herself say, in a curiously controlled voice, "Just drive me back to the station, Aunt Lily. I'll wait for a train to – somewhere. If you ever do find the restaurant wish everyone a happy new year from me…"

Lily gave a curious whoop and started the car with another violent jerk. "I can't do that. You can't miss… The family would never forgive… I'll try this road…"

"Couldn't we ask…?" Myrtle pointed to a figure in the middle of a field on their left, but even as she pointed she realised that they would get no help there. It was a scarecrow, incongruously and rather horribly dressed in a top hat and tailcoat. The tails flapped like wings in the bitter wind, and she half-expected to see it take to flight. Or at least to see that ridiculous hat blow off and reveal a foolish white turnip head … if that round white shape under the hat was a turnip … but that was nonsense. What else could it be? But the hat remained in place and the whole scarecrow swung round one arm pointing stiffly to the road ahead.

"It's this way, this way," Aunt Lily shrieked, as if she was actually taking directions from the scarecrow. The car leaped forward, stalled and leaped again, then roared down the road. Had Lily always driven so fast? Myrtle wondered. Or was she really so terrified of being late? And why? And this must surely be the wrong road. It wasn't really a road at all, just a track running across an empty moorland, brown with brambles. But

Lily drove on as if sheer speed would bring them to the right place.

"Are you sure this is the right way," Myrtle inquired nervously. "I mean – isn't the restaurant in a town?"

"It's a lovely little country inn," Lily said, "in a teeny tiny little village. So quaint! You'll love it."

Myrtle strongly doubted that she would. And suddenly her fears were confirmed.

It seemed they had arrived. Or at least there were buildings ahead, but on the other side of a bridge, an impossible bridge, a narrow arch of stone with no parapet, not even a railing – Myrtle closed her eyes as the car swooped up, expecting a wheel to nudge over the edge and send them crashing to the water below – but they swooped downwards again, and came to a sudden halt.

She opened her eyes. They were in a tiny moorland village, a few low houses under slate roofs and the most unwelcoming inn she had ever seen. Lower even than the houses around it, with no lights in the windows, no visible Christmas decorations – it looked to Myrtle as if it was hardly more than a mound of earth, a barrow…

"Come on, come on," Lily was shrieking. She scrambled out of the car and ran round to wrench open the door on Myrtle's side. "Come on … they're waiting."

And so they were. Her family was ranged in front of the inn. And then she knew

There was Uncle Eric. Grandmother hunched in her wheelchair. Her parents gazing at her with the same disapproval they had always shown when they were alive. A young cousin who had come off his motorbike one dark wet night, standing there in his leathers, the blood from his ruined head still running darkly over his jacket… Others she was less certain of, but all, certainly, dead.

She should have realised. Lily was dead too of course. That smell in the car. Her confusion at the crossroads. Suicides had once been buried at the crossroads in case they tried to get back home. The four roads confused them, as they had confused Lily (had she killed herself? Myrtle wondered, or had it just been the kind of silly accident Lily was prone too – the gas left on, a fire or an explosion, Lily stepping into the road in front of a car…) and they did not know which way to take, but the scarecrow image of Baron Samedi, Lord of the Dead, had sent Lily on her way. Then there was her wild driving ("for the dead travel fast") across the briary moor and the dreadful bridge and oh, she knew those too now, they were in that song that had always frightened her as a child:

*When thy life is gone and passed*
*Every night and all*
*To Whinnie Muir tha comest at last*
*And Christ receive thy soul.*

And once you had got over the thorny moor you came to the "Brig of Dread" – the dreadful bridge that formed the final frontier between the dead and the living. Well, they had passed that. So – she must be dead too. That certainly explained her thin coat, which now she looked at it more carefully was certainly a dressing gown. Under it she wore a winceyette nightie. And slippers. She wished she could remember just what kind of bed she had risen from this morning to come here. Was it a sterile white one in St Thomas's Hospital or a deeper darker one in Highgate Cemetery – or even her own warm bed in her Hampstead flat where she had died peacefully in her sleep?

But of course her family would never let her rest.

She tried to think – even if she were dead she might still have a chance. There must be a reason for Lily's desperate anxiety to drag her into the dark. It could mean she had a chance of avoiding it. She'd be damned if she was going to spend the afterlife in a dark inn with her dreadful family, eternally desperate for the bathroom, without a fight. Indeed, she very probably would be damned…

What did they say, the people who knew about these things?

Move towards the light? There wasn't much of that – the sky was dark already and the only spark of light in front her came from her family's glowing red eyes. But if she looked back... Yes! there, low on the skyline, but dazzling clear, the last of the sunset shone like a signal.

With a sudden decision she batted Lily's desperate hands aside, leaped from the car and began to run back, back towards the bridge, the moorland path back towards the station, towards that saving light. There were no instructions in the song for passing the bridge, but she had crossed it once and she could go back again. Perhaps her family could not follow her over running water. True, Lily had passed over easily enough and they might too, so she would have to run further and faster than she had ever done when she was alive, through the thorns of Whinny Muir in her nightdress and slippers. What did the song say?

> If 'ere thou gavest hose and shoon
> Every night and all
> Sit thee down and put them on...

Well, yes, she had given clothes to Oxfam in her time, even if only it was just more convenient to do that than to try to sell them on eBay. Perhaps that would count and her feet would be protected by her unwilling charity. But if the thorns did prick her to the bare bone she would keep going. And somehow she knew that every step would get easier. She would race down the roads they had travelled in Lily's car, and if she could only make it the station she was suddenly sure that there would be a train at the platform. Whether it would take her back to London, back to life – or to somewhere else entirely – she could not guess. But it would take her away from ... them. She might not make it. There were already sounds of pursuit behind her, pattering and barking howls that sounded more like dogs than humans, and more like hyenas than dogs.

She dared not look round to see what they had become.

But she ran.

# SCRUFFY THE VAMPIRE SLAYER

Scruffy dressed carefully for the first day of her new term at St Walburga's. She wanted to strike a balance between looking too cool, and so attracting the unwelcome attentions of the Griswold Gang, who did not believe in people getting ideas above their station, and looking too geeky, which would simply make her a target for everyone else. Scruffy was not, in fact, particularly worried by bullies. Her policy of hitting out and hitting hard when attacked usually stood her in good stead. Still, there was no need to borrow trouble. With this in mind she darted through the dreary concrete exercise yard in front of St Walburga's, where the Griswold gang were lolling about, comparing designer labels, and swapping the names of their probation officers, re-forging alliances, re-igniting feuds, and extracting the lunch money from the small and weak, and made briskly for the school library.

The Griswold gang would never be found in the library. Many of them probably did not even know where it was. Some of them were convinced that the whole literacy thing was a giant con-trick: people just pretended to find some meaning in those intricate patterns they called letters, specifically to annoy the Griswolds. Others were prepared to concede that reading was possible, though not necessarily desirable, but it was less a learned skill than a trick, which they had somehow missed being shown – perhaps they were playing truant on the day the class did it.

Scruffy slipped into the room and realised, at once, that something was different. Not the books themselves, certainly. They still looked like a collection of jumble-sale rejects waiting for the bin-men in a Nissen hut. Not the furniture, not... Scruffy gave a little squeak as she realised that she was being watched. Someone was sitting at the librarian's desk.

Her first thought that he was very good-looking, not in the pretty-boy-band way that she admired herself, but in the haggardly handsome style her mother preferred. Indeed, for a moment, she thought she might have seen him on the telly – in a commercial, perhaps? But no – telly people, unless they were reporters looking for soundbites on inner city decay, the failure of the government's education policy, or teenage immorality – were not likely to turn up at St Walburga's. Then she realised that she was staring at him, but it hardly mattered because he was staring at her as well.

"Scruffy?" he said, uncertainly. "Are you – er – Scruffy?"

He had the kind of accent that the Griswolds automatically associated with sexual deviation, but Scruffy's Nan, an unreconstructed East Ender, would have called him a gentleman.

"Yeah," said Scruffy, adding automatically. "I didn't do anything. We're allowed in here."

"Yes, I know. I've been waiting for you. I'm your Watcher."

"And just what," Scruffy demanded, her eyes narrowing. "Did you want to watch me doing?" She had heard about middle-aged men like this, but it was the first time she had actually met one.

"No, no, I mean – do you know what a mentor is?"

Here she was on safe ground. She had seen them in the Narnia films. "It's a half-man, half-horse, but…"

The new librarian sighed. You got the feeling that he was beginning to realise that things were going to be a lot more difficult than even he had bargained for…

~~~

Scruffy huddled in the shadow of a flying buttress attached to the Gothic soot-stained walls of St Elphege's church, trying to psych herself up to making her first patrol in her capacity as Vampire Slayer. She had eventually accepted that Mr Harris the

Librarian was for real and that she really was the Chosen One, the one frail bulwark between St Walburga's and its environs and the minions of Hell. She was also, unconsciously, acquiring a good deal of Mr Harris' vocabulary. Only a few weeks ago she would not have known what bulwarks, environs or minions were – well, she might have made a stab at bulwarks but she would have been wrong. She was yet to see a vampire, but she believed, partly because it was the only way to explain the presence of Mr Harris (MA, PhD Cantab) in St Walburga's library. Only some kind of supernatural intervention (or a really terrible crime in a previous life) would have placed a classics specialist there.

And if it was all true – Mr Harris: Watcher, Scruffy: Slayer – it meant that somewhere in the litter infested buddleia jungle that was St Elphege's churchyard lurked her legitimate pointy toothed prey. In spite of her crash course in unarmed combat, plus the use of club, sword, crossbow and stake, she was by no means certain that she was really going to be able to deal with them. Her main problem, even before the questions raised by the semi-immortality and superhuman strength of her opponents, was "What if I get it wrong, and try to stick a pointy piece of wood through a perfectly innocent civilian?" Quite apart from the embarrassment, might it not lead to a prison sentence? Mr Harris had been less than reassuring; well, he had insisted that she would always recognise a vampire. It came with the territory. If she met one, saw one, even heard or smelt one, she would know. And were she to make a mistake then they certainly wouldn't send her to prison. "Much more likely to remand you in custody for a medical report," he had added, rather spoiling the effect.

Well. There was only one way to find out. She stepped out of her shelter and began her patrol.

There was a full moon but this hardly mattered. The churchyard was permanently lit by the sodium lamp stands which lined the streets beyond, making it look like a sunny day in Hell. But even their light could not penetrate the deep dark shadowy places – and it was into these shadows that she would have to go. She took a deep breath, stepped forward, and tripped over a fallen gravestone, landing in a heap of unspeakable litter. She yelped, swore, massaged a grazed shin … and stayed on the ground. Just ahead of her she could hear a murmur of conversation. A man and a woman were talking. Oh right, she thought, a couple looking for somewhere quiet – or a working girl and her client agreeing terms. They'll think I'm a Peeping Tom … but … something in the sound of one of those voices raised the hairs on the back of her neck. Just as Mr Harris had said. She knew deep in her bones. One of the voices was human. The other, she was fairly certain … was not. Only a few metres away someone was being chatted up by a vampire.

She crept closer. Beyond the shadows was a little patch of open ground. A big boxy sort of tomb thing stood in the middle, and on the tomb sat a lady, in lacy Victorian gear, holding a sketch pad. Talking to … a vicar. Scruffy could clearly see his white dog-collar gleaming in the moonlight. Right. Or rather, not right. Because according to her finely honed Slayer senses the lady was human and the vicar was a vamp.

For two vital seconds she hesitated, not really trusting herself. And then there was a sudden ugly eruption of teeth and the vicar was lunging at his victim's jugular. Scruffy sprang forward, stake held in the approved jabbing position. She might have been too late even so, but the lady dropped her sketchbook and pulled a silver cross from under her high-collared blouse. It might not have proved a permanent solution, but it kept the vampire off for just long enough to give Scruffy a chance to jab her stake under his short ribs (Slayer Manual figure 3). Mercifully, instead of turning on her with the roar of an outraged Anglican cleric, he exploded in a cloud of dust.

"Well done, er – Scruffy," said Mr Harris, emerging from the buddleia. Scruffy realised that he must have been following her on her first patrol and wondered if she should feel touched or cross.

"Ah – er – good evening?" he added, turning to her rescuee. Even at this moment Scruffy could admire the way he could make a conventional greeting sound like "And what the … are you doing here?"

The lady stood up. Her lacy blouse and long flounced skirt were black (and slightly ragged when viewed close to) so Scruffy assumed that she was a somewhat elderly Goth. The sketchbook, which lay on the ground between them, showed a more than competent pencil drawing of St Elphege's church by moonlight.

"I'm Saffron," she said cheerfully. "Sorry about that, but my parents were hippies. I'm a free-lance artist and I've been asked to come up with some suggestions for a cover for a paper-back collection of horror stories. I thought I'd start with a few sketches of St Elphege's and … rather foolishly, I suppose, I wanted to catch it by moonlight—"

"And why you have remained so completely unperturbed by this vampire attack?" said Mr Harris.

"Ah – well, I was wondering if something of that sort might happen. I really am a freelance artist, but I'm also … involved with a sort of New Age Group. I've been sent here by my Chapter to check out some rather ominous signs."

"Like that?" Mr Harris asked, looking at the little heap of dust, surmounted, incongruously, by a clerical collar which was all that remained of the vampire vicar.

"Well, that as well – but we've checked the omens very carefully and they suggest that you're sitting on a Hell Mouth."

Mr Harris ran a hand through his already romantically tousled hair. "What a surprise!" he said wearily.

"Which is due to blow at any moment," Saffron continued. "Probably on Halloween, Hell being kind of traditional. When Hell will, quite literally, break loose and take over."

Mr Harris looked round at the desecrated churchyard, lit by the stark sodium glare. "And when it happens," he said, "how will we tell?"

~~~

It was Scruffy's mum's proudest boast that she had always been "there" for her daughter. More specifically she had been there with a nice cooked tea every evening on Scruffy's return from school. This state of affairs was achieved by her insistence on accepting only lunchtime engagements as an exotic dancer at such local venues as The Dog and Ferret, or the Marlborough Arms, with an occasional special evening performance contrived by enlisting the assistance of Scruffy's Nan as a sitter, at such times as she was not pursuing her own vocation as life model and Character Extra, but now that her daughter had reached the years of discretion, Scruffy's mum had decided to devote more energy to her own career, after all, as she informed her daughter almost tearfully, she only had a few years left before she joined Nan on the Ugly Register. With this in view, she had obtained an engagement as a table dancer at the House of Atreus Burger Bar and Grill Palace, a newly opened eating establishment of unusual opulence run by the handsome and charismatic Mr Atreides.

So Scruffy's mum now spent her evenings gyrating to loud music while wearing a red PVC bikini, glittery horns and matching tail, all of which, except the horns, were readily detachable when required. Although it must be said that Scruffy's mum was quite as stern an upholder of the "Look, Don't Touch" rule, as Mr Atreides himself who, jealous for his licence, patrolled his territory as nervously and regularly as Scruffy did hers, watching with simple pleasure when Scruffy's mum enforced his rules, if necessary, with that splendid right hook she had passed to her daughter. Indeed he seemed to take so much pleasure in watching her that her colleagues had begun to make jokes about love and even weddings which, Scruffy's mum maintained, with only a slight trace of wistfulness, was as likely as her appearing for her performance in full wedding dress and veil...

So there was no question of her interfering with Scruffy's

patrols, or with the long hours she spent in the library helping, or at least attempting to help Mr Harris and Mrs Walden (as Saffron, for some reason beyond Scruffy's comprehension, liked to be known) in their increasingly desperate attempts to find a way of capping the Hell Mouth. She could at least make coffee and do odd bits of photocopying when she was not staking vampires, and punching out demons.

There had been a moment when they thought they had cracked it. Mr Harris found a reference in an obscure document to a method of capping the Hell Mouth by filling it with "creatures moore eevil than thoose which essay to issue foorth". But there was no indication as to where these creatures might be found, and further research revealed that the author had been, in Mr Harris's unhappy opinion, "as mad as a box of frogs".

Time passed and no discoveries were made. Indeed the day came when Scruffy realised that St Walburga's Halloween Disco was scheduled for that very afternoon (no one was uncool enough to come to school in the evening) and there had been no breakthrough. Scruffy listlessly turned out a shiny red leotard, found some red tights, borrowed a spare pair of her mother's horns, and set off for school. Before going to the pumpkin-infested gym she paid a brief visit to Mr Harris, and found him deeply depressed, brooding over a pile of Latin primers.

"All I ever wanted to do was to teach Latin, you know," he told her. "And for all the good I've done as a Watcher, they might as well have left me to it."

"You couldn't have been a better Watcher," said Scruffy, then realising this sounded rather final she added, "maybe Saffron's got it wrong."

"No, she's right. All the signs are here—" he looked up and caught sight of the horns. "Have you adopted protective colouration?"

"Nah. I thought I ought to go to the disco. I mean, if anything is going to erupt it will probably be there."

"Again," he said bitterly, "how will you tell?"

On her arrival in the gym, Scruffy saw what he meant. A blasphemous heavy metal track blasted from the sound system. Someone had already spiked the fruit punch, probably not just with alcohol. Scenes that would not be out of place in the suppressed out-takes from the film *Caligula* were taking place under the fixed glares of paper pumpkins. Teachers seemed to be acting on the principle of joining those they were unable – in any sense of the word – to beat. For a moment Scruffy wondered if Hell was indeed erupting right there.

And then there was an unearthly cry from the corridor, a cry that over-rode even the Blood Beasts' rendition of Slaughterfest Five. Saffron was screaming – not calling for help, just screaming one horrible mad banshee note. Without hesitation Scruffy turned and pelted out of the gym. Unfortunately so did the greater part of the Griswold gang, bored already with simple depravity, and looking for stronger meat. Nevertheless she arrived ahead of them in the library and there she realised that she had been wrong. Hell was not about to erupt in the gym. It was erupting already in the reference section of the library.

Horrors in shapes so wrong that they hurt the eyes were boiling out of the floor. And one of them had wound a disgusting tentacle around Saffron. She was still screaming so Scruffy supposed she was still alive. Mr Harris having thrown his Latin primers at the monster without noticeable effect, was now jabbing at it with a pair of dividers.

Scruffy dived forward, attacking the tentacle with fists and feet. The touch of it made her feel sick but that hardly seemed to matter. "Drop her!" Scruffy shrieked. "I'm the Slayer! Leave her! Take me!"

Mr Harris was trying to push her aside, protesting that if Hell was going to cherry pick victims then he was the obvious choice … and the tentacle wavered. It was clearly not prepared to have victims struggling to throw themselves into its (his?) clutches. It wanted to grasp this unexpected bounty, but the Hell Mouth was not yet wide enough to get another tentacle through. To gather in Scruffy and her Watcher, it (she?) would have to release Saffron, if only for a moment. That momentary waver was enough to allow Mr Harris and Scruffy to wrench Saffron free and drag her back to the librarian's desk.

And then the entire Griswold gang piled into the room.

"Reinforcements for the Hell Mouth!" Saffron moaned.

"Possibly not—" said Mr Harris, a note of hope suddenly infiltrating his habitual tone of gloom.

There was a moment of stasis as Horrors met Griswolds. The front ranks of Hell, who could see (sense?) what was coming, came to halt. There was some evidence of a scrimmage behind them.

"But those behind cried 'forward', and those before cried 'back'," murmured Mr Harris.

The Griswolds, perhaps moved by simple curiosity, perhaps recognising kindred … Things … moved forward. And the Horrors fled back with eldritch cries which could very probably be translated as "…this for a game of toy soldiers. I'm off!" And the Griswolds flocked after them … and the Hell Mouth snapped shut. All that remained in the library were Saffron, Mr Harris, Scruffy, a scattering of the young and innocent who had been drawn after the Griswolds in the stampede from the gym, and a faint smell of sulphur.

One of the first-year pupils, too young to have been fully inoculated with the St Walburga ethos, began, helpfully, to gather up the spilled pile of books.

"Are these yours, sir?" she enquired.

"Eh – oh, yes. Latin books…"

"Latin?" several of the other first years peered over her shoulder.

Somehow, suddenly, they were sitting in a circle on the floor, with Latin primers on their knees. Saffron was briskly photocopying the opening pages for those who had not secured their own book.

Somewhere, so far underground that it must have been in

another dimension, there were strange sounds, sounds suggesting that … Things … were thrusting unimaginable articles into trunks and suitcases of shapes that defied earthly geometry, coaxing small tentacled monstrosities into pet-carriers of no mundane design, putting larger tentacled monstrosities into warm coats, and hurrying them out to unearthly vehicles, calling to each other to make sure that Auntie R'kshesta had got a lift, and that little Yog-S'bash had taken his travel-sickness pills – sounds, in other words, suggesting that the original inhabitants of the Hell Mouth were moving out as fast as possible to a more desirable location. But neither Mr Harris nor his Latin class payed any attention.

"Discipulis picturam spectate," said Mr Harris. "Now, look at the first word. What English word does it remind you of?"

"Disciples!" shrieked Caleb, who was excused religious instruction because his parents belonged to the small and rather obscure sect, the Church of Universal Damnation, and who, therefore, knew the Bible and Biblical language rather well.

"Quite right. And what are disciples?"

"Followers," said Caleb confidently. "People who follow —"

"And learn, perhaps?"

Caleb nodded

"So in this context perhaps we can translate this as 'pupils' or 'students'."

"Us!"

"Quite right. Now, 'picturam' is of course easy."

"Picture!" roared his class.

"Students, look at the picture!" yelled Said, romping ahead.

They had translated their first Latin sentence.

"Is it all as easy as that?" Kyeleigh demanded.

"No," said Mr Harris firmly. "Some of it is very difficult indeed."

They settled down happily. It was the first time that anyone had suggested that they were capable of difficult work. Scruffy, who had already been introduced to the concept, smiled wryly.

"Made the world safe for Latin lessons then, have we?"

"For the time being – and with the unwitting help of the Griswold gang," said Mr Harris. For a moment his haggardly handsome face looked just … haggard. And then, as he looked back at his pupils it softened again and he looked almost young and hopeful. "Would you like to join us?"

Scruffy hesitated for a moment then sat down. She had learned how to kill vampires. Latin should be a doddle. Saffron offered her some photocopied pages, and Scruffy noticed that her black blouse and skirt was now as white as a wedding dress, the ragged edges transformed to delicate lace. And as for herself, she saw, with only mild curiosity, that her devil costume had mutated into a very pretty bridesmaid's dress.

She took a moment to wonder if the same sort of thing had happened to her mother before turning her attention to a map of the Roman Empire.

While her mother hardly noticed the mutation of her own costume, busy as she was, sipping champagne as Mr Atreides announced their upcoming nuptials and the patrons roared approval.

# SITTING TENANT

"Basically, we did the chap a favour," Piers said, splashing some more wine into his glass, ignoring the way that Jessica's thinned lips and raised eyebrows were telegraphing disapproval both of his own drinking and his failure to offer top-ups to his guests. "To say nothing of the neighbours. And are they grateful? Just because he made a bit of a fuss when they took him away…"

Moments after he put the bottle down Jessica snatched it up again and swished around the room, mutely offering to fill up the glasses of Zoë and Clare and their partners (who changed with such frequency that she had given up trying to remember their names.) But Piers, who had not survived long years of business meetings by paying attention to body language, continued serenely with his monologue, only slightly impeded by a mouthful of washibi nuts.

"You should have seen the place! Well you can, of course, I took some pix. Jess, where did we put those 'before' pix?"

Jessica, wincing a little both at the shortening of her name and the slight spray of chewed nuts which accompanied it, extracted the disc with the required pictures and slipped it into the player. Piers seized the remote control and stabbed it at the screen. "Look at these! I can tell you, it's a good thing we've all had dinner!"

Zoë and Clare gave gratifying squeaks of horror, although no one was sure how much Clare could really see through the foliage of her newly implanted eyelashes. But the pictures, exposed in their full horror on a flat screen that took up much of the far wall, were certainly enough to make the least sensitive squeak.

"That," Piers announced with deep satisfaction, "is the room we're standing in right now."

But the pictured room was almost invisible under the heaps of rubbish which must have accumulated over many years. Newspapers were piled up to the ceiling dividing the room into narrow rat runs through which the owner could only have moved sideways, leaving long dark smears of grease and newsprint along the heaps.

"Eugh!" Zoë exclaimed, "what is that on the floor?"

"Would you like me to zoom in and show you a close-up?" Piers asked eagerly. "He never threw anything away. And I mean anything."

"Not a good idea, Piers," Jessica said hastily. "Show them the garden."

He punched the remote again and brought up a wasteland of buddleia with the carcase of some kind of vehicle enmeshed in it.

"But how did he get in and out of the house?" Clare wondered.

"I don't think he did," Piers said. "He was a complete recluse."

"He must have gone out sometimes. To buy food," one of the partners objected.

"The neighbours said not. There was a story that he trapped rats and—"

"Piers!" Jessica said warningly.

"But I think he went out at night and sorted through rubbish bins – that kind of thing. I dare say you could have found trails through the garden. If you'd looked."

"Bit eccentric, was he?" the other partner suggested.

"He was completely out of his tree. Been like that for years, apparently. Something to do with the war," Piers said, swirling the last of the wine round in his glass. "Fetch the bottle over here, will you Jess. I'm running a bit low. That's what I mean when I said we'd done him a favour. I said a few words in the right quarters. Did what the Social Services should have done years ago, and got him proper treatment."

"He's probably quite grateful now," Clare offered.

"I shouldn't think so, really," Jessica said. "He's dead."

The word fell flatly into the bright room, with its blond and shining wooden floor, its freshly painted walls, its swathes of curtain patterned in the curious modern fashion with images of street people, and took the gloss from it.

"Dead?" Zoë faltered.

"He must have been terribly ill, of course," Jessica affirmed shrilly. "I mean – not just mentally... but ... all those years of neglect."

"Like I said," Piers repeated. "Did the chap a favour. Died in a clean bed, didn't he? More than he'd have done here." He glanced round suddenly as if he had seen something out of the corner of his eye ... something in the corner of the room. But there was nothing there.

"They look after them so well in those places," Clare agreed vaguely.

"And we got the place at a rock-bottom price, didn't we?" Piers said. "Mark you, I knew what could be made of it the moment I saw it. It was just a case of getting the chap out."

"Getting him proper treatment," Jessica corrected. She too glanced round but her uneasy gaze focussed on the window...

Clare's partner sniffed suddenly. "I say – have you got a dog or anything like that?"

"No," Jessica said, shivering delicately, "nothing in the least like a dog. Why?"

He looked suddenly self-conscious. "No reason. Just thought – now you've got that big garden you might have..."

Then Zoë sniffed too but said nothing. And shortly after that everyone, somehow, found that it was very late and perhaps they should leave.

Piers remained sitting solidly on the sofa, finishing his wine while Jessica shepherded their guests to the door, wishing them a safe journey and begging them to come back soon, while Clare fluted at her from the gate that she must remember Thursday, and Zoë squealed again at the lines of retro gnomes holding lanterns on each side of the path.

Jessica returned to the television room carrying a can of room-freshener, and standing in the middle of the room she sprayed it into each corner.

"Suffocate me, why don't you?" Piers said. "What's wrong with you?"

"There's a smell in here," she said shrilly. "I knew we'd never get rid of that smell."

"Balls," said Piers. "We had the floors up and most of the plaster off the walls, and there's not a smell in the world that would survive that."

"Everyone could smell it," Jessica said. "That's why they went off so early."

Piers sniffed the air elaborately. "Paint," he stated.

"No. It's some kind of – I don't know – an animal smell."

He sniffed again, less confidently. "Perhaps something's got in," he said eventually. "I'll have a look round."

He searched the house but found no alien animals. He did notice, however, that the lights were not quite as bright as they should have been. Perhaps the output from the power station dropped in the evenings – and then he heard Jessica scream.

He went upstairs without any particular hurry and found her standing in the bedroom by the window, one hand on the blind as if she had frozen to it.

"What's the matter with you?" he asked.

"There's someone in the garden," she said.

He pushed her away, and peered out. After a moment the movement-sensitive safety lights came on in the garden. Everything sprang into sudden focus, the carefully chosen shrubs and trees, the high brick wall with its pretty climbers… And a mass of something in the far corner that looked, for a moment, like buddleia and then dissolved itself into shadows.

"What did you see?" he asked.

"Something moving through – through the bushes. As if he was crawling..."

"What bushes?" he said, staring at the wide spaces of shaved grass, the newly paved path.

"The bushes..." She faltered, looking over his should. "I saw them moving... I saw something moving."

"Hallucinations," he said, "are nature's way of telling us that we might be sniffing a leetle too much nose candy..."

She made a move to slap his face, but he caught her wrist and looked down thoughtfully at the veined and corded flesh on the back of her hand. "Pity we can't renovate people like we can property," he said.

But she ignored the implied insult. "They're not hallucinations. And they've got worse," she whimpered. "There's always a smell downstairs. And..."

"Oh yes," he said, "and you've seen the old rat eater, crawling through the garden, the garden that isn't there any longer."

She moaned and tried to pull away from him. "You really ought to get yourself together, Jess," he said softly, "unless you want to find yourself in the place where he ended up. Of course, they'll have a spare bed now. And they look after people so well in those places, don't they? They looked after him all right."

She shook her head helplessly. "Why are you being like this?"

"Jessica, Jessica," he said, shaking her backwards and forwards, "how much are we going to get for this house when we sell it on?"

"Don't know..." she whimpered.

"It could be a million, Jessica, couldn't it? It could be more. Now that's small change to you, no doubt, but I don't want to lose it. And I will lose it if ... if the place gets a reputation for being haunted. Because that kind of thing is worse than subsidence. Worse than a rumour that they're going to open a thirty-fourth runway just across the street. Worse than..." He shook his head. "So we have to stay right here. Right here. Until it's the best time to sell. And we never, never admit that there's anything wrong. Because there isn't anything wrong. It's all in your mind."

"Listen," she said. "Listen!"

She waited to hear, from downstairs, the dry slither and rustle of someone making his way through piles of newspaper, the squeak and scutter of rats, to catch the sick musty smell of a house that hasn't been opened to the air for decades, where nothing was ever thrown away. Not even the small, well-chewed bones of rats … or worse.

"But what if – what if he comes upstairs?" she whispered.

"There's nothing there. Nothing. Nothing!" he shouted.

And they listened, listened to the silence.

And then the lights went out.

# THE CHEST

"I never thought Dave would do it." Kelly wept. "Never. Never. Never."

"You told him to, babes." Her friend Caddy (short for Cadillac) measured a therapeutic dose of cold white wine into a glass and passed it to her. "You gave him the keys and told him to come and take anything he wanted."

"I never thought he'd *do* it though." Kelly took a mouthful of wine. "*And* he brought *her* with him."

"Course you didn't expect *that*, babes." Caddy filled her own glass. "You wanted him to come round on his own. Then you thought you'd get to talking about how you'd bought the stuff when you was all happy and lovey-dovey and one thing would lead to another and off you'd go to bed, and it would be all happy and lovey-dovey again." She shook her head. "Wasn't going to happen, babes. Men aren't like us. Their minds just don't work that way. I wouldn't be surprised if you *had* gone off to bed, and afterwards he'd gone off with all your stuff all the same, so be thankful he did bring her along. I expect she made him. She's a bossy little cow." She hitched herself onto the tall kitchen stool and began to rotate her left foot carefully, so many circles to the left, so many to the right. Then she did the same with the right one.

"What are you doing?" Kelly asked, momentarily distracted.

"My exercises. Slims the ankles and keeps the joints supple." She stretched out both her admirably slim and no doubt supple ankles. "It works too. See."

Kelly, semi-hypnotised by the movement, began to rotate her own left foot. Then she started to sob again. "They even took my chest…"

Startled, Caddy glanced at her friend's strappy top. Everything still seemed to be in place.

Kelly shook her head impatiently. "Not my implants. My goddess chest..."

"Good," Caddy said. "I never did like that thing. And just think, babes, it'll ruin her colour scheme. She's got it all black and white. She's minimalist."

"It was the first thing we ever bought together. It was my *Valentine* present," Kelly wailed, refusing to be distracted by details of interior decoration.

"It was a horrible thing, babes," Caddy said firmly. "As soon as I saw it I knew you and Dave weren't going to last. If ever there was a bad omen it was buying that chest. And what on earth it was painted with I don't know. It came off over everything. Ruined my pink Vivienne Westwood."

"It was covered in red ochre. It was ethnic," Kelly sniffed. "And..." a faint flash of the old Kelly surfaced for a moment "...that was never a Vivienne Westwood. I don't care what they said on eBay."

The goddess chest had once had pride of place in Kelly's bedroom. The walls were still painted a curious terracotta shade to tone with its background colour, the dull earthy red which, as Caddy had said, did indeed tend to come off on everything. On the front panel a rather clumsy hand had carved, in high relief, a female face surrounded either by wild locks of hair or, possibly, snakes. She was grinning and lolling her tongue in a way that suggested the last stages of strangulation or, again possibly, dementia, and painted in horribly garish colours of gold and green. No one was quite sure why Kelly had been convinced that she was a goddess, and not even she had ever decided which goddess she was, but the box had been called the goddess chest from the first moment of its arrival in the house.

"Anyway," Kelly said, draining her glass, "I want her back."

"Now, babes..." Caddy began nervously.

"I don't care about the other stuff. I don't want anything *she's* touched but I want my goddess back. And she wants to come back."

Caddy firmly put the cork back in the bottle of white wine, feeling her initial prescription might have been a mistake. Especially if Kelly had been seeking any other kind of chemical comfort before she got there. She was certainly in a funny mood. "I'll put the kettle on, shall I?" she trilled. "Nothing like a cuppa..."

"Are you still seeing that roadie?" Kelly asked. "The one with the van?"

"No," Caddy said without hesitation. And then, thinking quickly, she added, "He's gone abroad. Emigrated."

Fortunately Kelly was too wrapped up in her own troubles to inquire what country in the known world would have accepted him.

Caddy made a pot of green tea with the concentration she gave to every physical activity. She did not want to hear any more about Kelly's goddess. Kelly had been silly about that chest right from the start, attributing all kinds of opinions to it. According to Kelly the goddess liked yellow flowers, the brighter the better, and they had to be tied up with red wool. So there had always been at least one and often several bunches of marigolds, or tulips in particularly crude shades of yellow, in the bedroom, usually in various stages of decay because Kelly never changed their water. She had also, to Caddy's certain knowledge, taken to leaving a saucer of milk and honey in front of the chest and insisting that the goddess (or perhaps her snakes) drank it overnight. Caddy would not have been surprised if one of Dave's reasons for moving out had been the constant fear of putting his foot into a sticky saucer in his own bedroom. It was the kind of thing that puts a man off.

"You drink that up," she said, handing over the tea. "Now. Did you get your keys back from him?"

"Forgot to ask." Kelly whimpered.

Caddy leaned over and snagged the Yellow Pages from the

kitchen counter. She found "L" for locksmith and reached for the phone.

"But I've got his," Kelly said. She gave a weird little giggle.

Caddy's fingers froze on the first button. "What?"

"They were in his jacket," Kelly's voice no longer sounded plaintive. No longer – really – sounded like Kelly at all. "He took it off because he got quite hot moving all my furniture out. He just threw it down on the floor like he always does – did – and I hung it up for him like I always do – did."

"And while you did that you picked his pocket?" Caddy said, unbelievingly.

"He had my keys. I took his. Fair exchange." Kelly laughed. It was not her usual breathless giggle but a full-throated bay. It sounded like a much older woman's laugh. Possibly an older woman with serious mental problems. "So we could go round now and get my chest," she continued. "It's quite light. We can easily carry it outside between us, and get a taxi."

"A taxi driver's never going to have that in his cab, coming off all over his seats."

"Then we'll take it on the Tube. Dave and I did that when we bought it. I can't manage it alone or I'd have brought her home before."

"But Dave and *her* will be there."

Kelly shook her head. "No they won't," she said positively.

Caddy took a mouthful of hot green tea. "No," she said firmly. There were limits to friendship and breaking and entering definitely crossed them.

Kelly usually pleaded and pouted and whined when she wanted you to do something. She had never before, in Caddy's experience, picked up a large knife from the display on the kitchen wall and presented it point forwards to her friend – in a roughly jugular direction.

"Come on," she said.

And Caddy, her perfectly toned and admirably supple ankles trembling slightly, followed her friend out of the flat. The knife, by then, was tucked into Kelly's handbag but Caddy wasn't going to risk anything.

She was hoping that she might see someone she could ask for help but it was the middle of the afternoon. The streets were more or less empty (there were certainly no policemen visible) and the Tube station was apparently unmanned. Kelly steered them carefully towards an empty carriage and no one, except an old lady who looked quite as mad as Kelly and would probably have joined the expedition, rather than going for help if appealed to, got on.

By the time they reached their station, Caddy was resigned to going as far as Dave's flat. Somehow, once there, she was going to part Kelly from her handbag, and then run screaming. After all, Kelly would have to put the bag down when she picked up the chest.

Dave's new flat was in a pleasant, leafy – empty – street.

Both women walked up the steps to the front door, and Kelly took the keys from her bag and unlocked it. The hallway was, as Caddy had said, all black and white. The walls and ceiling were white, a black lacquered table stood against the wall (piled with post, Caddy noticed, as if no one had had time to open it) and there were big black and white marble tiles on the floor. There was also, rather unexpectedly, a broad red trail running right across the middle of them.

"I said that chest would ruin her décor," said Caddy shakily. "They must have dragged it across the floor."

"That's not red ochre," said Kelly. She bent down and dabbled her fingers in it. Then she stood up and licked them deliberately, one by one. "It's not red ochre at all."

Caddy looked at her for a moment, watching her friend's mouth spread into a wide mirthless grin while her tongue lolled out, impossibly long and red... Then she turned and ran, screaming down the steps into the pleasant leafy street, while behind her she heard Kelly – screaming too.

Or was she laughing?

# A STRAIGHTFORWARD PROCEDURE

Destiny (born Doris) signed the contract without hesitation – not even reading it through properly. The thought that her husband would have been so angry at her rashness only added a naughty spice to the transaction.

Now she sat in front of the mirror in the pretty pink room in the shockingly expensive nursing home, lifting the loosened flesh around her chin and neck with her thumbs while her fingers tightened and tautened the skin over her cheekbones.

*Soon she would have her own face back, even better than it had been when she was young. She would be smooth and flawless as a porcelain doll, just like the pretty nurse who was standing by, waiting to take her for her first treatment – a perfectly straightforward procedure, the girl had assured her, she had had it herself…*

There *were* drawbacks – but Destiny had ignored them. Who *wanted* to spend her life baking herself leathery under a hostile sun? As for having to wear sunglasses all the time, so what? She'd buy a whole wardrobe of designer sunglasses.

"Are you ready?" the nurse asked.

Destiny, not just ready but barking for it, looked blank, then remembered and unclasped the chain from her neck. Something about the metal interfering with the treatment, something else she hadn't listened to. Wondering why the stupid girl hadn't taken the thing off for her she dropped the small silver cross onto the dressing table – and turned from the mirror to see her surgeon who, strangely, had been standing just behind her.

But he had not been reflected in the mirror. And neither, now she came to think of it, had the nurse…

And then they both smiled.

Her last coherent thought was that she was quite sure no one had told her about the *teeth*...

# NIGHT OUT

Mrs Padgett gave a final glance round the kitchen, mentally ticking off her list of tasks: cat's tray? Filled with clean litter. Cat's bowl? Filled with fresh food. He wouldn't eat anything, of course, but she had to be on the safe side. Casserole? In the oven, keeping warm. Fruit salad? In the fridge, keeping cool. And some plain yoghurt to go with it, not cream. She had read, somewhere, that cream was bad for you, though her own mother, still very much alive, and a force to be reckoned with, had eaten a bowl of porridge with cream (and white sugar) every day of her life. Or so she said. Perhaps there was some ingredient in porridge that cancelled out the evil effects of cream.

Mrs Padgett brought her mind back firmly from scientific speculation and checked the bread bin. A whole fresh loaf. Good. But could that be all? Doubt paralysed her for a moment. How could she be sure that she had thought of everything? But then she gave herself that mental bracer that had proved so effective in the past.

"Buck up, Muriel," she told her middle-aged self silently, just as she had once told her much younger self, about to walk down the aisle in her white dress to become the bride of an almost unrecognisably younger Mr Padgett. And just look what that had led to!

And now all she had to do was to give her family their last-minute instructions, check her handbag (compact? door-key? purse?) and walk out the front door.

Everyone has an evening out alone sometimes.

She said, "Buck up, Muriel," again, aloud this time, and went into the sitting room.

Mr Padgett was watching the news. Timothy, her youngest

(he had been quite a surprise, almost an embarrassment, at first although it was quite funny now to remember how shy she had been at those ante-natal classes with girls young enough, some of them, to be her own daughters), was doing his homework. Neither of them looked up when she came in. Her middle child, Sara, soon to walk down the aisle on her own account, was out doing some necessary shopping, but she would be back in time for dinner. Mrs Padgett waited until the weather forecast came on.

Then she said, "I'm off now. You know about the casserole, don't you? Don't burn yourself when you get it out of the oven – you'll find the oven gloves hanging right next to the stove…" They always hung right next to the stove but last time Mr Padgett had searched through all the kitchen drawers and found a lace tablecloth to muffle his hands, ruining it, and very nearly his fingers, in the process. She suppressed that memory firmly.

"There are some jacket potatoes as well, and I don't expect Sara will want one…"

No, she certainly would not. She intended to wear a wedding dress that was a mere slip of white satin (Mrs Padgett's mother had said she'd worn a bigger nightie than that on her wedding night, never mind what she'd worn to church) and it would contour itself to every mouthful of potato. It seemed so unfair. Timothy, who was never likely to wish to appear in public in a white satin slip, seemed to eat twice his own weight in starch every day and never put on an ounce.

Remembering Timothy's appetite she said, "There's heaps of bread as well. Don't leave anything for me – you know we get a lovely meal. Oh, and if any children should knock…"

Mr Padgett, withdrawing his gaze from the television screen for the first time since she had come into the room, stared blankly at her and she hastened to explain, "It's Hallowe'en, dear. They may come round asking for sweets. Trick or treat, you know. Well, there are some bags of sweets and things all ready on the hall table."

Mr Padgett thought about this for a moment, and came to a suitably managerial decision. "I'll leave all that to young Sara," he said firmly.

"Yes dear," said Mrs Padgett. "Now, you will be all right, won't you?"

"We'll be fine," said Mr Padgett, who had never cooked a meal in his life. "We're used to fending for ourselves, aren't we, Tim? You go off and enjoy yourself. You don't often get out on your own."

Four times a year, Mrs Padgett thought, with uncharacteristic sharpness. I must manage it about four times a year. And I'm not surprised when I have to plan everything like a military campaign. Three times as much work beforehand and heaven only knows what my kitchen will look like when I get back. For a moment she wondered if it was all worth it. She was tired, and no wonder, and she had a slight, but nagging, headache.

Perhaps it would be better just to go upstairs and lie down.

Timothy looked up. "Are you going out, Mum?" he asked.

Mrs Padgett was saved from anything she might have said by her husband saying, "She's having a night out with the girls. Aren't you, Mu? At least that's what she tells us. I bet we'd be surprised at what she really gets up to."

Mrs Padgett smiled nervously. "Are you sure there's nothing you need, before I go?" She hovered, fighting with those awful guilt feelings, waiting to see if her husband and son had any last requests, but Mr Padgett had gone back to the television and Timothy to his book. If she was going, and it seemed as if she must be, there was no sense in being late.

She went up to her bedroom. Now … coat, gloves, handbag. A quick glance in the mirror to check her neat but timid bob and that pink lipstick she could never quite get used to. Her elder daughter, Melanie, living a life of married bliss in Pinner, who could drive, and went out alone in the evenings two or three times a month, had persuaded her to abandon her old-fashioned red lipstick, but she was still not sure about it. After all, if red lipstick was so completely out of fashion why were they still making it? For a moment she hesitated in front of the mirror, thinking not of her lipstick but of Melanie. No sign of ante-natal classes for her and yet she seemed happy enough...

Perhaps she should phone her – no, not tonight.

"Buck up, Muriel!" she said quite loudly and fiercely to her reflection. "You know you'll enjoy it once you get going."

She picked up her handbag and, calling a cheerful goodbye to her son and her husband, she went out closing the front door carefully behind her.

The garden was dark and smelt of wet leaves. If Mr Padgett or Timothy had looked out of the window and seen her walking, not down the drive but across the lawn to the tool shed, they would have been surprised. They might even have been a little disturbed. But the sitting room windows were tightly curtained. Still, Mrs Padgett moved quietly. She had oiled the hinges on the door earlier that day and it opened with barely a whisper. The cat, who had been waiting in the shrubbery, hurled himself forward with a squeak of excitement but Mrs Padgett hushed him firmly. Very, very quietly she took the garden besom from its rack and carried it outside.

Decorously she sat herself astride the handle while the cat leaped up behind her. Guilt was forgotten in a flood of glorious excitement. She recited her spell and the broom rose smoothly into the air. She pointed its head in the direction of their meeting place and set off for the greatest witches' festival of the year.

The broom banked high over the house, skittish after its long confinement. Mrs Padgett, feeling the wet wind rush through her hair, took a firm grip on her handbag and shrieked aloud her delight and anticipation.

Far below Mr Padgett roused himself momentarily from his television programme, catching the echo of that eldritch cry. He turned to his son. "Do you know, I could have sworn I heard someone shriek 'Buck up, Muriel'," he said.

But Timothy was reading.

# DIVERSION

It was a very hot day in that early summer heatwave we weren't ready for so when the bus took us into an avenue of deep green shade, I was grateful. My next less-grateful thought was the council really should cut back those heavy branches scraping the vehicle's roof, single-decker though it was; my last, the abrupt realisation that we were not driving down a tree-lined street at all but through a tunnel of trees standing thickly on each side, their branches interlacing overhead. And there was no asphalt under our wheels. We were on a forest path.

The bus *could* quite possibly have been diverted from its usual route without informing the passengers. Or a new driver could have got himself lost. But we were in the depths of Epping Forest. Could he really have wandered so from his route without anyone noticing? True, it had been a fraught journey. Somewhere in the bus a child had something – a toy? – which sounded unfeasibly heavy. Every so often he would drop or throw it with a resounding crash then shriek to have it back, and his mother would scream that she'd said if he did it again she'd take the thing away and he couldn't have it, upon which he would scream so piercingly that she did return it, and we waited tensely for the next inevitable crash and shriek. This wait was enlivened by a young woman sitting behind me. She was a large girl whose figure suggested that sometimes Epstein worked from life, and she shouldn't have worn skin-tight leopard-skin leggings. She was shouting a long monologue into her phone, recounting a series of domestic disasters enough to make the average member of the House of Atreus tremble and go pale, while a lady in a hat and coat in the seat opposite to mine shook her head, tutted and sighed, and I cringed, waiting for her to remonstrate with the girl, provoking a flood of protest and very possibly Language.

The one touch of humanity came from a very small girl one seat ahead of me, sitting in silence, contemplating her silver sandaled feet. I was wearing silver shoes as well although of a considerably larger size, and once we exchanged small grave smiles, silently congratulating each other on our excellent fashion sense. I suppose, with these distractions, I might have failed to notice our departure from the beaten track but I didn't really think so.

The lane narrowed alarmingly and I was just about to resign myself to being trapped for hours and determining to confiscate whatever that child was playing with, and damn the consequences, when we burst out into a wide woodland glade. And stopped. There was a moment's perfect shocked silence. Then the child dropped the thing again and everyone broke out in questions and protests. I was near the front, and determined, and I got to the driver first.

"Where are we?" I demanded. "This can't be Epping."

You might say one forest glade is pretty much like another, but spring and summer are quite different in the woods, and it was summer when I got on that bus. But here the trees wore the light green of spring, the grass was fresh and starred with primroses. Beyond the large pool of water, a pond, perhaps even a small lake, that glittered in the middle of the clearing, I glimpsed a tide of bluebells lapping the trees like another, lovelier lake

The driver peered at me from under his peaked cap, which our bus drivers didn't wear. It was crammed down over his ears, as if to hide them. There was so much that wasn't right here that I was hardly surprised to see his face was disturbingly beautiful, like a young and wicked choir boy who knows enough to hide his evil knowledge with a mask of innocence.

"It's Another Part of the Forest," he said. "A diversion," he added shiftily. "Er. Why not disembark. Get some fresh air. We won't be here long."

I might have stayed and argued if Princess Silverheels hadn't caught sight of the water and flashed past me, out of the bus and across the grass.

"I'm only going to paddle," she shouted as she went.

The woman with her shouted despairingly, "Channel! No!" – then appealingly to the rest of us, "I can't swim."

I could. And remembering that children can drown, if they are really determined, in a few inches of water, I jumped down to follow Channel (surely *Chanel*, my Inner Editor protested) while the woman stood in the door, blocking the exit, accidentally but very effectively, and wailing, "Chaaaaaaanel! Come back!"

Channel paused briefly to jettison her sandals and her dress, then streaked across the little beach into the pool, ran splashily and – disappeared under the water. I kicked off my shoes, ripped my skirt off, and followed, discovering the reason for her disappearance immediately when the beach shelved abruptly under my feet and I found myself up to my shoulders in horrendously unforgivably icy-cold water. As I coughed and gasped, the child's wet head bobbed up beside me like a sleek little seal.

"Isn't it lovely," she said and plunged below the surface again.

Actually, once you got used to the chill, it was. My body had reacted to a few days of unaccustomed heat with rashes and alarmingly swollen mosquito bites, but these discomforts floated away in that first icy shock, and now the temperature seemed quite pleasant. The child emerged again further off and I swam after her.

"Be careful. There could be all sorts of things under the water…"

She laughed, a little trill like a bird. "There aren't. Look."

There weren't. The water was clear as gin; you could see right down to the shining stones at the bottom. It trembled slightly, suggesting it was fed from a spring which ran away somewhere, probably accounting for its clarity and chill. No danger of getting trapped in the weeds here. Although couldn't you catch Weil's Disease from fresh water contaminated by rats? I couldn't imagine rats widdling in this crystal bath, but with rats you never knew… Still, we were both in now and there were more immediate complications to worry about, such as, would we be allowed back on the bus still soaking wet, and anyway travelling in soggy knickers would be most uncomfortable, plus there would be an embarrassing wet patch spreading on the back of my skirt. But the skirt was black and the wet probably wouldn't show. Much. In the meantime I might as well enjoy the sensations of floating in cold fresh water instead of baking in a bus.

I relaxed a little and glanced back to see what my fellow passengers were doing. I was surprised to see that the driver hadn't yet had to lock himself inside the bus while a potential lynching party hammered on the windows. Far from it. He'd disembarked and was sitting on the grass, leaning against the front wheel, reading the paper. All I could see of him were his little brown hands gripping the paper's edges, suggesting that, impossibly, he had got smaller since I spoke to him…

The hat-lady was walking carefully across the grass looking for just the right place to settle, but no one else had taken advantage of the opportunity for a little fresh air.

I turned back to keeping an eye on Channel (Chanel?) who was performing some solo synchronised swimming. One of her moves brought her round to face the glade and she gave a squeak of surprise.

"Oh, look, that lady's taking her clothes off!"

I gasped, floundered and looked. The hat-lady had removed the hat, revealing sparse grey hair ridged into meticulous waves, after which she took off her outer clothes, then with a small fastidious gesture she turned her back on us and undressed completely, then lifted her arms above her head.

And began to turn into a tree.

Channel and I trod water and watched the whole process breathlessly. Her white bony feet elongated and writhed into the grass, pushing their way deep into the ground as if she were burrowing them into a pair of comfy slippers. Her legs fused into a single trunk encased in silvery bark which ran over the rest of her body as her arms became branched and twiggy, until in less time than it takes to tell, a graceful tree, a little taller than she had been, but still carrying the suggestion of a slender female shape stood where the hat-lady had been a moment before. The branches trembled and broke out into a shower of yellow leaves, bright as fresh-minted pound coins, just as if she had burst into delighted laughter at her successful transformation.

"Ooooh," said Channel, "do you think she *meant* to do that?"

"It certainly looked like it."

"Oh well, that's all right then." She performed a dolphin-like spring from the water, flourishing her arms.

But was it? Could this place offer other transformations? Did the sunlight catch a faint patterning of iridescent scales on the child's arms? Or were they water drops? I squinted down at my own skin. No scales but was my hair feeling longer and heavier? Could we be turning into naiads? Undines? Rhine Maidens? I tried a few Wagnerian "Wallala! Lalaleia! Leialaleis!". They resonated over the water disturbingly.

Channel turned round giggling and waved at me. Was that a tiny frill of webbing just starting between her fingers?

"Erm. What's your name?" I asked, trying to sound casual.

"Princess Polyanthus," she said without hesitation. "What's yours?"

"Mnemosyne Niobe Nelia Twistleton-Fogg."

We smiled at each other, each knowing how important it is to guard your true name.

"That's a good one. What are you called for short?"

"KittyKitKit, but you can call me Kit. Are you a Princess or a Polly?"

"Polly's nicer."

"Well, Polly, I think we should get out of the water now."

"But it's lovely."

I didn't want to frighten her. Or indeed encourage her. She might think that transforming into a water nymph would be lovely too. "Yes but – I think we ought to dry off a bit in the sun. Otherwise they might not let us back on the bus."

She was a nice child because she said agreeably, "All right."

Once on dry land I gathered up our clothes, and insisted we both put on our sandals. They might not be comfortable on wet feet but they would protect our toes from accidentally digging too deep into the soil and rooting us. The Princess stepped into hers and, while I was still struggling with the buckles of mine, I heard her exclaim, "Oh look, they're having a picnic."

And they, or at least five elderly people I had noticed at the back of the bus when I boarded it, were. Its route ran through the grounds of the local hospital and I had assumed they had been coming away from medical appointments – perhaps a clinic they all attended. But they might just as easily have been bound for Central London to attend the Five Hundredth Annual Meeting of the Mystics and Magicians Society. Perhaps they were. Now they were sitting round a table, very obviously enjoying a meal. I did not even ask myself where it had all come from. Swimming gives you an appetite and my priorities were different. So, evidently, were Polly's.

"Do you think…" she wondered.

"We can but ask."

I led the way boldly up to the group. There was a lot of spare chairs and unused china but I half expected them to shout "No room, no room" like the Hatter and the March Hare in *Alice in Wonderland,* and with a lot more excuse than those rude creatures had. Unlike Alice, we were dressed in little more than soggy underwear. But an elderly lady and an old gentleman jumped up before I had even formulated my request, and fussed about finding us suitable seating. I was offered a shabby comfortable chair with large flat human feet carved at the ends of its legs, and Polly had a solid wooden seat suitable for the kind of acrobatics that even the politest children like to perform at the table.

I hesitated, wondering belatedly if this was fairy food, but the old gentleman, a dapper silver-haired man with a fine beard, who looked more like an Elizabethan Wizard than anyone wearing a corduroy jacket with leather elbow patches had any right to do, seemed to read my thoughts.

He winked at me and said, "Don't be afraid to eat. We're not quite *there...*" [by which I supposed he meant Faery] "...yet."

"Oh no indeed," said the lady. "Or I should not have asked you to join us."

Of course, if they *were* fairies that is exactly what they *would* say, to tempt and trap us, but when she poured me a cup of tea, hot and strong and stewed, so precisely how I like it, I took it gladly and looked round for something to eat. They catered for all tastes. Beardy man had a wooden trencher heaped with slices of beef, and a leather jack probably filled with beer because every time he took a pull from it, it left foam on his moustache, while the lady next to me was eating a soft-boiled egg with dippy toast which she abandoned to help Polly find her favourite cake, which, I heard her say, must be of a very particular sort.

"NO nuts and no yucky bits," she specified firmly. "And pink but not strawberry."

I left them to it and foraged for myself. When I raised the cover of the dish in front of me I found a glass bowl heaped with glossy caviar nestling in crushed ice and surrounded by all the traditional accompaniments. Obeying an impulse which seemed the right one I offered it round the table, and although my companions all seemed to take some very little had gone when it was passed back to me, and I settled down to eat as much caviar as I wanted, an unusual but deeply satisfying experience.

Whenever one of my companions found a special dish of their own they offered that round as well, so I had such titbits as a particularly delicious kind of small sausage, serrano ham, a slice of savoury omelette, and some delicate sushi to go with my fish eggs. There was little conversation apart from the odd "please" and "thank you" and "you really must try this", but there was a persistent sound, softened by distance into something no more annoying than the crooning of pigeons, coming from the young woman in the bus still pursuing her telephone monologue. When I had eaten precisely as much caviar as I wanted, I filled a plate with treats and took them to her, with a cup of tea. It seemed the right thing to do. When I laid them on the seat beside her she acknowledged me with a flick of the hand and a "Thanks, babes" and continued describing an incident involving CCTV cameras, an off-licence, and a cousin, which clearly couldn't end well, especially for the cousin. Everyone else on the bus was sound asleep. There was no sign of the mother and child duo who had made the journey hideous. I wondered where they had gone.

As I returned to my place I heard another sound, faint and far away at first, but coming closer until it was unmistakeably the noise of jolly singing. It was that traditional drunkard's anthem, "Nelly Dean", but intermingled with the sounds of the sistrum, of reed pipes and cries of "Evoe". Abruptly the monologue from the bus ceased and the young woman appeared at the door. She looked rapt, and as she listened the phone fell unheeded from her hand. Her face grew blank and beautiful. Her hair loosened itself from a savage ponytail to tumble over her shoulders, now covered with an actual leopard skin, over a white tunic. Her limbs were still large but they were shapely now – she had become a model for Praxiteles not Epstein.

The singing drew nearer and suddenly the Bacchic rout of Maenads, fauns, and old Silenus on his donkey, had filled the glade. I caught Polly's hand, not sure if I was reassuring her in case she was afraid, or fearful she might run off and join them. The feet of my chair shifted as if it wanted to dance off itself and join the crew. They had already gathered some modern worshippers on their way. Besides the classic Maenads in their leopard skins and the furry-trousered fauns, I saw a whole rugger team, complete with supporters, a group of girls in brief dayglo shorts and t-shirts extolling drinking establishments in the Balearic Islands, and some Goths. None of them (with the possible exception of Silenus and his donkey) were really drunk, just jolly with singing and dancing. They fell into reverent silence as the chariot drawn by four leopards, bearing the young Dionysus, beautiful as any Instagram model, swept into the glade and halted beside the bus.

He and she gazed at one another. He stretched out his hand. She took it and leaped up beside him. There was a sigh of sentimental appreciation from the revellers, a burst of "Evoes", rattling sistra, and, surprisingly, a chorus of "True Love", sung, rather well, by the rugger fans. A ragged line of rugger boys, holiday girls, Maenads, fauns and Goths joined arms and began an impromptu can-can to the music of Offenbach, from *Orpheus in the Underworld*, set for panpipes, voice and sistra. Boots, both Gothic and sporting, polished hooves, and bare feet, flew into the air as they high-kicked across the glade while others decorated the chariot, passengers and leopards with wreaths and garlands of orange blossom, singing an a cappella version of "I'm Getting Married in the Morning". I hoped this meant Dionysus intended to Do the Right Thing by the young woman. I could not work my way through the tangled genealogy of Olympus to find if he had a wife already, but probably that didn't matter much to a god. And perhaps the girl *was* his wife, or had been in another life.

The chariot moved out of the glade, heading the procession of merry makers, now all singing something both Greek and antique.

"Ah," said Beardy man, "the Epithalamium – the wedding hymn.".

"*Well*," said one elderly lady, "I hope she knows what she's doing."

"I very much doubt it," said another, "but I expect she'll enjoy it. What's the matter, Catty, not jealous, are you? Surely you don't envy her, stravaiging through the woods with an upstart like young Dion, at your age."

"Stravaiging never was my style," Catty said austerely. At the time I thought her name must be Catherine. Only later did I wonder if it was Hekate…

Beardy man looked up from his almost empty trencher and grinned. "Nonsense, Catty, you stravaige with the best of us under the full of an autumn moon."

Catty tried to look stern but blushed, looking quite pretty for a moment.

"But we are shocking our young guest, I fear," he added.

I hoped he meant Polly, but for myself I disclaimed the slightest touch of shock and a strong preference for a nice cup of tea over a Bacchic romp any time of the day.

"Quite right," he said, and reached for the huge brown teapot suddenly at his end of the table. "Shall I be mother?" he said, turning to an assembly of mugs which seemed to have come with the teapot although I had not seen them arrive. "Now," he smiled at Polly, "this is a rather unusual teapot. It doesn't always pour tea. What can I pour for you?"

"Lemonade," she said promptly. "Proper lemonade. With ice."

The ice sounded like a challenge but he only laughed and tapped the pot with a teaspoon. "Iced lemonade for the Princess, if you please." It was indeed proper lemonade. I could smell the sweet sharp scent from halfway down the table. The ice cubes were small and had some difficulty with the spout, but there they were.

This was clearly a well-known game. There were requests for camel's milk, honey-dew gathered from the grass of Hymettus, "a beaker full of the warm South" all of which were provided without a blink (the honey-dew smelt of fresh grass, honey and heaven) while a lady who had been nibbling health biscuits, the texture and probable taste of compressed straw, unexpectedly wanted breakfast tea with a shot of rum in it, and a man with glasses who had been perfectly silent during the meal brightened up and asked for hot chocolate. I requested my customary builders' tea, which came from the spout with the milk added, precisely to my taste. At the end of the demonstration Beardy man pulled the flags of all nations from the teapot until the table was heaped with vivid silks, then clapped his hands. The silk flew upwards turning into a multitude of brilliant butterflies as it did so, while the teapot became a cuddly brown rabbit.

We all applauded, Polly and I perhaps more energetically than the others who had, I suspected, seen this kind of thing before and were more tolerant than amazed. Nevertheless Beardy man stood up to take a bow.

"Ah, gets them every time," he said, winking at me. "From Rudolf of Prague to the Glasgow Empire on a wet Wednesday."

The rabbit lolloped across the table and nestled in Polly's arms.

"What will you call him?" Beardy man asked.

"You mean, he's mine?" she squeaked. The rabbit seemed to give her more surprise and pleasure than anything else that had happened.

"Well, he thinks so."

The rabbit was certainly gazing up adoringly at Polly.

"His name is Benjamin Bowmaneer," she said with perfect assurance.

"Did you really play the Glasgow Empire?" I asked.

"I did. And the end of the pier at Skegness. And Butlins. I even did children's parties, dressed as Drumbledrawers…"

"Dumbledore," Polly corrected firmly.

"No, it really was Drumbledrawers – something to do with copyright. Anyway that didn't last. There was an Incident involving white mice and my agency had to let me go."

"What happened?"

"I'm not proud of it. It was stupid machismo on both sides.

Some small boys, wretched little beasts as they all are at that age, just too old for make-believe and too young to put up with it for the sake of the food and the presents. They started shouting that I wasn't a real wizard and I – well, I proved I was."

"*So* wrong in *so* many ways, Magister," said Catty.

"I know." He looked downcast for a moment then added, "But *sooooo* satisfactory. For a few minutes at least. Less so when I realised I'd thrown away that particular source of income."

"But... If you can do real magic you could just turn lead into gold, or whatever, and have all the money you wanted without working."

"What, and give up show business?" he said, roaring with laughter at what was clearly an old joke. When he had his laugh he said, quite seriously, "But where's the *fun* in that?" I think he would have said more but Catty raised her long forefinger to her lips.

"Can I trouble you for a tot of tiger milk, Magister? My thumbs are pricking," she said.

He took a shot glass filled with a white creamy liquid from behind her left ear, with a conjuror's flourish, and she downed the drink in one. Everyone stopped eating. Polly and I pulled on our respective dress and skirt.

The air brightened, like a second more glorious sunrise, and filled with golden effulgence, as a woman walked into the glade. She was not beautiful. She was Beauty itself. It made your eyes swim to see her splendour. I knew even before I saw the lovely winged child beside her, that this was Aphrodite. She stood for a moment in her own golden light letting us worship. And then she opened her perfect mouth and screeched like a fishwife.

"Where izzzzit?"

Even Benjamin cowered in Polly's arms.

"My little boy, my Cupid was playing with – with a trinket on the bus. He dropped it when we stopped and I thought it had rolled off into the grass, being as it's tricksy, but we've hunted high and far and not found a sniff, so one of you must have pocketed it. Hand over!"

"My dear Lady," Beardy man said, "I'm sure if anyone has, inadvertently…"

There was a rustle from beside the bus as the driver attempted to wrap himself in his newspaper. Cupid flew at him quite literally, zipping across the glade like a hummingbird, and tore the paper away revealing a child almost as beautiful as he was, a little street urchin dressed in withered leaves, with pointed ears pricking through his dark curls. A Puck, but an Essex Puck. As Cupid began shaking him he whined, "I never, swipe me pink and hope to die, I never saw your rotten apple…"

"Apple!" Aphrodite launched herself at him. "You know it's an apple then, you little monster…"

He pulled something from the folds of his leafy shirt and bowled it overarm across the glade into the pool. We watched the golden apple turn in the air pursued by Cupid, who had almost grasped it when the waters rose up to snatch it from him, and plunged down so the pool became a fierce stream, then a river that broadened and flowed away through the bluebell woods. Puck danced after it, skipping on the surface of the water and singing something sounding like a rude version of "Where the Bee Sucks", the words luckily obscured by a strong Warwickshire accent.

"Ah. The Apple of Discord," said Beardy man.

"You mind your own business," she snarled, then, to my amazement, turned on me. "It's *your* fault. You've ruined my story by singing Wagner in a magic pool! Now we'll have evil dwarves, and Norse gods, and dragons too, I wouldn't be surprised. I should…" She raised her hand but Catty stepped between us.

"You should take yourself off, you baggage! I don't know what mischief brought you travelling incognito on public transport with a Dangerous Magical Object, but you've only got yourself to blame if it's gone wrong. All these people have had their journey interrupted and now you've lost us our driver, and

I don't know what we're going to do…"

Laughter-loving Aphrodite actually backed away as Catty advanced on her until she picked up her skirts and ran, plucking Cupid from the air as she went. Before she plunged into the trees, she did shake her fist at me and squalled, "You haven't heard the last of this."

But you could tell her heart wasn't in it.

"Don't worry about the driver, Catty," said Beardy man picking up the peaked cap from the grass. "I've got the hat. I'll drive us."

"But – Magister – *can* you drive?"

He turned and winked at us both.

"How hard can it be?"

~~~

And there my artistic instincts tell me to stop. But no, I must add that Beardy man got us to Walthamstow Bus Station at exactly the time we should have arrived if there had been no diversion. He must have negotiated time as well as space to do it, and it didn't take long. Polly, Catty and I sat in the back seat, and Catty just had time to explain to Polly that "Magister" meant "master" – as in "schoolmaster", she added sniffily – and Beardy man was either a wizard pretending to be a stage conjuror or the other way round. She, Polly, could decide, but as she was clutching a live rabbit which had started life as a teapot the answer seemed fairly evident.

To me she explained why so many Greek gods had turned up in an English forest – there always had been an overlap.

"Young Will's Fairy Queen was called Titania because she was a daughter of the Titans. And Old Geoffrey tells a story where the King and Queen of Faery are Proserpina and Pluto. Venus comes into that story too, causing trouble as usual."

When I thanked her for her for protecting me from Aphrodite's revenge she sniffed again and told me to thank the tiger milk. "You may still have some trouble with her. She could make you fall in love with someone quite unsuitable or vice versa. But with any luck she'll be distracted by a lot of Norse gods, and good luck with that. I'd back the Magister against Odin any day, and I'd quite like to meet Loki again." She smiled, reminiscently, I thought. "I'm a complete fangirl of his, like the rest of my Chapter. Well ... a handsome – whatever he *is* – with a sense of humour. Who likes women better than fighting. Not many of those about. And it would do him good. Take his mind off making ships from dead men's toenails, or whatever peculiar hobby he's up to these days. Well – take care."

I realised that the bus had stopped in the bus station and people were getting off. The driver had vanished (possibly literally), Catty and the others had gone, and a familiar voice was calling, "Channel! Channel! Hurry up do. And don't forget Benjy, although what people think about a big girl like you carrying a toy rabbit about…"

No. I'm not going to say I had fallen asleep in the heat and had a very silly dream, muddling the people on the bus with bits of myths and memories of a *Midsummer Night's Dream*. Or that Princess Polyanthus was only an ordinary little girl with a plush bunny.

As Polly got up to join the woman (mother? Aunt?) she turned to me and winked.

So did Benjamin.

# A TRICK OF THE DARK

"What kind of job finishes just at sun-set?

Margaret jumped slightly. "What a weird question, darling. Park keeper, I suppose." Something made her turn to look at her daughter. She was propped up against her pillows, looking, Margaret thought guiltily, about ten years old. She must keep remembering, she told herself fiercely, that Maddie was nineteen. This silly heart-thing, as she called it, was keeping her in bed for much longer than they ever thought it would but it couldn't stop her growing up... She must listen to her and talk to her like a grown-up.

Intending to do just that she went to sit on the edge of the bed. It was covered with a glossy pink eiderdown, embroidered with fat pink and mauve peonies. The lamp on Maddie's bedside table had a rosy shade. Maddie was wearing a pink bed-jacket, lovingly crocheted by her grandmother, and Maddie's pale blonde hair was tied back with a pink ribbon... But in the midst of this plethora of pink, Maddie's face looked pale and peaky. The words of a story she had read to Maddie once – how many years ago? – came back to her: "Peak and pine, peak and pine." It was about a changeling child who never thrived, but lay in the cradle, crying and fretting, peaking and pining ... in the end the creature had gone back to its own people and, she supposed, that the healthy child had somehow got back to his mother, but she couldn't remember. Margaret shivered, wondering why people thought such horrid stories were suitable for children.

"What made you wonder who finishes work at sunset?"

"Oh – nothing." Maddie looked oddly shy, as she might have done if her mother had asked her about a boy who had partnered her at tennis, or asked her to a dance. If such a thing could ever have happened. She played with the pink ribbons at her neck and a little, a very little, colour crept into that pale face. "It's just –well – I can't read all the time, or –" She hesitated and Margaret mentally filled in the gap. She had her embroidery, her knitting, those huge complicated jigsaws that her friends were so good about finding for her, a notebook for jotting down those funny little verses that someone was going to ask someone's uncle about publishing ... but all that couldn't keep her occupied all day.

"Sometimes I just look out of the window," she said.

"Oh, darling..." She couldn't bear to think of her daughter just lying there – just looking out of the window. "Why don't you call me when you get bored? We could have some lovely talks. Or I could telephone Bunty or Cissie or..." It's getting quite autumnal after all, she thought, and Maddie's friends won't be out so much, playing tennis, or swimming or... You couldn't expect them to sit for hours in a sickroom. They dashed in, tanned and breathless from their games and bicycle rides, or windblown and glowing from a winter walk, and dropped off a jigsaw or a new novel ... and went away.

"I don't mind, mummy," Maddie was saying. "It's amazing what you can see, even in a quiet street like this. I mean, that's why I like this room. Because you can see out."

Margaret looked out of the window. Yes. You could see a stretch of pavement, a bit of Mrs Creswell's hedge, a lamppost, the post-box, and Mrs Monkton's gate. "It was not precisely an enticing view, and she exclaimed, "Oh, darling!" again.

"You'd be amazed who visits Mrs Monkton in the afternoons," Maddie said demurely.

"Good heavens, who..." she began, but Maddie gave a reassuringly naughty giggle.

"That would be telling! You'll have to sit up here one afternoon and watch for yourself."

"I might," Margaret said. But how could she? There was always so much to do downstairs, letters to write, shopping to do, and cook to deal with. (Life to get on with?) She too, she realised, dropped in on Maddie, left her with things to sustain or amuse her. And went away.

"Perhaps we could move you downstairs, darling."

But that would be so difficult. The doctor had absolutely forbidden Maddie to use the stairs, so how on earth could they manage what Margaret could only, even in the privacy of her thoughts, call "the bathroom problem"? Too shame-making for Maddie to have to ask to be carried up the stairs every time she needed – and who was there to do it during the day? Maddie was very light – much too light – but her mother knew that she could not lift her, let alone carry her by herself.

"But you can't see anything from the sitting-room," Maddie said.

"Oh darling—" Margaret realised she was going to have to leave Maddie alone again. Her husband would be home soon and she was beginning to have serious doubts about the advisability of re-heating the fish-pie. She must have a quick word with cook about cheese omelettes. If only cook wasn't so bad with eggs. "What's this about sunset anyway?" she said briskly.

"Sunset comes a bit earlier every day. And just at sunset a man walks down the street."

"The same man, every night?"

"The same man, always just after sunset,"

"Perhaps he's a postman?"

"Then he'd wear a uniform," Maddie said patiently. "And the same if he was a park-keeper I suppose – they wear uniform too, don't they. Besides he doesn't look like a postman."

"So – what does he look like?"

"It's hard to explain," Maddie struggled for the right words. "But – can you imagine a beautiful skull?"

"What! What a horrible idea!" Margaret stood up, clutching the grey foulard at her bosom. "Maddie, if you began talking like this I shall call Dr Whiston. I don't care if he doesn't like coming out after dinner. Skull-headed men walking past the house every night, indeed!"

Maddie pouted. "I didn't say that. It's just that his face is very – sculptured. You can see the bones under the skin, especially the cheek bones. It just made me think – he must even have a beautiful skull."

"And how is he dressed?"

"A white shirt and a sort of loose black coat. And he has quite long curly black hair. I think he might be a student."

"No hat?" Her mother was scandalised. "He sounds more like an anarchist! Really Maddie, I wonder if I should go and have a word with the policeman on the corner and tell him a suspicious character has been hanging about outside the house."

"No mother!" Maddie sounded so anguished that her mother hastily laid a calming hand on her forehead.

"Now darling, don't upset yourself. You must remember what the doctor said. Of course I won't call him if you don't want me to, or the policeman. That was a joke, darling! But you mustn't get yourself upset like this... Oh dear, your forehead feels quite clammy. Here, take one of your tablets. I'll get you a glass of water."

And in her very real anxiety for her daughter, worries about the fish pie and well-founded doubts about the substitute omelettes, Margaret almost forgot about the stranger. Almost but not quite. A meeting with Mrs Monkton one evening when they had both hurried out to catch the last post and met in front of the post-box reminded her, and she found herself asking if Mrs Monkton had noticed anyone "hanging about".

"A young man," Mrs Monkton exclaimed with a flash of what Margaret decided was rather indecent excitement. "But darling, there are no young men left." Margaret raised a hand in mute protest only to have it brushed aside by Mrs Monkton. "Well, not nearly enough to go round, anyway. I expect this one was waiting for Elsie."

Elsie worked for both Mrs Monkton and Margaret, coming in

several times a week to do "the rough", the cleaning that was beneath Margaret's cook and Mrs Monkton's extremely superior maid. She was a handsome girl with, it was rumoured, an obliging disposition, who would never have been allowed across the threshold of a respectable household when Margaret was young. But nowadays... Mrs Monkton's suggestion did set Margaret's mind at rest. A hatless young man – yes, he must be waiting for Elsie. She might "have a word" with the girl about the propriety of encouraging young men to hang about the street for her, but, on the other hand, she might not. She hurried back home.

~~~

Bunty's mother came to tea, full of news. Bunty's elder sister was getting engaged to someone her mother described as "a bit nqos, but what can you do..." Nqos was a rather transparent code for "not quite our sort". The young man's father was, it appeared, very, very rich, though no one was quite sure where he had made his money. He was going to give – to give – outright, Bunty's mother had gasped, a big house in Surrey to the young couple. And he was going to furnish it too, unfortunately, according to his own somewhat ... individual taste.

"Chrome, my dear, chrome from floor to ceiling. The dining room looks like a milk bar. And as for the bedroom, Jack says–" she lowered her voice "–he says it looks like an avant garde brothel in Berlin. Although how he knows anything about them I'm sure I'm not going to ask. But he's having nothing to do with the wedding," she added, sipping her tea as if it were hemlock. "I wonder my dear – would dear little Maddie be well enough to be a bridesmaid? It won't be until next June. I want to keep Pammy to myself for as long as I can." She dabbed at her eyes.

"Of course," Margaret murmured doubtfully. And then, with more determination, "I'll ask the doctor."

~~~

And, rather surprising herself, she did. On his next visit to Maddie she lured him into the sitting-room with the offer of a glass of sherry and let him boom on for a while on how well Maddie was responding to his treatment. Then she asked the Question, the one she had, until that moment, had not dared to ask.

"But when will Maddie be – quite well? Could she be a bridesmaid, say, in June next year?"

The doctor paused, sherry half-way to his lips. He was not used to being questioned. Margaret realised that he thought she had been intolerably frivolous. "Bridesmaid?" the doctor boomed. And then thawed visibly. Women, he knew, cared about such things. "Bridesmaid! Well, why not? Provided she goes on as well as she has been. And you don't let her get too excited. Not too many dress fittings, you know, and see you get her home early after the wedding. No dancing and only a tiny glass of champagne…"

"And will she ever we well enough … to … to … marry herself and to…" But Margaret could not bring herself to finish that sentence to a man, not even a medical man.

"Marry – well, I wouldn't advise it. And babies? No. No. Still, that's the modern girl isn't it? No use for husbands and children these days—" And he boomed himself out of the house.

Margaret remembered that the doctor had married a much younger woman. Presumably the marriage was not a success … then she let herself think of Maddie. She wondered if Bunty's mother would like to exchange places with her. Margaret would never have to lose her daughter to the son of a nouveau riche war profiteer. Never … and she sat down in her pretty chintz covered armchair and cried as quietly as she could, in case Maddie heard her. For some reason she never asked herself how far the doctor's confident boom might carry. Later she went up to her daughter, smiling gallantly.

"The doctor's so pleased with you, Maddie," she said. "He thinks you'll be well enough to be Pammy's bridesmaid! You'll have to be sure you finish her present in nice time."

Margaret had bought a tray cloth and six place mats stamped

with the design of a figure in a poke bonnet and a crinoline, surrounded by flowers. Maddie was supposed to be embroidering them in tasteful naturalistic shades of pink, mauve and green, as a wedding gift for Pammy, but she seemed to have little enthusiasm for the task. Her mother stared at her, lying back in her nest of pillows. "Peak and pine! Peak and pine!" said the voice in her head.

"Do you ever see your young man, anymore?" she asked, more to distract herself than because she was really concerned.

"Oh no," Maddie said, raising her shadowed eyes to her mother. "I don't think he was ever there at all. It was a trick of the dark."

"Trick of the light, surely," Margaret said. And then, almost against her will, "Do you remember that story I used to read you? About the changeling child?"

"What, the one that lay in the cradle saying, 'I'm old, I'm old, I'm ever so old?'" Maddie said. "Whatever made you think of that?"

"I don't know," Margaret gasped. "But you know how you sometimes get silly words going round and round your head – it's as if I can't stop repeating those words from the story. 'Peak and pine!' to myself over and over again." There, she had said it aloud. That must exorcise them, surely.

"But that's not from the changeling story," Maddie said. "It's from 'Christabel', you know. Coleridge's poem about the weird Lady Geraldine. She says it to the mother's ghost: 'Off wandering mother! Peak and pine!' We read it at school but Miss Brownrigg made us miss out all that bit about Geraldine's breasts."

"I should think so, too," Margaret said weakly.

~~~

Autumn became winter, although few people noticed by what tiny degrees the days grew shorter and shorter until sunset came at around four o'clock. Except perhaps Maddie, sitting propped up on her pillows and watching every day for the young man who still walked down the street every evening, in spite of what she had told her mother. And even she could not have said just when he stopped walking directly passed the window and took to standing in that dark spot just between the lamppost and the post-box, look up at her...

"Where's your little silver cross, darling?" Margaret said suddenly, wondering vaguely when she had last seen Maddie wearing it.

"Oh, I don't know," Maddie said, too casually. "I think the clasp must have broken and it slipped off."

"Oh but—" Margaret looked helplessly at her daughter. "I do hope Elsie hasn't picked it up. I sometimes think—"

"I expect it'll turn up," Maddie said. Her eyes slid away from her mother's face and returned to the window.

"How's Pammy's present coming along?" Margaret asked, speaking to that white reflection in the dark glass, trying to make her daughter turn back to her. She picked up Maddie's workbag. And stared. One of the place mats had been completed. But the figure of the lady had been embroidered in shades of black and it was standing in the midst of scarlet roses and tall purple lilies. It was cleverly done: every fold and flounce was picked out ... but Margaret found it rather disturbing. She was glad that the poke bonnet hit the figure's face... She looked up to realise that Maddie was looking at her almost slyly.

"Don't you like it?" she said.

"It's – it's quite modern, isn't it?"

"What, lazy daisies and crinoline ladies, modern?" How long had Maddie's voice had that lazy mocking tone? She sounded like a world-weary adult talking to a very young and silly child.

Margaret put the work down.

~~~

"You will be all right, darling, won't you?" Margaret said, rushing into her daughter's room one cold December afternoon. "Only I must do some Christmas shopping, I really must."

"Of course you must, mummy," Maddie said. "You've got

my list, haven't you? Do try to find something really nice for Bunty, she's been so kind…"

And what I would really like to give her, Maddie thought is a whole parcel of jigsaws … and all the time in the world to see how she likes them. She leaned against her pillows, watching her mother scurry down the street. She would catch a bus at the corner by the church, and then an underground train, and then face the crowded streets and shops of a near-Christmas West End London. Maddie would have plenty of time to herself. She knew (although her mother did not) that cook would be going out to have tea with her friend at Mrs Cresswell's at half-past three, and for at least one blessed hour she would be entirely alone in the house.

She pulled herself further up in the bed, and fumbled in the drawer of her bedside table to find the contraband she had managed to persuade Elsie to bring in for her. Elsie had proved much more useful than Bunty, or Cissie, or any of her kind friends. She sorted through the scarlet lipstick, the eye-black, the face-powder, and began to draw the kind of face she knew she had always wanted on the blank canvas of her pale skin. After twenty minutes of careful work she felt she had succeeded rather well.

"I'm old, I'm old, I'm ever so old," she crooned to herself. She freed her hair from its inevitable pink ribbon, and brushed it sleekly over her shoulders, then she took off her lacy bed-jacket and the white winceyette nightie beneath it. Finally she slid into the garment the invaluable Elsie had found for her (Heaven knows where – although Maddie had a shrewd suspicion it might have been stolen from another of Elsie's clients – perhaps the naughty Mrs Monkton). It was a nightdress made of layers of black and red chiffon, just a little too large for Maddie, but the way it tended to slide from her shoulders could have, she felt, its own attraction.

All these preparations had taken quite a long time, especially as Maddie had had to stop every so often to catch her breath and once to take one of her tablets … but she was ready just before sunset. She slipped out of bed, crossed the room, and sat in a chair beside the window. So. The trap was almost set (but was she the trap or only the bait…). Just one thing remained to be done.

Maddie took out her embroidery scissors and, clenching her teeth, ran the tiny sharp points into a blue vein in her wrist…

~~~

The bus was late and crowded. Margaret struggled off, trying to balance her load of packages and parcels, and hurried down the road, past the churchyard wall, past Mrs Monkton's redbrick villa, past the post-box – and hesitated. For a moment she thought she had seen something – Maddie's strange man with the beautiful skull-like face? But no, there were two white faces there in the shadows – no … there was nothing. A trick of the dark… She dropped her parcels in the hall and hurried up the stairs.

~~~

"Here I am, darling, I'm so sorry I'm late… Oh, Maddie – Maddie darling … whatever are you doing in the dark?"

She switched on the light.

"Maddie. Maddie, where are you?" she whispered. "What have you done?"

# CASUALTIES OF THE SYSTEM

"There is such a thing," said Mr Scroggins heavily, "as having *too* much of a good thing."

Mr Witherspoon peered at the papers Mr Scroggins had placed before him on the highly polished table. "Ah ... do you think so? Hm – hm – I suppose excess is always bad. 'Medio tutissimus ibis' as – er – Ovid has it."

Mr Scroggins looked at him with bulging eyed incomprehension and he translated, kindly, "The middle road is the safest way – moderation in all things. But is it *possible* to have an excess of good? An interesting philosophical question." He smiled hopefully.

"We are not here to discuss philosophy, Mr Witherspoon," Mr Scroggins informed him. "We are here to discuss the record of your Young Persons Rehabilitation Department."

"Ah," said Mr Witherspoon. "Well, in that case I think we had better have some coffee."

"I have ordered some, Mr Witherspoon," said Mrs Taylor. She was a soft-faced apparently rather nervous lady who currently represented the Probation Department. Mr Scroggins had instantly tabled her as being Not Up to the Job, which made her record all the more extraordinary. And suspect.

"Splendid, splendid," Mr Witherspoon was saying, "we can always rely on you, Mrs Taylor."

She looked as if she would be about as useful as a lace parasol in a thunderstorm, thought Mr Scroggins, and then mentally amended that to a lace parasol with a long metal tip. Dangerous as well as useless. She would Break Down Under Stress. And that, as far as he could see, went for the lot of them. Mr Witherspoon maundered on like an elderly classics master –

from Central Casting. He wouldn't last five minutes in a real school. Mr Hornbeam must be well past retirement age, plus he seemed to be deaf, or perhaps he was just not sufficiently interested in the proceedings to listen.

Mr Scroggins was an emissary from the new Department of Political Awareness, and occupied a position roughly corresponding that that of the late Witchfinder General, being employed to sniff out backslidings and failings to take cognisance of the new climate of ferocious political correctness. He was not accustomed to people who did not listen to him. The rest of the rabble sitting round the table was just that. Rabble. One of them was ACTUALLY LOOKING AT HIS WATCH.

Mr Scroggins opened his mouth to administer a magisterial rebuke. At precisely the same moment the door also opened and an unbelievably ancient woman (surely she must be past statutory retirement age as well? He must look into their retirement policies – it was amazing what appalling derelictions you found in places like this when you just lifted one stone...) came in with a trolley. No group of people can have coffee poured for them without a whole babel of "milk?" "Sugar?" "Very weak/strong for me, please." "Is there any tea?" "Could you pass the biscuits?" And even, horrifyingly, "Just touch my cup Mabel, you'll make it sweet enough for me," from someone surely old enough to know better than to indulge in what could well be construed as sexual harassment, and the moment passed. Even Mr Scroggins realised this. He waited with barely concealed impatience until everyone was coffeed to his or her satisfaction and the awkward one provided with a cup of tea. Then he tore into the matter closest to his heart.

"You have too many successes," he announced.

Half-a-dozen faces turned towards him. They did not, he noticed, look at all surprised. They simply looked mildly inquiring, like cattle peering over a hedge.

"Over the past year," Mr Scroggins said in tones of direst foreboding, "the rate of youth crime in this district has fallen–"

he almost said disastrously but changed it in time to "–unbelievably. Every male person remitted to your department is now either in full or part-time education, training, or gainfully employed. Or a combination thereof. One–" he frowned down at the paper he had retained "–is married *as well* as being in full time employment; and two appear to have entered a seminary." He coughed, not sure whether these should have been counted as failures. He certainly did not consider they were either being educated *or* trained, but he decided to leave them for later and to attack his main objective: "But there are three who seem to have vanished from your books entirely."

"Jason Doakes, Wayne Trenchard, and Hannibal Toop," murmured Mrs Taylor.

"Hannibal?" Mr Scroggins repeated incredulously.

Mrs Taylor cleared her throat nervously. "His mother was a great admirer of a cinematic production, I believe, dealing with, er…"

"Murder and cannibalism," Mr Witherspoon murmured rather apologetically.

"Yes," said Mrs Taylor. "Well, with a start like that…"

Mr Witherspoon shook his head sadly. "One of our failures," he agreed.

"Yes, but what *happened* to him?" Mr Scroggins demanded. "And to the other two, Jason and Wayne?"

"Doakes and Trenchard were, I am afraid, casualties of the system," said Mr Witherspoon.

Mr Scroggins bristled. That was one of his own phrases. It meant, in his terms, simply young offenders. Not young offenders who had vanished into thin air.

"They were some of the early entry," said Mrs Taylor. "We've – learned things since then."

"And so have the little scrotes remitted to the department. Didn't care for the idea of being casualties of the system themselves," Mr Hornbeam rumbled unexpectedly. "Stories seem to have got about – somehow." He grinned, showing a set of horrendous brown pipe-smoker's fangs. "Did us no end of good."

"What system?" Mr Scroggins roared.

"Well—" Mr Witherspoon and Mrs Taylor began simultaneously, then courteously waved the other to go on. This, inevitably, resulted in an awkward silence broken only by the sound of a digestive biscuit being ground between Mr Hornbeam's teeth.

"I don't care who tells me," said Mr Scroggins, now entering his quieter – and more dangerous – phase, "just so long as somebody does."

Mr Witherspoon cleared his throat. "Well, I suppose it's *our* system. Although we *are* in discussion with other authorities who are hoping to adopt it. You see, at the beginning of this year we experimented with the system of sending some of our worst cases on – er—" He hesitated.

"Safari," Mrs Taylor supplied.

"Precisely. On safari. To – er – to find themselves. And it has been successful beyond our wildest dreams."

Mr Scroggins' eyes narrowed. It was the last thing he had expected from this backward-looking conservative mob, and he did not believe it for a moment.

"You've been sending these unfortunate lads on foreign holidays?" he said.

"Not quite holidays," Mr Hornbeam said robustly. "I'd call it work experience myself."

Everyone at the table nodded gently. "It *was* at your suggestion," Mrs Taylor reminded him gently.

"And you managed to *lose* three of them?"

"Not – *lose* – precisely," said Mr Witherspoon. "We do know exactly what happened to them."

"Look, you can't go pushing these lads out of your district to clutter up other peoples' lists. We could all do that and it wouldn't help."

"We didn't," Mrs Taylor protested. "Hannibal Toop *wanted*

to stay."

"One of our failures," Mr Witherspoon repeated sadly.

"Refused to come back," Mr Hornbeam bellowed unexpectedly. "Got himself a job. Well, good luck to him, I say. *And* he'll need it. Don't suppose Mr Wilde will put up with him for long."

"So he took a job with a Mr Wilde. I hope this Wilde character went through the proper checks," Mr Scroggins said. "Where is his business?"

"Lewknors Lane, off Drury Lane," said Mr Hornbeam promptly. "At Jonathan Wilde's Lost Property Office. Ugly customer, Wilde. But then so was Toop." He cackled. "And good luck to *you* if you want to check on Wilde's suitability to – er – mentor young people. What did he call that six-year-old boy that was tried at the Old Bailey for stealing an oyster woman's rings "A young game cock of my own breeding?" He carried him out of the court on his shoulder when the judge acquitted him out of pity. Don't see him doing that with Toop. More likely to collect the forty-pound hanging fee on him."

Mr Scroggins ignored these senile maunderings, and jotted down the address. "But if he's working in London at a known address, then he must appear in your records. And if, by some unpardonable carelessness he does not, a phone call should find him."

"You won't find Wilde in any telephone directory. He lived in *eighteenth*-century London," said Mr Hornbeam. "He finished on the gallows of course. With any luck so will – or has – Toop."

Mr Scroggins opened his mouth but no sound emerged.

"Now Doakes was an arsonist," said Mr Witherspoon "He set fire to his school, amongst other buildings."

Mrs Taylor dabbed her eyes. "The school-keeper."

"The school-keeper went back for his cat. Saved it too, but he'd inhaled too much smoke. Died in hospital."

"I took poor Ginger in," Mrs Taylor said. "Of course he misses Harry but he really has settled down very well. Such a *brave* old boy..."

"What happened to Jason?" Mr Scroggins gritted.

"His mother, as they so often do," said Mr Witherspoon, "said he was no angel but he wasn't a bad boy, really. He got blamed for things he hadn't done, she said, and he was easily led. He'd set fire to the school because he was bored. He was only really interested in dinosaurs."

"So we sent him where he'd find plenty of dinosaurs. But I rather think they found him first," said Mr Hornbeam. He slid a folder in front of Mr Scroggins. It contained some colour photographs. The keynote colour was red. They were either astonishing examples of special effects ... or they were not.

"And Wayne Trenchard?" Mr Scroggins croaked, looking away quickly.

"Trenchard mugged old ladies," Mr Witherspoon said. "You don't make huge amounts of money from that, of course. A purse with a few pounds. Perhaps a ring, almost worthless except as a treasured memento of a dead husband. But of course old ladies don't on the whole fight back. And if they do ... well, there *were* two deaths. But it was probably fear and shock rather than actual injury, and very hard to bring home to the perpetrator... And his surviving victims were often too frightened and confused to identify him."

"Sent *him* back to the Vikings," said Mr Hornbeam, with senile relish. "Lasted three days. Someone hit *him* on the head. Good riddance."

"And then, of course, word got round," said Mr Witherspoon. "Offences, as you have noticed, began to drop quite dramatically. If you know you risk spending even just a few weeks as a powder monkey on *The Victory*, for instance, or a drummer boy at Waterloo or even just in a Marylebone workhouse in the 1850s – well a lot of crime probably doesn't seem worthwhile. It even seems a better idea to stay sober if you know you can't control yourself when you're drunk – or at least to stay at home to do it if you must drink to excess."

"And for the milder cases there's always nineteenth-century Eton," said Mr Hornbeam. "They think it's a soft option. But they learn…" He cackled reminiscently. "Terrible food. Ghastly accommodation. Greek. Latin. Swishings … and I believe it was worse back then."

"Or they can take a course in pyramid building. Healthy outdoor life, plenty of exercise, splendid diet consisting mainly of lentils with lots of garlic and onions…" Mr Witherspoon offered.

"*And* those overseers with whips," said Mr Hornbeam, jovially. "Still, you only have to *mention* the Black Death to have them blubbing and begging for the pyramids. Although I have a theory that we're all descendants of the ones who *survived* the Black Death, so we've probably got natural immunity, but no one yet's had the guts to give it a try. Even when I offered an incentive of half-a-crown and a week off their sentence," he added in an aggrieved tone. "No backbone, lads, these days. No sense of adventure."

"So," said Mr Scroggins in the tones of one humouring several possibly dangerous loonies. "You send your young offenders back in time." They nodded. "And how do you do that?"

"Witchcraft, dear," said a voice from the end of the table. He realised that the lady with the trolley had remained for their discussion. She was sitting down, leaning her elbows on the table in a way Mr Scroggins found unnecessarily familiar. "The further back you go the easier it is. Can't do the twentieth century at all, which I suppose is a good thing. Can't have people going back and interfering with the timelines. Anything earlier and any changes you make seem to iron themselves out – over the years."

Mr Witherspoon nodded. "We are very lucky to have, in Mabel, a most proficient psychic practitioner – I think Mr Scroggins would prefer that term to "witch", Mabel – who has discovered not only how to manipulate the time portals with remarkable precision, but how to set up surveillance cameras so that we can keep an eye on our clients' progress. And record it, of course."

He passed Mr Scroggins a whole pile of folders. He leafed through them. The photographs were beautifully crisp and clear (they had been rather too clear in the case of Jason Doakes – those prints left no doubt at all about his fate). Of course they were stills from films. He could have them identified without any difficulty – and pictures of the youthful clients of the Rehabilitation Department had simply been photoshopped into them (although how they had managed it with the … the *fragments* of Jason Doakes, he could not think). He was quite sure that everyone in the room was either quite mad or indulging in a very silly and elaborate hoax. The department would be closed. There would be sackings – there would be … a detail occurred to him which would destroy the whole silly tissue of lies at once.

"Your rehabilitation centre is always full. Where do the – er – residents come from?"

"We have a reciprocal programme," Mrs Taylor said

"We do indeed," said Mr Hornbeam. "Get an intake of work'us boys, feed them up, teach them about the rights of man – and woman – and you'd be amazed how they jolly things up for the authorities when they go back."

"But how," Mr Scroggins inquired cunningly, "do you persuade them to go *back?*"

"Most people want to go home however bad that home may be. Some have mothers whom they discover that they love, sometimes much more than they realised. Many have friends and families – and sweethearts," said Mrs Taylor gently. "Hannibal Toop was quite a surprise. Perhaps he had no one."

"*That* wouldn't be a surprise," Mr Hornbeam muttered.

"We have kept a few. Mrs Taylor, for instance, has adopted two little refugees from the Thirty Years War," Mr Witherspoon said.

"Hansel and Gretel," Mrs Taylor agreed. "We really–" her

voice broke a little "–really couldn't send them back. They had seen things you could not *believe*. Except of course we know that they were true. Are true. I have had to become vegetarian. Little Gretel cannot *endure* the smell of cooking meat…"

Mr Scroggins glared round. "Hansel and Gretel is about right," he snarled. "Because I think you lot have been telling me a lot of fairy tales."

"Their names are not really Hansel and Gretel," Mrs Taylor said with a sudden accession of quiet dignity. "They couldn't tell us what their real names were. The little boy has only just started to speak. The little girl gave me two German words that could be roughly translated as Chops and Steak. I think they may have been called this as a – a – joke on the part of the … of whoever had been holding them prisoner."

"There is a surprising amount of truth hidden in fairy stories," said Mr Hornbeam with sudden gravity. "Think – but not too hard – about why a child could have been frightened so badly by a simple kitchen smell. She and the boy, by the way, were being kept in a kind of chicken coop. They could barely move, and they were filthy … but they were being well fed." He paused then added, "One of our lads found them and got them out. We brought the lot of them back, remitted the rest of his sentence and found him a job. Deserved it."

"Supposing – just supposing – I were to believe this farrago of nonsense," said Mr Scroggins, trying not to suppose any such thing, "how do you justify your treatment of these unfortunate children?" He thumped his palm on the photographs to make it clear which unfortunates he was talking about.

Mr Witherspoon rose up. "But they were not children. Doakes, Trenchard and Toop were, by any standards except yours, young men. The State itself concedes that they were old enough to marry. My grandfather was serving his country at their age. Doakes was taller than I am and certainly a good deal stronger. He was capable of work but he chose to make his money by robbing the most vulnerable people in our society, women, elderly and frail *women* – like our mothers and our grandmothers – who are entitled to our help and protection – to our *respect* – by any standards. We sent him to a society where he could have thriven but he chose, instead, to continue his attacks upon the old and frail. And he paid the price. Trenchard was quite sane but he was ridden with hatred, hatred for the school which tried to teach and control him, for the homes he did not own – reckless of human life, he killed a better man than he would ever have become to feed his mindless appetite for destruction. And he finally fed an appetite greater although more innocent than his own. And Toop – Toop has found his master in Wilde, thief and thief taker, a murderer who used the law to carry out his murders for him, and who died at last by his own instrument of murder, the hangman's rope."

Bur Mr Scroggins could bear no more. He stood up. "Very well. Very well, Mr Witherspoon," he said, "you will be hearing from me shortly."

He strode to the door.

"No dear," said Mabel, "this way."

She had opened another door, a door in the blank wall. A door that was not, could not be there. Beyond it was darkness and a hot swampy smell. And he could hear things out there – huge things lumbering through the dark. Mr Hornbeam, showing a surprising turn of speed, tipped him through the opening before he had even thought of taking evasive action.

And it closed behind him.

# "IT'S WHITE AND IT FOLLOWS ME"

Dean Swift tells of a kind of witty game called "Selling a Bargain", much played by the maids of honour to Queen Anne – a game perhaps more witty than decent – for it consists in the seller "naming his or her hinder parts" in answer to the question "what?" which the buyer is artfully led to ask. As a specimen, take the following instance: A lady comes into a room full of company, apparently in a fright, crying out "it is white and it follows me!" On any of the company asking "what?" she sells him the bargain by saying "mine arse". And the company laughs heartily.

Only this victim – and Lady Mary – do not laugh. Lady Mary's face is painted white and red, with the scarlet mouth and bright rouged cheeks of a Dutch doll, as is proper for a fine court lady, but under the paint she has a pale skin with a faint gold-dusting of freckles, like her Highland mother, and her eyes are not round and black but long and sea-green. And there are those who will tell you that she wears her silk stockings even to bed, to hide the toes which still show the marks where the midwife clipped the webs that joined them together when she was born, and that those webs are the legacy of her great grandfather, who was a seal-man from Sule Skerry. Of course everyone has her detractors and the Court is a hotbed of gossip. But it cannot be denied that Lady Mary has strange blood

"Lady Mary does not care for such wit," says old Lady Ramillies, the most recent victim of the jest. Her tall fontange quivers with anger and she cracks her fan like a whip, for she takes no more pleasure in being laughed at than any common body, and the latest bargain-seller has a mother who, as her

Ladyship has been heard to say, was well content to walk out in Moorefields a-Sundays in a cherryderry gown faced with calico, for all her daughter has come to be such a fine lady, making sport of her betters in her damask hoop.

"It is never good to make-sport of such things," says Lady Mary and bites her painted lip. But the old dowager is talking of indecency and backsides, and Lady Mary, who has a pawky tongue of her own, is not.

Lady Mary's family is good enough (if you discount or disbelieve in the seal-man). There are few at court who know more of the Highlands than they do of Russia or the South Sea Islands, and just as any visitor from such out-of-the-way places may come to court and pass as a prince, so Lady Mary's mother had the name of a great lady when her husband brought her home and presented her to merry King Charles. Whatever the truth of that might be, there are certainly no calico-trimmed gowns made of mixed silk and cotton in her family. She has her share of beauty too, but such money as the family had has been spent upon the young heir.

Lady Mary is lucky to have a place at court, but she must save and contrive and stretch her credit to pay for her own damask hoops and high lace head dressings, and somehow she must set out her beauty to sell herself as a bargain to some rich man before that beauty fades. She has no support in this venture because her father is dead, and her mother is – strange. She was once one of the sights of Whitehall, with her lovely face and her fine head of red-gold hair – and her empty eyes that stared at sights which no one else could see, while her lips moved in an endless conversation with her unseen companions. At last Lady Mary found two strong maids to watch over her and now she keeps to her apartments. She still has her lovely face, for time's ravages pass such creatures by, and her blank mad beautiful eyes. And the young heir is in Europe following Marlborough, it is said.

Lady Mary sits in her mother's apartment, so close to the roof of Kensington House that it is almost an attic, mending her stockings by the light of the fire, to save coin on candles. On the other side of the hearth sits her mother, playing with an old broken bead necklace that she slides between her fingers as she croons and mutters.

"What does she say, my Lady?" asks one maid curiously.

Lady Mary decides that she will dispense with that one's services as soon as a good replacement can be found.

"I do not know," she snaps. "She has gone back to the speech of her childhood and I have no Erse."

She is safe enough there, for the maids have no Erse, nor Latin either, and they will not recognise the *Aves* that her mother murmurs and if they catch her repetition of the name Maria, they will think she talks of her daughter. Or *to* her, for all she hardly seems to realise that Lady Mary is there.

Lady Mary breaks off her silk thread with a sideways grind of her strong white teeth. It is late and the maids are yawning. She tells them to go to bed if they will, for though her mother hardly needs to sleep and will not lie down, it will be safe enough to leave her alone for she has a fear of flames and will not meddle with the fire. As for Lady Mary, she must go about her duties. Day or night there must always be ladies awake and ready to wait upon the Queen, should she need them. She turns away from the curious stares of the maids to slide her mended stockings on her feet, but swings back to the fire to roll them to her knees and tie her garters, and they wonder if the stories about her toes are true. Then she puts on her buckled shoes, takes her fan in her hand, and goes out. They hear her heels clip-clocking along the corridor, down the stairs, and away.

But Lady Mary does not go towards the Queen's apartments. She turns instead to the Orangery, where no oranges can ripen because, apparently, it did not occur to either Hawksmoor or Vanbrugh, learned architects as they were, who were both concerned with its structure, to provide it with a glass roof. But this does not matter. The Queen is happy enough to use it as a banqueting house and a few hours ago it was glittering bright with candles. Now it is dark and empty – but not quite empty. Someone is waiting at the far end amongst the fruit trees that will never bear fruit. She sees the glint of a white shirt in the gloom and hurries towards it.

Moments later she is wrapped in strong arms, and all her artfully applied face-paint is being kissed away. But only too soon for Lady Mary, her lover lifts his head to gasp out the same old song of "if you loved me you would…". But he is not begging for what is quaintly called "the last favour", a favour Lady Mary is willing enough to grant, when time and place allow, but something quite other.

"How could I go with you?" she protests breathlessly. "What of my mother…"

"We'll send for her as soon as we are safe in France." And some remnant of common sense reminds him that she is not likely to be an ornament to the court of the King-in-Exile and makes him add, "surely some convent would take her in."

How like a man, she thinks, picturing a secret flight with her reckless lover, leaving her mad mother behind. They would never reach France. They would probably never get clear of London and he would be hanged for the spy and Jacobite agent he is, and what would become of her?

"They would never let her go. I could not leave her to be a hostage for me…"

"If you loved me, you would…"

And perhaps she would. She is not one to cry "all for love and the world well lost". Already she begins to think that she was a fool to begin this affair. It was the fault of her blood, the same blood that no doubt sent her great grandmother walking along the seastrand on moonlit nights, looking for seal-men and finding, perhaps, a ship-wrecked foreign sailor…

"If *you* loved *me* you would not ask it," she protests. "You know well how well I love you. I have proved it often enough." And she clings and cries and kisses and they prove their love for each other amongst the white blossoming trees kept prisoner in their pretty china pots.

Her lover goes away, only half-satisfied, at last, and she mends her face and smooths her laces so she is fit to show herself amongst the Queen's maids. They look at her bright eyes and the flush on her cheeks that all her arts cannot hide and whisper to each other. But Lady Mary has a sharp tongue, and a ready hand too, and no one as yet cares to risk either by affronting her directly.

~~~

There are high doings at Court, a victory to celebrate perhaps or a treaty signed, an alliance made sure. The sad Queen, who has no heir and never will have now, who has lost seventeen children in the course of her long life, and who now perhaps consoles herself with brandy, and the Duchess of Marlborough (there are few who can blame her for that, though, in the case of Sarah Churchill they might question her taste), presides over magnificent celebrations. The banqueting house blazes with light again, and a splendid dessert is set out on the long table: great pyramids of fresh-picked fruit, small dark sweet strawberries and shiny cherries, black and white and red, that reflect and refract the candle flames standing on each side of a stream that runs the length of the table, spilling from a tiny fountain, supported by cherubs. Red and gold fish swim in the stream as real as life – perhaps they are alive indeed.

Lady Mary sits on her fragile chair watching while a dark man in a coat of green brocade and a shirt trimmed with such quantities of fine Flanders lace that the price of it would buy a farm, piles her plate with cherries. It seems that she has found her buyer, a man so rich he can afford a penniless wife. And for good measure he is already provided with an heir, through the good offices of his first – dead – wife, so he need not trouble himself about bringing seal-blood into his family. Should there be any seal-pups (and he intends to spare no efforts in that direction) they will, of course, be provided for, but they will have no share in his house or his estate.

Lady Mary should be blissfully happy. He has given her an emerald ring "to match her eyes" and it blazes, green as jealousy, on her finger as she lifts her hand, loaded with more jewels and dripping with cherries, to her lips. He watches her as she encircles the shining cherries with her glistening cherry mouth, watching him in her turn, and smiling, and he laughs at her audacity. But there is enough sour within the sweet to pucker her mouth whenever she thinks of it.

Her predecessor, the heiress, the mother of those pure-blooded heirs, is said to have died in childbirth, along with her last baby. But there are other darker stories. The lady was left much alone upon that great estate in the country while her husband amused himself (and who else?) at Court. There was a young tutor, a poor relation, employed out of pity who did not have enough to do. His pupils were still too young for much formal teaching and he grew bored – and dangerous. The danger was of course as much to himself as to the lady. He set traps for her baited, no doubt, with the sugared notes of "if you loved me, you would…" and both fell into them together. Perhaps, when her guilt became all too evident (how long had her husband been away? Oh, more than three-quarters of a year, but here she was, near her time) he had begged her to run away too with the old song of "if you loved me, you would…"

But she would not. Would not leave her children or cast herself and her unborn child unprovided on a hard world. And he, who had brought them to this desperate pass, could not bring himself to flee alone, to save himself and leave her. But neither he nor she understood just what kind of a man she had married.

There were spies in the household. His Lordship knew just when to return, to find her ladyship lying in her bed weak from her labour, her bastard in its cradle beside her, its father in the library half-stupid with brandy… According to those dark stories, he made a clean sweep. If anyone had looked under those decent burial clothes, linen, and fine linen at that in defiance of the law, that clothed the lady as she lay in her coffin they might have seen certain marks upon her throat that are not usually associated with death in child-birth. They might too have wondered why her husband kept his hands hidden in those rich embroidered gloves throughout the funeral as if to cover the deep and bloody scratches from the nails of a desperate woman fighting for her child's life, if not for her own. But she lay in the great hall of her husband's house, and it was filled with his people. No one was going to pry under that white linen cloth, or look too closely at that pathetic bundle lying on her breast. No more than they would suggest that a search should be made for the young tutor – so mysteriously missing. Perhaps if they had dragged the lake, that was one of the beauties of the fine gardens, they might have found him with those same ugly marks upon his neck. The little body of the baby might be there too, for rumour said that bundle that was laid with the lady in her coffin was just that – a bundle of shawls, for her husband would not allow the bastard a place in his family's tomb.

Lady Mary has heard these stories and sometimes she thinks they may be true. Indeed, they might be said to work to her advantage. If the man wants a pretty well-born wife then he is going to have to pay well for one, for he is no great bargain himself. It is not that which troubles her. A man prone to such fits of murderous jealousy would not be pleased to hear of her latest liaison. Her lover has gone to France carrying intelligences, but sooner or later he will come back to London – perhaps with intelligences too, for he may be a double agent, taking gold from both sides. And when he does return he will expect to see her... She is not afraid that her prospective husband will kill her if he discovers that she is still playing whore to a Jacobite spy, but that he will simply cast her off and she will lose what must be her last, her only chance of sealing her bargain. So she sits and nibbles her fruit, and smiles boldly up at him while she thinks, desperately, of what she can do.

And when she receives a letter through certain unofficial channels, a desperate letter, begging her not to marry this monster, threatening to stop the wedding by all or any means – threatening in fact to tell all – then she knows.

Lady Mary is writing letters while her mother prattles and croons. The maids understand that she is writing to the young heir, to tell him of her wedding plans and to urge him to send his consent with all the speed he can, and they stare at her with a kind of frightened pity. They have heard the stories too, how the poor murdered lady ran for her life down the long gallery, screaming for her lover to save her, and how her screams can still be heard on winter nights. And when her husband followed her coffin to the church, you could see the blood drip from it at every step.

Lady Mary finishes her letters, scatters sand on them to dry the ink, folds and seals them with her ring, and tucks them briskly into her bosom. And no doubt the letters are duly sent, and duly received too, for in time an ill-spelt scrawl arrives from the heir consenting that his sister's bargain shall go forward. And a young man is landed secretly at night on the Essex coast – and walks not into the arms of his anxious lover but those of the Riding Officers who have – somehow – had news of his expected arrival.

He is surprised to find that he is not surprised. He knows that he has been betrayed of course, but he realises that he has always expected betrayal. When he sees the levelled muskets he greets them almost cheerfully and goes with his captors to an inn nearby where they drink smuggled liquor, pledging the queen and the Chevalier St George in turn. His only fear is that Lady Mary, who was to meet him, has been taken too, but he sees no sign of her. And he hears nothing of her either as he travels with his escort to London, and tells himself that means that, somehow, she has escaped. Perhaps she will send him some help...

Lady Mary buys her bride clothes and makes ready for her wedding. It will be a quiet affair. Her brother will hardly be able to leave his regiment and her mother must keep to her apartments, but such private weddings in these times are more common than otherwise. A far more public ceremony is in preparation for Lady Mary's lover, though that too is often described as a wedding and many of the participants dress as bridegrooms for their last journey in the hangman's cart. The gaolers notice that (unlike Lady Mary) he is uncannily calm. Perhaps he believes that Lady Mary really will come to his rescue, as he begged her in the letter that one of his visitors smuggled out of goal for him. He knew she received it for she sent him a token: a little sprig of orange blossom.

Perhaps he believes in her right up to the last, for he carries the blossom in his hand as he rides to his death at Tyburn, in his white shirt...

Lady Mary hears of his death on her wedding morning. The ceremony is to take place that evening in a private room in Kensington House. And now nothing can prevent it, Lady Mary should feel happy enough. But as she dresses, with the reluctant help of some of her fellow ladies in waiting, she seems very ill at ease.

"What is that perfume?" she demands, looking about her.

"What perfume?" asks her hairdresser impatiently.

"I don't know. There are no flowers here..."

"No indeed," says one of the ladies. "I smell nothing."

"Orange blossom," Lady Mary mutters. "I can smell orange blossom..."

But no one else does.

Her hoop is on, her fine damask gown pinned in place, and her head is dressed. The ladies hover around her, putting the last touches to her head, but she sends them away. She needs time, she tells them, to compose herself, so she sits alone before her mirror, slipping the cold heavy rings onto her fingers, the great emerald last, burning green as poison in the candle-shine. And then she glimpses something in the mirror behind her...

The bridal party are assembled, the clergyman is already beginning to tap his foot, when the door opens and the bride comes in, wide and wild eyed, crying out, "It's white and it follows me…"

Indeed.

# TEA DANCE

"He's one of them asylum seekers," Mrs Flynn stated. She was one of those who make up for lack of research with perfect confidence of utterance.

"Asylum." Mrs Freeman felt the word stirring echoes in her mind. You couldn't say that word at all once. Not out loud. "That place," they said but you knew what they meant. They were talking about the huge redbrick building at the top of the hill, with the great big gardens, like the park, only – from what you could glimpse through the iron gates – nicer. They took poor Mr Makepeace there when he decided he was the New Messiah and wanted to go off to the Front to stop the fighting.

Where he made his mistake, Mrs Freeman's mother had maintained, was starting his healing mission *before* he went off. Doctor had decreed that little Effie Mullins was going to die of her TB and he was quite put out when Mr Makepeace cured her. Particularly when, to all intents and purposes, she *had* died when Mr Makepeace took her by the hand and said, "It's not your time, yet, my dear. You must wake up." And she sat up and asked for a bit of the cake she could smell baking, which was supposed to have been for her funeral.

"Doctors don't like you interfering," her mother had said, "even if it's for the good. But I reckon they should have let him go to France."

But he had stayed in "that place" instead, casting demons out of the more violent patients, and sitting in the garden in the summer telling stories to whoever would listen – often only the birds and squirrels. (People had seen them, sitting round his chair, gazing up at him "as if they understood every word".) Very much missed he was, when he died, sudden-like, in his early thirties. Mrs Freeman remembered one of the nurses sitting in her mother's kitchen, drinking tea, and telling her the demons had come back with a vengeance after Mr Makepeace passed.

"She's gone off again," she heard Mrs Flynn say. "Goes into a world of her own, she does. And she was looking forward to the Tea Dance. She got a special invite, she did." She bent over her friend to adjust her corsage of mink roses, a discreet move aimed at making sure Mrs Freeman had not left them permanently for quite another world, without making too much of it.

"No, Bridie, I heard you," Mrs Freeman said mildly. "You're talking about the new Entertainments Manager. He gave me the invite."

Mrs Flynn straightened up sharply and Mrs Brightwell exchanged glances. Just like a child, their looks said, Bessie heard much more than you ever gave her credit for.

"I think he's very nice," she added.

"He's foreign," Mrs Flynn stated, as if the two statements were incompatible.

"I dare say he can't help that," Mrs Freeman murmured. "He's got ever such sad eyes."

"He looks like that Rudolf Valentino," said Mrs Flynn. "And we all know about *him*." She folded her lips as if to suppress any further discussion of *what* they might know. It was obviously better not repeated.

"He's a lovely dancer," said Mrs Freeman.

"Wasn't that Rudolf *Nureyev*?" said Mrs Brightwell.

"He was ballet," said Mrs Freeman, "Valentino did the tango." She drifted off again, seeing a dark and dangerous man with mascaraed eyes. Then she drifted back. "But I was talking about the Entertainments Manager," she said. "He dances lovely."

"Them foreigners do," said Mrs Flynn, shaking her head. There was obviously no limit to the things foreigners were capable of.

Mrs Freeman caught, from the flotsam of her memory, a fiercely beautiful Tartar face. "He might have more a of look of that Nureyev, though," she allowed.

"He comes from around there," said Mrs Flynn

"What, Covent Garden?" gasped Mrs Freeman, her mind still on ballet. Did people need to seek asylum from Covent Garden now? Anything was possible these days.

"I thought he was Hungarian," said Mrs Brightwell

"Same thing," stated Mrs Flynn inaccurately. "Besides I reckon he's a gyppo."

Mrs Freeman had a sudden crystalline memory of her mother's voice, scolding: "Look at you Bessie, and your frock only clean on today. I swear I'll give you to the Gypsies, it's all you're fit for." And every time the Gypsies stopped on Low Heath little Bessie had confidently expected his mother to take her by the hand, lead her to the camp, and hand her over. But every time she had been disappointed.

"He don't wear earrings," she objected.

"Well they don't, not now," said Mrs Brightwell. The other women looked at her in surprise wondering how she came to be so positive about the changes in Gypsy custom and practise. But she did not stoop to explanations.

"He might *of* done, once," said Mrs Flynn, her tone implying some kind of discreditable cover-up. "You take a look at his ears next time you have a dance with him, Lou. See if they've been pierced."

Mrs Brightwell gave her an old-fashioned look. "I can't go peering at men's ears. Not at my time of life."

"They're pointed," said Mrs Freeman.

"They're what?" Mrs Flynn exploded.

"Pointed," Mrs Freeman said positively. "He's got pointed ears."

"He never has!" said Mrs Flynn.

"You mean – like that elf?" said Mrs Brightwell, thoughtfully. "Now he *is* a good-looking man."

"Elf!" Mrs Flynn exclaimed. "Honestly, between the two of you I really wonder where I am sometimes."

Another memory, as plain as the picture of her young mother scolding her for dirtying her dress, floated up into Mrs Freeman's mind. The last time she had seen an Elf... Or he could have been an Angel. She'd been going home alone through the fields late one lovely summer's evening and she'd seen him, walking across the corn field, leaving no footprints but a train of shining poppies behind him. Beautiful enough to be an angel, but no wings that she recalled. She'd learned, by then, not to talk about such things at home so she kept the vision to herself. And as she got older she'd stopped seeing things like that. Once or twice, when the babies were young, she'd thought that they might be seeing things too ... the way she would hear Cassie laughing and babbling when she was quite alone ... and Alfie, the youngest, who played so quietly by himself except for those times when she'd heard him talking to a friend who wasn't there. But they grew out of it. Except Alfie, who never did live to grow up. Perhaps she shouldn't have *let* him talk to – whatever it was. Perhaps her mother had been right not to encourage her...

"The elf in that film," Mrs Brightwell was saying patiently. "*You* remember. Leopold Bloom."

Her two friends looked at her with mild surprise. "That's a funny sort of name," said Mrs Flynn

"Well, it's probably not his real one. They have to change their names, don't they, when they go into films? I mean, I don't suppose that Valentino was really called Valentino either," said Mrs Brightwell.

"I wonder what the Entertainment's Manager's real name is," said Mrs Freeman dreamily.

"But we *know* his name," snapped Mrs Flynn. "Remember when he was introduced to us: 'Roman – call me Roman'. That's what he said."

Mrs Freeman closed her eyes and saw that wild beautiful face, with its pointed ears, and sloe-dark slightly slanted eyes.

*"You* know my name isn't Roman," he had murmured. "You may not know my name, Bessie, but you know who I am. Will you dance with me, Bessie, dance with me…"

"Dance?" Mrs Freeman repeated.

"Ah, Bessie," Mrs Flynn murmured, looking down at her friend in her wheelchair, "in faith, your dancing days are done."

"Tomorrow," that soft voice had murmured, "tomorrow it is my dancing day…"

"My dancing day," Mrs Freeman repeated softly.

Mrs Flynn and Mrs Brightwell exchanged uneasy glances. The room had begun to fill. Mr and Mrs Friedland were getting ready to give their exhibition tango.

"Wonderful for a couple in their eighties," Mrs Brightwell said automatically.

"Nonsense!" Mrs Flynn snapped. "They'd be wonderful at any age."

Mr and Mrs Friedland, dipped and stamped and swung, effortlessly conjuring the spirit of a South American brothel in the recreation room of an Old People's Home in a seaside town on a grey autumn afternoon in England. A patter of genteel applause followed a performance that should have been greeted with the stamping of booted feet, and "Brava's!" from voices hoarse with whiskey and cigar smoke… More couples moved onto the floor. Mrs Flynn and Mrs Brightwell, who had grown up in a time when women often danced with each other if they danced at all, swung off together into a neat foxtrot. Mrs Freeman sat still, her hands loose in her lap. She was not sure he would come. She was not sure she wanted him to … and then she looked up and he was standing beside her.

"It's time then?" she said tremulously.

"It's time," he said, holding out his hands.

She looked carefully at his ears as he bent towards her. There *were* small gold rings in the lobes. Perhaps they had been hidden in his hair before. Then she stretched out her own hands, and let him lift her up.

"Are you Death?" she asked softly.

But he only laughed, and she laughed too, and laughing like a young girl she danced away with him.

# EXTENDED FAMILY

Angela wriggled her shoulders. Sweat pooled between her breasts, sopped into the waistband of her good skirt, gathered clammily under her armpits. The air-conditioning in the room cooled without drying, making her skin itch. As soon as this was over she would go back to the hotel, strip everything off and stand under the cold shower for hours and hours. Or no, perhaps she wouldn't even wait to take her clothes off, but just kick off her shoes and shower fully dressed. Of course it would ruin her skirt but she would never wear it again. She wanted nothing to remind her of this afternoon. Or any of this holiday.

As if he sensed what she was thinking James gripped her arm suddenly. "Mum. You won't leave me here, Mum, will you?"

He had lost years, all of a sudden, regressed from cocky teen to frightened little boy. She remembered how much she had once wanted that little boy back. Now she wanted the teenager. She wanted things to be normal.

"No, of course not," she said bracingly. "Anyway, I don't expect they'll want to keep you for long. They've given your stomach a good rinse and you've had all the shots you need."

But what had the doctor told her about Weil's disease? Something about rats. You got it from contact with water that had been contaminated by rats' urine. God only knew what the brown waters of the klong that James had fallen into were contaminated with. Rats' urine was probably the least of it. Bile burned the back of her throat when she thought of his head rising screaming from the filthy water. God only knew what he must have swallowed. Those unnameable floating lumps of… She gulped herself. She mustn't be sick. She mustn't frighten James.

"Now," she said with determined brightness, "I phoned Dad. He's on his way. As soon as he gets here, and the hospital says it's okay, we're all going home."

"All?" he said. "Not Ting? She's not coming with us, is she?"

"Of course your sister's coming home too." Angela put her hand on his forehead, frightened that this was the start of the fever and hallucinations she had been warned about. Or was he really regressing? She remembered that plaintive little boy's voice: "Can't we send her back, Mum?" She hadn't listened to him all those years ago, she mustn't listen now. "I should try to get some sleep," she told him.

"But you won't go off while I'm asleep, you won't leave me?" he repeated insistently. "You won't leave me with Ting."

"Well, I'm certainly not staying here," the girl's voice broke in unexpectedly. She had been so quiet that Angela had almost forgotten she was still in the room. "I'm hungry. As soon as Dad comes we're going off for some dinner. Mum can stay with you all night if you like. If you're scared without her, little boy."

The boy's eyelids fluttered and fell. Angela turned to look at her daughter. "I don't think he really knows what he's saying," she said defensively. "He's had such a shock. And he could be starting a fever. The doctor said…"

"Oh yes, leptospirosis. I wouldn't worry about that. He's much more likely to have poisoned the rats."

Angela thought suddenly, I always told people that the children really liked really – loved – each other. They might fight like cat and dog but that didn't mean anything. It'll settle down as they get older. And even now, James wouldn't let anyone else hurt his little sister … and I was lying, wasn't I? Lying to myself as much as to everyone else.

There was a soft knock on the door and she swung round, hoping against hope to see her husband, and knowing it couldn't possibly be. Not yet. And of course it wasn't. It was one of those very pretty nurses, girls whose very prettiness made it so much harder to tell them apart. The nurse stood hesitating for a moment, then catching a glimpse of the younger girl she smiled with relief and said something in Thai.

"What is it?" Angela asked shrilly. She had laboriously learned something of the language but it had all deserted her now.

"She wants to know if we'd like some tea," her daughter said impatiently.

"Oh no, no, we don't want to be a bother…"

"I do." She turned back and spoke to the nurse who smiled brightly again and went out. "You'll feel better when you've had a cup of tea," she told her mother.

Angela winced. How many times had she said that to her daughter when she came home from school crying? When that dreadful comedy programme was so popular and the girls at school had decided to re-name her Ting Tong Macadandang, after an ugly transvestite because the name Angela had chosen so carefully for her – Galaya, which meant "beautiful girl" as she had once proudly told her class – was, they said, so obviously not right for her.

"But you *are* beautiful," Angela had said. "Dry your eyes and have a cup of tea. You'll feel better…"

Only she hadn't. And the social worker's suggestion that Galaya should laugh right along with the other girls, and pretend that "Ting" was just an affectionate nickname, hadn't really helped either. "Nicknames are a feature of Thai culture. You can know someone for years without ever using their real name," she had pronounced authoritatively. But Angela knew now that shouldn't have gone along with it. She should have tackled the head mistress and demanded she put a stop to it, and she should have stopped James using it right from the start, because there was nothing affectionate about it. If Galaya *had* to have a nickname they should have chosen something nice. She wondered why she had never thought of it that way before.

There was another knock on the door and she jumped again, but this time it was only the tea. Yet another pretty girl smiled and put the tray down and left, tiptoeing with exaggerated care for the sleeping boy. Galaya filled two cups. It wasn't the straw-coloured fragrant tea that Angela had been expecting but an English brew, black as tar and almost as thick. It must have been kept brewing all day. And the milk had been boiled. It was still faintly warm with a skin on it. But someone must have gone to a lot of trouble to get it for them. She stared into the cup Galaya filled for her and thought that she must try to drink it. There was a faint scum of milk on the surface. She thought of that brown water again. Luckily she made it to the bathroom before she was desperately hopelessly sick. Even then, she tried to heave as quietly as she could so as not to wake James.

When she came back Galaya was sipping her own tea. "Better?" she asked. "Or do you want me to call a nurse?"

"No, no, thank you." She dropped into her chair, dabbing at her wet face with a tissue.

Galaya shrugged and got up to pour her a glass of water from the jug beside the bed. It was still cold, tinkling with ice, and Angela drank it gratefully.

"I wish your father would come," she said. "I just want to go home."

"If we were in London James would still be lying on a trolley in a hospital corridor somewhere. And *none* of us would understand what the nurses were saying."

"Oh I know, I know," she said quickly. "Poor James. Poor little Jimbo. He couldn't have had better treatment. And it's so *clean, everywhere*— I didn't mean…" But she wasn't sure what she did mean, except that everything would be all right once they were safe at home. It would be cool. And James would be well again.

"I never wanted to come here anyway," Galaya said.

"Yes," Angela said. "I know. I'm sorry."

But she had arranged this holiday with the best of intentions. It wasn't her fault that everything had gone so dreadfully wrong. She was beginning to have a terrible fear that things might have begun to go wrong a long time ago. More than twelve years ago… She remembered James looking disdainfully at the baby in her arms.

"What's wrong with her eyes, Mum?"

"There's nothing wrong with them … look she's smiling at you. She's saying, 'Is that my big brother? He looks nice'."

James ignored this. "But her eyes do look funny," he said.

"That's what called an *epicanthic fold,* James. Everyone has it before they're born but she's kept hers because her mummy was from Thailand. Doesn't it make her look pretty and special?"

"David Prewitt says she's a mong."

She felt dizzy with rage but she forced herself to say, "That's not a nice word, James. I think David means that *he* thinks the baby has Down's syndrome. But she certainly doesn't. Not," she added hastily, "that it would matter if she did. We would love her just as much."

James looked unconvinced. It was then that he had asked, "Can't we give her back mum?"

It had been just the wrong time to adopt, she knew that now. James had been an only child for too long to welcome a rival, but he was too young to understand. Too young to even pretend to be pleased. But what else could she have done? As soon as she had seen the baby her heart had broken with love. She had so longed for a little girl. Of course she loved James just as much as ever but if she could she would have given him half-a-dozen brothers and sisters. And she hadn't been able to. But this little one had dropped into her arms. Literally.

It had been a family scandal at first. Her uncle Robert, ages older than her father, almost as old, she had always thought ridiculously, as her grandfather, had gone to Thailand and come back with a wife. Family gossip, of course, maintained that she had been a bar girl (at the very least), that he had bought her from her family (or her pimp) for ten dollars, that… But no one really knew. He certainly did not introduce Maelaenee to any of them, or bring her to family celebrations – not that he came to them himself either. But then he never had. And he did not welcome visitors to the extent of refusing to open his door to them. The whole family waited almost hopefully to hear that his bride had emptied his bank-account and run off with the milkman, but instead they were stunned by the news that she had died in childbirth. No one in the family had even been told that she was pregnant. And he had chosen to make the announcement by arriving on Angela's doorstep with a tiny baby in his arms and a carrier bag containing a packet of formula milk, a feeding bottle, a large economy-size pack of disposable nappies meant for a much older baby, and an envelope containing a birth certificate. He had thrust the baby into Angela's arms, dropped the carrier on her doorstep, turned on his heel, and walked away. And she had taken the baby in. What else could she have done?

She had half-thought that he had been on his way back to Thailand to pick up a replacement wife, but perhaps she had been unfair to him. Instead he had gone home, written a will leaving custody of his daughter to Angela, and died. For a while she had assumed that he had killed himself. It was only later when, desperate to find *something* about her new daughter's background, that she had contacted her uncle's doctor and discovered that he had died of heart failure.

"What they used to call a broken heart," said the doctor, who was a young man and still something of a sentimentalist. "You often find that with widowers. The wife dies and they just give up. Of course he hadn't been looking after himself, poor old chap. Not what you'd call well-nourished."

"I expect he'd got used to her doing the cooking," Angela had said, somewhat sharply. She found it really hard to believe in Uncle Robert's broken heart. She did not think he had looked grief-stricken when he handed over the baby. Thinking about it now, she thought she remembered that he had looked *frightened*... But that was ridiculous. Unless it was the responsibility that terrified him so much, he couldn't wait to drop it into someone else's arms.

"Oh, he'd been cooking all right. He died in the kitchen. There was a heap of ingredients cut up on the table. Luckily a neighbour heard him call out – got there too late to help him but at least she turned the gas off…"

She had visited the neighbour, clutching a bunch of flowers, offering thanks for her timely intervention. And trying discreetly to learn something about Maelaenee. But it turned out that the neighbour knew very little.

"We said good morning. If we saw each other. But we didn't – socialise. She seemed a nice woman," she added meaninglessly. "Very quiet. He was really upset when she died, of course." She dropped her voice then. "He used to *talk* to her. Every night. You could hear him."

"Talk to her?" Angela repeated, hoping to hear more. But the woman had nodded, tight lipped, taken the proffered flowers and shut the door. And Angela went home to fight Authority for the possession of her daughter.

When she first held the baby everything had seemed simple. But of course it wasn't. In spite of the will. Perhaps Uncle Robert had thought he needed to do no more than undergo a marriage ceremony of doubtful legality to give Maelaenee English nationality, but he had been wrong. A meticulous search of his house turned up the dubious marriage certificate and some blurred photographs – of the ceremony perhaps, showing Uncle Robert and a young woman staring gravely at the camera. The girl had a flower in her hair. But she might not have been Maelaenee at all, but Angela thought she must be. The photographs were in an envelope with Maelaenee's long expired visitor's visa.

Angela found herself being treated more as if she was the baby's kidnapper than her rescuer. She really believed that if the Authorities had been able to find any information about Maelaenee's family, and that family had shown the slightest inclination to take her baby, she would have been shipped off to them. But Angela had clung and fought and accepted the most shocking intrusions into her private life. She had changed the baby's name from the father's choice (Shirley, for no reason that she could imagine – perhaps it was the first female name that came into his mind when he registered her birth) to the prettiest Thai name that she could find. She had – with considerable difficulty – set up a network of Thai families who would support her in her determination that the child should never forget her mother's homeland. She had tried, pathetically, to learn Thai herself so the child would grow up bilingual. And at last she had been given her reward. She had her little girl.

But where had James been in all this? Again she had taken advice and again she realised now that advice had been wrong. James had been told that the new little sister was a gift for him. They had gone to all this trouble for *him*. So that he would have a little sister. When he protested that he would much rather have had a puppy they had laughed tolerantly and repeated it to visitors who laughed too. Of course he *couldn't* have a puppy. The Authorities didn't think dogs and young babies went well together. He had to make do with a sister. And he didn't want her. He *really* didn't want her. He never had. His mother had done it all for herself. Her husband was willing to go along with things if it made her happy, although he protested occasionally, asking questions like, "Why not call the child Shirley? For all they knew Robert had chosen it after long discussions with his wife. She did know of course that Maelaenee *was* a western name, didn't she? Version of Melanie, according to that list of Thai names of hers. Perhaps the girl *wanted* to be English, and wanted it for her daughter too..." But fortunately he had never said it in the hearing of the Authorities.

But though Angela could change her daughter's name, and see that she learned her mother's language, and played with children from her mother's background whenever it could be arranged, there had been one thing she could not do. She could not find out anything about her mother, she could not take her back to see her mother's home. Oddly, it had been James who had made the breakthrough. Perhaps he was still hopeful that there *was* a family somewhere who would take Galaya back and restore him to his rightful place as only child. Perhaps it was simple curiosity, but using the scanty information on that marriage certificate and the growing powers of the internet he had finally traced a village that might have been her mother's home, and relatives who might belong to her. And Angela had promptly dragged Galaya and James with her. "It'll be an *adventure!*" to find if it was true.

It had been a good thing, of course, that she had taken them to a hotel in Bangkok first, while she checked and double-checked. It would have been so embarrassing if they had gone straight to the village and discovered – as she had been told so kindly and politely yesterday – that Maelaenee's relatives would much rather *not* meet her daughter.

"But why?" she had demanded desperately from the so kind, so polite official who had given her the news. "Is it – I mean – were they *ashamed...*" She choked on the idea that family gossip might have been accurate, that Maelaenee's roots could be discovered in the Patpong district rather than in some idyllic village. But he had shaken his head, still smiling, not understanding, and said something about superstition. So she had gone back to the hotel. It was still early. People liked to get business done before the worst heat of the day set in, although she was already sweating. She had told her children that there was a hitch, a problem, perhaps they wouldn't make a long journey to see a village which did not remember Maelaenee, but they could do some site-seeing instead, just as if they were tourists.

That was how they had found themselves at the temple. And it had been horrible. Galaya had translated the story in a bored voice, the story of Mae Naak, whose gilded statue dominated the place. Her husband had gone off to fight someone or other and had been badly wounded. By the time he recovered and returned to his village his wife had died in childbirth ... or so his neighbours had tried to tell him. But he hadn't believed them because he had found her and their child living in his house, just as he had expected. And nothing would persuade him that she was not a living woman. Not even that those neighbours who tried too hard to persuade him that she was a ghost all suffered grisly deaths could shake his belief in her.

"Drowned, disembowelled," Galaya recited, as if she was reading off a shopping list. It was only one evening when she was preparing a meal and dropped a lime that he realised the truth... Impatient, forgetting the need to keep up appearances for a moment, she had reached for the fruit and her arm had lengthened, and lengthened, and at last he saw she was a ghost and ran for protection to the temple.

"It's supposed to be romantic," Galaya said. "She was faithful through death."

She rolled her eyes.

The narrative became a bit muddled after that, or perhaps Galaya was too bored to go on with her translation, and by this time Angela was feeling faint and she couldn't remember anything more until they were outside although it was so hot it still felt as if they were shut in a hot steamy bathroom, and someone suggested it would be cooler beside the klong, and they walked down there and a group of small boys had run past them, screaming, playing the Mae Naak game, and one of them must have pushed James into the canal.

He had been pulled out very quickly before Angela had time to think of crocodiles, or complications from dirty water... But as they pulled him out he had clutched at her and muttered, "She pushed me. Ting pushed me."

And she knew that Galaya had been behind her. Six feet away at least. So even before she had seen the doctor and heard him talk about hallucinations and Weil's disease she had known there was something terribly wrong.

"I know you didn't want to come," she said again. "But don't worry. Daddy will be here soon. He's moved heaven and earth to get a flight out to us, and he'll do the same to get us home."

She blundered to her feet and went to the window as if she might see and recognise her husband's plane coming to land. But it was dark by now and all she saw was the room behind reflected with mirror-clarity: James tossing in his feverish sleep in the clean white bed, Galaya slumped in her chair, Galaya reaching for a magazine lying on the table, stretching out her arm to pick up a magazine on the table, stretching and stretching out her long, long arm.

# THE FETCH

"You really ought to have a ghost," said Felicity, tilting her long-stemmed wineglass so that the yellow wine glittered in the candlelight.

"Do you mean we should buy one? Can you recommend a reliable stockist?" Ambrose asked lightly.

"Harrods, I should think. I'm sure they'd get you one, even if they don't carry a stock. Or you could try Habitat for something trendier but more middle market. If you did go to them, of course, you'd have to be prepared to find a copy of your ghost in someone else's Blue Room. Like seeing endless replicas of your pine veneer dresser in other people's kitchens."

Emily had been listening, admiring, but bewildered, to the nonsense her friend and her husband were talking. She said, rather plaintively: "But we haven't got a pine veneer dresser" – and realised at once that it was the wrong thing to say.

Felicity smiled her little pussy-cat smile at Ambrose and glanced again at the exquisite dresser they did have, a perfect piece of furniture polished by generations of farm wives to a rare blue bloom. She envied Emily her new house, her money, her jewels and her clothes, though never her looks or her husband; but she felt she could have killed her just for that dresser.

She made herself say, "That's just what I mean. You have everything so perfect here, so right that you must have a really special ghost. A unique spectre. If you haven't got one then you must advertise."

"I'm sure there's an agency that could help us," Ambrose said, "they can probably be found in *Time Out*, calling themselves RentaWraith, or GhoulsaPlenty."

"But we have got a ghost," Emily said softly.

Conversation stopped abruptly. Felicity watched Ambrose's big deceptively jovial red face become almost black with a sudden rush of dark blood. He seized the wine bottle and filled their glasses. She noticed that his hand was shaking.

"How exciting," said Felicity. "What sort of ghost, Emily?"

"It's all rubbish. A delusion. People will think … all sorts of things if you start describing your hallucinations, you know," said Ambrose.

Emily often told Felicity that she liked to have guests because Ambrose was so nice to her if other people were there. Felicity wondered how badly he behaved when they were not. There had been a scandal not long after he married. Easily hushed up, with his money, and Emily's, but very nasty. Something about a girl and violence that stopped only just short of murder. And there had been that unpleasant business with the hunt saboteur. Lucky for both of them there had been someone to stop him…

But there *had* been a death once. A younger boy had been killed while Ambrose was at school and he had left very soon afterwards. Ambrose had never officially been blamed for that. At the worst it had been rough horseplay, perhaps a little bullying that went too far. But the school did not want to keep him.

Felicity wondered if he ever hit Emily. She found the idea rather exciting. She smiled encouragingly at her friend, who was looking quite crushed by merely verbal violence, and said, "What sort of ghost is it? A headless nun? Or something utterly non-human with green and dripping scales?"

"No," said Ambrose, answering for his wife as he so often did. "She's rather a disappointment even if you choose to believe in her."

"It's a female ghost then?"

"Yes, so they say. Rather pathetic, really. She stands under the pines at the end of the garden. It's supposed to be a youngish woman with brown hair pulled back or piled up, wearing a long blue dress with a high neck. The funny thing is, she's supposed to look a bit like Emily. I think she was some dim little Victorian slavey who used to wait for her boyfriend there, under the pines, and he stood her up. In the end, she pined away, if you'll excuse the pun, and died, as they did in those days, and she's just too dim to move on. That is, if there really is anything there, which I strongly doubt."

Felicity suddenly thought, but he has seen her too. Aloud she said, "Perhaps the boyfriend went off to the war and got killed. One evening the ghost of a soldier in a red coat will come limping up the lane and they'll float off together, hand in hand."

Emily struck in, sounding more confident than usual. "I'm not sure that she did just die. Naturally, I mean. There's something round her neck. It could be a red ribbon, but it could be – something else."

"D'you mean you've really seen her?" Felicity squeaked.

Emily nodded. Her slightly bulging eyes bulged still more with importance. "Several times. The first time I thought she was real. You know, those Victorian dresses used to be fashionable. Well, I went up to her and I was going to ask what she wanted, tell her she was on private property, but when I got right up to her she wasn't there."

"You mean, she vanished?" Ridiculously, Felicity felt gooseflesh creep up her bare arms.

"No," Emily frowned, trying to explain. "It was like one of those puzzle pictures. You know, one way it's just blobs and splashes of paint, but if you catch it from the right angle it's a face. Or sometimes," she added, to herself, "it's a face, but if you look again it's a skull. Suddenly I was at another angle and she wasn't there."

"But did you know there was a ghost before you saw her? Had you heard any local stories about her that could make you, well, imagine things."

"But there were no stories," said Emily. "No one ever saw anything until we came here."

For some reason that seemed the weirdest thing of all. There was a short uneasy silence, and then Ambrose said, "Our char's seen her."

Felicity felt this was a neat way of devaluing Emily's psychic pretensions, but Emily accepted the supporting testimony, with one mild protest. "Mrs Beacham doesn't like being called a char, dear. But she has seen her. She thought it was me, she said, until she got close, and then suddenly she wasn't there anymore."

"It's all your imagination," said Ambrose roughly. "You haven't got enough to do."

Emily, who ran a large house and an extensive programme of entertaining for Ambrose' business friends, with the assistance of Mrs Beacham three mornings a week, smiled and said nothing.

Felicity swallowed the last of her wine and stood up. "Well, it's been lovely but now I must catch my beastly train."

"Ambrose will drive you to the station," said Emily. "Can't you stay a bit longer?"

"No, really I have to be up early. Working woman, you know."

They talked themselves into the hall and Felicity gathered up her wrap and her bag.

"You must really come and stay with us," said Emily. "You could have a nice rest. We've got masses of room."

"I tell you what," said Felicity, leaning forward to kiss her friend. "I've got some holiday owing to me. I'll come down and organise a lovely housewarming party for you. You remember my famous parties."

No doubt Emily did remember from the days when they had shared a flat. She looked uneasy as she remembered but Felicity smiled and got into the car beside Ambrose.

"A lovely party for a lovely house!" she called to Emily as the car swept her out of sight.

"You really do like the house, don't you?" Ambrose said. He sounded amused.

"It's beautiful," Felicity agreed. Envy almost choked her.

"More your sort of place than Emily's, really," Ambrose said, twisting the knife. "Funny that. Her having the money and you having the style. Not to mention the expensive tastes."

"Very funny," she said resentfully. But she let her shoulder and thigh drift against his.

"Sometimes, you know, I ask myself how long I can go on with Emily."

He might have meant to sound pathetic, to give a new twist to the old line "my wife doesn't understand me". In fact he sounded violently angry. Dangerous.

Felicity wondered what he might do, someday, if he got angry enough.

"What time does your train really leave?" he asked.

"In forty-five minutes," she replied precisely. "You can always tell Emily it was late and you had to wait with me on the platform."

"Why should I tell Emily anything?" he sounded genuinely puzzled.

Felicity did not answer. He turned off the main road into a tree-lined lane. She endured the interlude that followed by thinking of Emily's money, the money that must come to Ambrose if she should die. Of the house. And the housewarming.

It was late when Felicity got back to her London flat. She shared it with two other girls, who were in bed and asleep when she got there, but she rattled about the kitchen, making herself tea, not caring if she woke them. She hated them, hated the flat that never felt properly warm, never looked tidy, or even clean, hated Emily who had everything she wanted, hated Ambrose who had handled her very roughly. Most of all she hated herself.

She had always envied Emily, ever since they had met at that very expensive boarding school where Felicity's aunt had taught English. When Felicity was left an orphan, and a very poor orphan at that, her aunt had persuaded the headmistress to give her a place in the school where she could keep an eye on her. She was not, of course, a boarder. She alone, of all the girls, had gone at the end of the school day, well, not home but to her aunt's flat to sleep. She alone, of all the girls, had no rich relations. Under those circumstances it was very difficult to make friends, which is how she came to be involved with Emily. Emily was so plain and shy that it cancelled out any advantage in having rich parents. The only girl who could be bothered with her was her fellow outcast.

When they left school, Emily's parents had bought her a flat in London, and for a while Felicity was reasonably happy. She shared the flat with Emily, paying no rent, borrowing her clothes, and giving parties with her money. Emily was reasonably happy with this arrangement. She hated the parties, but it was a nice big flat and she could always go to bed with a book.

Then her parents took her to meet Ambrose.

At first Felicity could not understand why both families seemed so anxious for Emily and Ambrose to marry. They were both so rich. It seemed absurd to hoard money like that when they could have made two poor people really happy. And Emily obviously had no appeal for Ambrose at all. It was only later, as she got to know him, and to hear the gossip about him, that Felicity realised what a very unattractive commodity Ambrose had been. He had been lucky to get Emily, a nice quiet girl, who would give him at least the appearance of a respectable marriage, tell lies for him when necessary, and bail him out whenever his taste for violence got too much for him. He had been lucky, too, in being born rich. Amongst the poorer classes, who have little influence with the judiciary, and a distressing tendency to call a spade a spade, Ambrose might have been called at least a sadist, at worse a dangerous madman. He might even have been locked up.

Sitting at the sticky kitchen table, sipping her tea, Felicity thought about Emily. She thought about the ghost, hallucination, apparition that Emily (and the char) had seen in the garden. And she made a decision.

Next day, after work, she went to see a friend.

Felicity was one of those people who always know where to find an expert, and this friend was an expert in what some people call paranormal phenomena and others, black magic. She outlined the situation to him crisply, giving all the details but no names.

"What you have there," he told her, "is a fetch. A co-walker. For reasons I shall never understand it's quite often called a Doppelganger, even in England. It's the ghost of a living person. Of your friend, in fact. There was a case in the eighteenth century, I think. A young girl met herself one evening, walking in her father's grounds. It's Holland Park now, by the way. The apparition was just like her in every detail, except that it was pale, and I think it was carrying withered flowers. The girl died soon afterwards."

"Then," Felicity suggested, hesitantly, "it could mean death. It's dangerous."

"Yes, I think it probably is. Not in itself, but it does suggest that a rather nasty psychic field has been set up."

"Could it be a warning?"

"Yes, indeed, yes."

"So, if my – friend – did something to change her fate, left her husband, or got him to move house, something like that, then she might save herself?"

"Perhaps."

"But if, on the other hand, she did something really crazy, like dressing like the apparition and walking under the pines herself, she could … make the disaster happen."

"If she was crazy enough to try it, yes. Almost certainly. Has she got a dress like the one described?"

"No."

"Good. If she had I would have advised her to burn it."

Felicity frowned. "Can you avoid your fate?"

"Perhaps. Perhaps not. I should certainly advise her to move right away from the neighbourhood, leave her husband, who sounds like a boor anyway, and hope for the best."

"Yes," said Felicity. "I see."

She finished her tea, thanked him, and went home. Once there she sat down to make a list. It began with a reminder to buy a length of blue cotton print, either from Laura Ashley or from Liberty's.

It took more than one visit to persuade Emily that a combined housewarming and Halloween party, with all the guests in fancy dress, was a good idea. But Felicity was all girlish enthusiasm, and Ambrose was quite encouraging, and in the end they brought her round. Felicity was to do all the decorations, the pumpkins with grinning faces, the plastic cobwebs and the polystyrene bats, and she would provide costumes for herself and for Emily. No one, she promised, as she took her friend's distressingly ample measurements, would know about them until the evening of the party.

"I feel quite excited, really," Emily lied timidly, trying to enter into the spirit of things, as they addressed invitations and made the necessary follow-up phone calls.

"It's got to be fancy dress," Felicity insisted, making call after call from Emily's phone, "And not just a silly mask and a sheet either. If you're not in costume I promise they won't let you in."

"That's right Felicity, you tell them," said Ambrose almost cheerfully.

It was a pity that just before the event Felicity had to go back to her office for three days so that the bulk of the preparations suddenly fell on Emily. Ambrose lost a lot of his good humour while Felicity was away, and when she came back, with her parcels and her bottle of wine, on the night of the party, she found her friend very close to tears.

"Never mind," she told her, "the house looks lovely. Quite terrifying. Come and put your costume on."

She unwrapped her parcels in Emily's bedroom. Hers held a white filmy nightdress and phial of stage blood; Emily's a blue print dress, long skirted and high necked, complete with choker made from a narrow piece of red satin ribbon.

Emily leaped back as if from a snake. "Oh no. I couldn't wear that!" she exclaimed. "I really couldn't"

Felicity let her mouth droop. "But I thought it was ideal! Your very own ghost! I made it specially for you! It was supposed to be such a lovely surprise."

"I just couldn't, Felicity," said Emily, with uncharacteristic firmness. "I'd feel awful."

Felicity held up her vampire costume, so the light shone through it. "We could swap," she suggested.

Emily gasped at the thought of exhibiting herself to her guests in that nightdress and gave in. Indeed she caved in completely, putting herself passively into Felicity's hands, as if she had no will left. Felicity buttoned her into the dress, tied her sash, fastened the red ribbon round her neck, and then sat her in front of the mirror to pile up her hair in a fanciful Victorian style. As Felicity studied her friend's reflected face she wondered just what she was doing. Perhaps Emily had been doomed from the start like the girl who met herself in Holland Park, with her bunch of withered flowers. Perhaps, after all, Felicity was doing no more than give a nudge to something quite inevitable. She smiled at Emily's reflection.

"It's going to be a lovely party," she said.

"You've been very clever with your makeup," said the innocent Emily. "You look just like a real vampire. Really evil!"

Felicity, who had made no change in her usual party makeup, smiled again.

The party went with a real swing. Felicity, which had carried realism to the extent of wearing nothing at all but her nightdress and a few dabs of blood, was very popular. Some people may have noticed that their host was drinking rather a lot, and seemed in a worse temper than usual. But perhaps that was because his costume, Jack the Ripper, in black cloak and top hat, with a great blood-stained knife sticking out of his pocket, proved less original than he had thought it would. There were at least four other Jacks. How careless of Felicity to have suggested the same idea to so many people. The hostess too seemed unhappy. As her friend, Felicity said later in her sworn statement, she had complained of a headache at around midnight and gone for a stroll.

She was not seen again by anyone at the party until the next morning when they found her under the pines at the end of the garden. There was a red ribbon of blood round her throat.

There was quite a lot of scandal about that.

One or two of the guests, those who had sold their stories to the Sunday papers, gave a quite wrong impression of the kind of party it had been. The police somehow gained the idea that there had been some sort of drug orgy going on. They never ever managed to trace the movements of all the guests, some invited, some not, some masked and all in some sort of disguise. The fact that five people were in identical costumes did not help. The story of the ghost got out and a prominent psychic announced that poor Emily had been struck down by forces from the Beyond because of her foolish mockery of that pathetic revenant.

Ambrose helped the police with their enquiries for a few days but his previous experience with such affairs was a positive advantage and eventually they had to let him go. He got a small flat in town and Felicity moved in with him. In the summer they got married and began to think of what they should do about the house.

Felicity was determined that they should live there. After all, everything she had done (if she had done anything; she was not prepared to admit even to herself that she had) had been done to get the house. And a murder and a haunting made the place virtually unsaleable. Besides, moving in would be an excellent way to face down scandal.

Fortified by these and other rationalisations, she drove down one summer's day to see what would have to be done before they could move back. A quick look round told her that it would be perfectly habitable after a good clean and she decided to call on Mrs Beacham in the village to see if she would oblige.

As she left the house she glanced, almost without intention, at the pines. What she saw sent her running down the drive and out into the lane, too frightened even to think of trying to get into her car. It took a lot of deep breathing, and the repetition of her mantra "there's nothing there, there can't be anything there," before she could go back. This time there was nothing.

She got into the car and drove to the village.

She had pulled herself together by the time she got there but Mrs Beacham's sharp eyes detected signs of shock.

"You've been up to the house, then?" she said.

"Yes," said Felicity. "We shall be moving in shortly. So we'd be grateful if you could see your way to going in and giving everything a thorough clean."

Under Mrs Beacham's knowing eye she began to babble. "You'll probably want to take someone with you … to help … it's a big job. I'll pay you what you like, of course…"

"I don't want paying more than the going rate," said Mrs Beacham. "I don't have cause to worry about no ghost."

"Mrs Beacham," said Felicity, trying to control her trembling lips, "there is no ghost there."

"Well, maybe it isn't exactly a ghost, not yet. It's not the last Mrs Edwards, that's for sure. It looks more like a blonde lady though it could be a redhead."

She looked steadily at Felicity, who lowered her eyes, knowing that Mrs Beacham had what she had seen.

It was Felicity herself who now stood under the pines, blood running through her long blonde hair.

# THE BUS

Mrs Fortescue shifted from numb cold foot to cold numb foot and peered into the murk. There was no sign of the bus. She wondered if she dared put her shopping bags down and try to rub some life back into her fingers. Of course, if she did the bus was sure to arrive and she would never be able to gather her things together in time to get on, and she would hold the whole queue up. She sighed thinking of the days when buses were big and red, and had conductors who would sometimes jump off to give some help to over-burdened elderly ladies. Now the buses were small, more like vans really, and only had drivers who not only expected you to have the right change but to know what your fare was. And you had to jump out of your seat and ring the bell when you wanted to get off. Mrs Fortescue, used to bus-stops, tended to forget and gave herself an unnecessarily long walk at the end of her journey. She sighed again, reminding herself how much she disliked people who went on about the good old days, and how she had always promised herself that she would never be one of them. But nothing was as it should be anymore.

It was these shopping trips that were depressing her, she thought. She had once overheard her daughter-in-law Melanie telling one of her friends that they were so *important* for her. They made her feel *useful* and stopped her *frowsting* about the house and *imagining* illnesses for herself. But her arthritic knee wasn't imaginary. The doctor had said so. And the fact that Melanie never gave her the money for any of the rather expensive purchases she asked her to make wasn't imaginary either. Occasionally she said vaguely, "Oh, we must settle up, Mother Fortescue," (and how she hated being called Mother Fortescue, it made her feel like some kind of mad nun), but they never did settle up. And once when she'd asked outright for her money Melanie had looked at her in that wide-eyed way she had, and said, "But darling, I gave you the money before you went out. Surely you remember. Oh dear, I hope you're not starting to have memory lapses … it could be terribly dangerous. I mean there's the gas … and the bath…" And Mrs Fortescue had never dared bring up the subject again.

And she had never mentioned her brooch at all. It had been a birthday present from her husband Fred, much too precious to wear but nice to look at, sometimes. It had been in a locked jewel-box beside her bed. She had taken it out one Friday evening and cried over it a bit, then she put it back in its cotton-wool nest, but when she had opened the box again on the Sunday it had gone. And Melanie had bought herself that very expensive outfit for her friend's wedding on the Thursday. And no one could tell Mrs Fortescue that the two events were not related. But she had never had the courage to tackle Melanie about it. Well, she might as well face facts. She was terrified of her daughter-in-law.

"What can she do?" her friend Mrs Fraser had demanded. That was before Melanie had been so rude to Mrs Fraser that she never came to the house again, and they were still having cosy talks over a coffee. "You stand up to her! She can't eat you!"

Well no, but Mrs Fortescue wasn't afraid of being eaten. She was frightened of having to go into an old people's home, and that was where Melanie wanted to put her. Sooner or later she would get her way. Sooner really. Only too soon now, when Mrs Fortescue was just not able to make herself useful any longer by running Melanie's errands and doing the bits of housework that Melanie didn't like to ask the home help to do, then Melanie would persuade her husband that his poor old mother would be far better off in a home. It was Mrs Fortescue's own fault of course, she told herself. She should never have given them her house. She had not really listened to Clive's complicated explanations of the benefits; she had signed everything he put in front of her because she loved and trusted him. He was after all her only son. And he had betrayed her to Melanie. Tears misted her eyes briefly but she blinked them away. She must pull herself together. Eventually the bus would come and for today, at least, she would make herself a cup of tea in her own kitchen and go up to her own comfortable room to drink it in peace. And tomorrow, perhaps, she would suggest that Melanie did her own shopping. And she would ask her where that brooch had gone…

And she would put those bags down. The queue would just have to wait while she picked them up again when the bus finally appeared. She dropped them and examined her hands. The skin had turned a nasty blue-grey between the red lines scored across her palms by the bag handles. And then of course the bus was there. She had not even seen it coming, and there it was, with the doors open and a young man helpfully urging her up the steps.

"My bags," she wailed, "my bags—"

"You don't need those, old girl," he said. And suddenly, thankfully, she knew that she didn't. She just didn't want to carry them any longer. Let Melanie tell everyone her mind was failing. She could just hear that breathless, little-girl voice spreading the glad news amongst her horrible friends: "Do you know, she came home without the shopping?" But she knew she could not bear to drag those bags a step further. Gratefully she sank down into a seat by the door and looked up to thank the young man. And then she knew that Melanie was vindicated. Her brain had gone. She was hopelessly senile. Because the young man bending over her was her husband Fred, not Fred as she had last seen him in the hospital but Fred as he was when they married, young and jolly, with his hair neatly cut and a flower in his buttonhole. She gave a faint weak moan.

"That's all right, old girl," said the young man. "It's me all right."

"But you're dead," said Mrs Fortescue helplessly. She looked round the bus, as if she could find a clue there to what was going on. It was not really a bus, she realised. It was much too big and clean and comfortable. It reminded her of those big coaches – what did they call them? – charabancs, that was it, that they had gone to the seaside in when she was a child. But … there was something odd about the driver…

"Yes," Fred was saying, earnestly. "I'm dead all right. But you see, old girl, so are you. We all are. We came to pick you up."

He gestured round the bus. Mrs Fortescue began to recognise the passengers. There was Auntie Conny, who'd had such a good time with the Yanks during the war, until her special sergeant got himself killed, right at the end, in Normandy, and she was so cut up because she couldn't even wear black for him. Well, there she was, sitting next to her sergeant and looking as jolly as jolly. Mrs Fortescue wondered, briefly, where Auntie Conny's husband was but decided it would be politer not to ask. And wasn't that her mum, younger than she'd ever known her, smiling with all her own teeth, and such a lovely colour in her cheeks; and Fred's mum, and … and come to think of it, she couldn't feel any pain in her knee at all, and there was a wonderful loose feeling in the rest of her joints. She touched her fingertips to her cheek and felt smooth young skin. As if she knew what she was thinking Auntie Conny leaned over and gave her a compact mirror so she could see her own face, gone all young and pretty again, framed by her own glossy brown hair with a nice bit of perm in it.

"Well," she said, "I will say death does wonders for your looks."

"That's right, old girl," said Fred. He reached into his breast pocket and took something out. "Remember this?"

"It's my brooch," she said, softly.

He pinned it to the lapel of her jacket, because somehow she was now wearing the smart navy costume she and her mother had chosen for her honeymoon. Her going-away suit, they'd called it then. She glanced out of the window so that Fred wouldn't see that she was crying for pure happiness. For a moment she saw the wet cold street and a flurry of people bending over the body of a poor old woman on the pavement, then it flicked away and she was looking out at a summer lane, glittering with sunlight.

"Where shall we go then?" said Fred. "Last one in chooses."

They all looked at her.

"Could we go to the sea?" said Mrs Fortescue tremulously.

"Course we could! You'll like the seaside here, old girl."

"It's heavenly," Auntie Conny agreed and they all laughed.

Fred sat down beside her and put an arm over her shoulders. The charabanc swished along green lanes overhung with honeysuckle, past summer fields studded with white sheep and placid cattle, and picture-book villages. Auntie Conny began to sing that she did like to be beside the seaside, and soon all the other passengers joined in. So did the driver. He had a nice voice, Mrs Fortescue noticed, and a really smart uniform, besides a lovely pair of white feathery wings.

Which was, of course, just as it should be.

# THE CO-WALKER

Martin hadn't wanted to go out that night. He told Mike so when he phoned but he knew he sounded too weak, as if he was making excuses not to see them. "I don't feel too good. I'm going to get an early night."

But Mike had come round, he'd brought the car round with Chris and Sue and a girl Martin didn't know and they were all laughing and making Mike lean on the horn, until he came out before the neighbours called the police, and they almost dragged him into the car.

"We'll come back here after closing time," Sue told the strange girl. They'd been drinking somewhere already and Sue was giggly and expansive. She told the stranger: "We'll show you Martin's flat. Martin's got a fantastic flat but he never invites anyone up to see it."

"I do," said Martin weakly, feeling in the wrong because he was still sober.

"You're turning into a hermit. You shouldn't let things get on top of your like this," Chris shouted at him, though there was no need to shout in the crowded car.

"As the actress said to the bishop," said Sue and they laughed and Martin tried to join in and told himself that he'd feel better when he'd had a drink.

The strange girl was pressed up against him in the back seat. Her hair smelt of something perfumed and smoky, and he didn't want to breath in that smell, he was afraid he'd get breathless again, and have to ask Mike to stop the car.

"I hear you've been ill," she said suddenly, as if she knew what he'd been thinking.

"I had what they call a breakdown," he said shortly. "I don't like talking about it." Then, afraid that he'd been too abrupt: "People get so dreary when they go on and on about their health. I don't want to turn into a medical bore. I'm terrified of that."

But he could just as easily have said, "*I'm terrified.*"

"Don't talk about it if you don't want to," she said and smiled.

He was too close to see her properly but her voice sounded quiet. Soothing. Gentle.

Mike was stopping the car, and Sue was shrieking, "No, no, we can't go to that pub, not after last time!" – and Chris began to shout with laughter.

"Where do you want to go, Martin – it's your night out?" Mike said.

"I don't know." Martin felt the breath catch painfully in the back of his throat. Anywhere, he wanted to shout, anywhere as long as I can get out of this car. But he had no breath to shout. What was that smell in her hair? Hash? She didn't seem the type. Incense? At the thought of incense his ribs seemed to squeeze together. He clawed at his chest, but then the girl was leaning across him, rolling down the window, telling him he'd be all right, telling Mike sharply to drive to that quiet pub by the river…

The pressure on his throat relaxed. He took two good gasps of air, petrol scented, dirty, tired with the summer heat but still wonderfully reviving. After two more he was able to say: "I'm all right. Sorry. Sorry. I'm all right."

Everyone was suddenly quiet. They were uneasy and embarrassed. He was sure they were already regretting their invitation.

Chris said, "Haven't you any pills? Or a spray or something?"

"No." He was still hoarse. "The doctor said it was purely psychological. And I won't take tranquilisers."

Sue said, "Gin is the best tranquiliser" And Chris, suggesting something even better, seized the chance to laugh raucously again, and everyone joined in gratefully.

~~~

They came to the pub by the river. It had chairs and tables on the terrace, under a roof of vines. Martin sat next to the strange girl and learned that her name was Alison. Chris bought a round and then Mike. Martin drank two gins quickly and felt better.

"Look at the sunset on the river. It's so beautiful," said Sue sentimentally.

"It's a cliché," Chris grunted. "Nature is full of clichés."

Alison stared at the red sky and shivered a little. "The nights are drawing in already," she said quietly.

"We only had a few long summer evenings. And now it's starting to get dark soon after eight."

"Aren't you looking forward to the long winter evenings, in front of the fire? On the rug?" Sue said.

"I thought you liked it outdoors, Sue" said Chris.

"I like it anywhere," she said.

"If I had the money," Martin said abruptly, "I'd follow the sun. I'd spend the Northern summer in Iceland, or wherever it is that they have white nights, and then I'd move on. Where, where would I go? Does Australia have long days when ours are short?"

They agreed, after some discussion, that it must for the sake of balance, but no one else was very interested in the question. Chris began to talk about what could be done in the dark. Martin stared at the blackening water and the darkening sky.

"Let's have a big party," said Mike. "I feel like breaking out. Come one, everyone must ring at least two friends and invite them along to Martin's flat after closing time."

"Not Simon." Sue was giggling and protesting. "No one is to dare ring Simon."

"Friends, I said, not your local sex maniac," said Mike. "Come on. Two calls each. Tell them we're all taking bottles back to Martin's place and they can meet us here – someone check the name of the pub – or they could go straight there, but no one will be around to let them in until about half-eleven."

People began stabbing numbers into their phones.

"What about you?" Mike said. "Come on, Martin. You must know *two* other people."

"I left my mobile at home," he said, feeling absurdly guilty.

"Never mind. You can borrow mine. Right, get on with it. Call two people, preferably gorgeous women."

"Are you sure you don't mind?" Alison asked Martin.

"No." He smiled and the smile turned into a cheerful grin with very little effort at all. "I mean, yes I'm sure, and no I don't mind. Let them all come. Even Simon. Whoever he is and whatever he's done."

He stood up. The evening was quite dark now. It was no longer evening, he thought. It was night. People were talking excitedly into their phones

Mike and Chris rang off, laughing and punching each other.

"Nurses," Mike explained. "We've got half-a-dozen coming."

"Each?" one of the other men asked hopefully.

"Go on, Martin," Mike said. "What are you waiting for?"

Martin, suddenly nervous, said, "I can't think of anyone to ring. I've been out of circulation for too long."

"Then you can ring my flat-mate," said Alison. "I think there must be something wrong with my phone. I can't get through."

"Not fair…" Sue began, but Mike cut in quickly.

"He can ring anyone he likes, it's his party. Go on Alison, tell him the number digit by digit. He's hopeless with any machinery as complex as a push-button phone."

Everything began to seem very funny. Alison gave him a printed card with a number on it and he punched the numbers in clumsily, not paying much attention to what he was doing. It was only when he heard the ringing tone that he realised what he had done and then it still seemed very funny. He clutched the receiver, laughing too much to speak for a moment, and then he gasped out, "I've rung my own number!"

And then he heard the receiver being lifted at the other end, and a man's voice said, quite clearly, "Martin Patterson here.

Who's calling?"

Martin dropped Mike's phone so that it crashed and shattered on the floor. Then he was also lying on the floor, fighting for breath, tearing at the bands of iron which seemed to have been snapped round his chest, tears of fright and pain spilling out of his eyes.

They got him out to the car under the curious and unsympathetic eyes of the other drinkers. Someone brought him a glass of brandy. Chris phoned the police and asked them to check the flat for a possible intruder. Then Mike drove them all back. He insisted that the only thing to do was to go on with the party.

"If there is someone there, he's a burglar and he'll have messed the place up so you might as well let us finish the job. If there isn't anyone there, you'll want to celebrate because you haven't had a break-in," he told Martin firmly.

He was unable to protest. He wasn't even sure he wanted to. It might be good to have a party. To have as many people around him as possible, people who would know his name and call him Martin Patterson. Because he was Martin Patterson. He must hold on to that. He was Martin Patterson and whatever had answered his telephone that evening had no right to the name.

When they arrived in the neat little mews they found a police car and a rather puzzled policeman. "No," he told Martin, "there's no sign of a forced entry. Yes, the doors were locked. No, the neighbours had heard nothing and, with it being a nice evening, they'd had the doors and windows open. The woman in the flat next door was prepared to swear that she hadn't even heard his telephone ringing all evening."

And there it was.

Mike drew the policeman to one side and Martin could imagine their conversation:

"Nothing to worry about, officer. Just thought we ought to check. Be on the safe side. He's just getting over a breakdown. Probably all a mistake. And – you know – a break-down –

well…"

He saw the policeman nod and glances towards him with that odd mixture of sympathy and contempt that the healthy offer the sick. "I understand, sir … a breakdown…"

Martin stood in the mews looking wretchedly up at his own lighted window, feeling outcast and forlorn.

Mike left the policeman and gripped him by the arm.

"Come on, you're giving a party."

They went up the narrow stairs.

~~~

The next day Martin woke with a very convincing hangover and the feeling that he had made an utter fool of himself. He'd got drunk, dialled a wrong number and someone, by an odd coincidence, with a name very like Martin Patterson or, by a less odd coincidence, with a name that sounded just like that to a drunken (frightened) man, had answered, and he had panicked.

Everyone at the party, not to mention those who'd been told about it since, must be laughing themselves sick, or pitying him. He couldn't really make up his mind which was worse. And Alison, nice, quiet Alison, with the shiny smoky hair, would never want to speak to him again. By the afternoon, guilt and sorrow had receded a little. Mike phoned and told him everyone had enjoyed the party and that Sue and Chris were giving one on Saturday. So he'd pick him up about nine and they'd get a couple of drinks in before they went.

"When did you and Chris joined the Samaritans?" Martin asked suspiciously.

"What? Oh God, the boss has just come in. Around nine, Saturday, okay?" and Martin was left holding a buzzing phone.

Then he found the card Alison had given him. He must have stuffed it into his pocket instead of dropping it. It was a posh little printed card, engraved with the telephone number and two names, Alison and her flatmate, and for once he was in luck. The flatmate was a girl. As he dialled, later that evening, he wondered for a moment how he had come to make the mistake of last night. It was nothing like his own number. Then he shook himself. That was the point. He hadn't phoned his own number. He couldn't have phoned his own number.

His throat went dry when he heard the ringing tone and he nearly put the receiver down, but it was a woman's voice that answered.

"Alison?" he croaked.

"Speaking."

"It's Martin here," he made himself say it, "Martin Patterson."

"Oh, hallo. I didn't recognise you." Her voice sounded cool. But not frigid.

He blurted out, "I'm sorry I spoiled your evening last night. Can I make it up to you some time?"

And she said, "How about tonight?"

~~~

It was a good evening. The first time he'd actually been out with a woman since before … since before he was ill. Alison was gentle, quiet; she let him talk about unimportant things, she chattered about her work when he grew silent. She was simple and utterly wholesome. He must have imagined that sick sweet smell in her hair. Perhaps he had imagined the voice on the telephone too.

Strangely enough, that was a soothing thought. He would rather believe that he was going mad than that there really had been something in his flat to answer the phone. He found himself, incredibly, talking about it to Alison.

"I'm sorry I collapsed like that. But when I heard – when I thought I heard – my own voice saying my own name, it terrified me. It really did."

"It would," she agreed softly.

"You see–" he twisted his wine glass between his fingers "–I did something silly. That's why I had my breakdown." He stopped and stared over her head into the darkness outside the windows.

"Don't talk about it, if you don't want to."

"But I do. I can tell you." He dragged his gaze away from the night and looked at her pale pretty face instead. Dear, ordinary Alison. "I joined a black magic circle," he said in a rush.

She did not say anything but leaned over and gently took the glass out of his hands and poured him more wine.

"I am – I was – a journalist. It was for a story. One of those sensational Sunday paper things. My editor heard about it. It was … silly. Like a game. I had to sit in a certain pub reading one of those lurid paperbacks on witchcraft, holding it up so the cover showed, waiting for someone to sidle up to me and ask if I was interested in that sort of thing. I could hardly keep a straight face. But I did it. And someone did come … and then … I thought it would be a giggle. You know. Fat WI ladies prancing about with nothing on. But it wasn't."

"You don't have to tell me," said Alison again.

"Oh, it's all right, I won't describe any horrors. But there were horrors. And there was a man. He looked like, like a suburban bank manager. He was so – ordinary – Alison, I can't explain. So commonplace. But he ran the whole thing. He was a diabolist. Really, truly. He was a murderer too, but that was nothing. People won't believe me. They think it's part of the illness. Even my doctor. But this man, he found out that I was a journalist. He called me to his house one night. No, it wasn't at night, not midnight, not anything like that. It must have been around eight o'clock. He called me round for coffee but I knew he'd found out about me. And I couldn't keep away. I had to go. It was a semi in – I can't tell you where. He took me into the sitting room. It was all so ordinary. There was a hooked rug on the floor. I remember it because I kept staring at it. It was roses, red and pink roses on a fawn ground. Oh God, it sounds so stupid!"

"I understand," she said. "Go on."

"He just sat there and told me. My real name, the paper I was working for, and I sat and stared at the roses. I thought he'd have someone there, you know, a hit man, to kill me. He knew people like that. But all he said was 'look up', just casually. And I looked in the mirror. There was a plain mirror over the mantelpiece. I didn't want to look but I did. I couldn't help it. There was nothing in particular there, just this ordinary room and me. Then, the thing, the reflection moved. My reflection moved although I was still. I was standing quite still. It turned its back and started to walk away. And all – the man – said was, 'You'll hear from him soon.' So I went home. And on the way I collapsed. I couldn't get my breath and doctor said it was nerves and I should rest, but all the time I've been waiting to hear. Last night I thought I had."

His eyes slid back to the darkness beyond the windows. "Do you think I'm mad?" he asked hopefully.

"I think you are very badly frightened," she said softly. "But you frighten yourself."

It was only later that he thought that reassurance might have another meaning that was far from reassuring. That was when he got back to the mews. He had not asked Alison to come back with him. After his long rambling confession he felt embarrassed with her. It would be a pity, he thought, to have spoiled anything they might have had going but he had relieved his mind. He'd have to see how things went.

He dropped her at her door and left the taxi there. He walked back to his flat, testing himself to see if he could face the dark streets. He did very well until he turned into his own mews and saw that he had left his lights on. Until he saw them go out as he was still half-way to his door.

This time he fought the breathlessness. He walked up to his door and opened it. He forced himself up the stairs. The flat was empty. There was no one under the bed or in the wardrobe, though he looked everywhere, frightened and ridiculous, like an old maid who has heard noises in the night. But there was nothing. Only an indefinable sense of disturbance, a feeling that the flat had not been empty for long. Only some cigarette ends in an ashtray that he thought he had emptied, a CD left in the player that he could not remember buying. He sat down. There were no mirrors in the house. He'd made sure of that. He could not tell how ill he looked. On the arm of the chair someone, he himself, had left a book. Part of occult reading he had done for his article. It fell open in his hand and he read: *Some men have told me they have seen a double man, or the shape of some man in two places. They call this reflex man a co-walker, every way like the man as a twin brother and companion, haunting him as his shadow. This copy, echo, or living picture, goes at last to his own herd.*

He said aloud, "He goes at last to his own herd," and shuddered at the sound of his voice in the stillness.

"You frightened yourself."

Alison had said that. He frightened himself. He haunted himself. Perhaps he could find a priest who would exorcise himself from himself, send himself back to his own herd. He began to laugh. After a while he drank a lot of whisky and fell asleep at last, sitting up in his armchair, trying to remember if he had emptied that ashtray.

When he woke he could not find the passage in the book.

He persuaded his neighbour that he had a bout of summer flu and couldn't get out. She did his shopping for him, and she would have cooked his meals if he'd let her, but he wanted to be quite alone in the flat, to be quite sure that whatever moved in any room moved because he had touched it. Once, late at night, he thought he smelt cigarette smoke drifting in from another room and sat for an hour too frightened to move. But when he finally made himself get up to look there was nothing there. Once, reading casually late in the hot night, he came across a story about a girl meeting her own double in Holland Park, and was consumed with terror. He was sure that too would have vanished from the book next morning, but it had not. Several times the phone rang. But he would not answer it.

Mike came on Saturday night, about nine as he had promised. Alison was with him. They knocked for a long time while Martin hid in the bedroom. Then his neighbour, who'd taken his spare latchkey "just in case", went down and let them in.

"You look terrible," said Mike frankly, "I think we should take you to casualty, not to a party."

"You're not taking me anywhere," said Martin, but he lacked conviction.

"I wish you would come." Alison was still gentle, still wholesome, but woefully puzzled now. "I really thought you were getting this out of your system when you talked to me that night."

"Talked!" Mike exploded. "Look, if you spent the whole night talking to a girl like Alison you must really be sick!"

"It wasn't all night," said Martin weakly. He found himself overborne by Mike's sheer weight of health and good spirits.

"Well, it shouldn't have been. You don't mean you let her go home."

Alison had gone into his kitchen to make them some coffee. Mike leaned forward to whisper to him, "You'd be well in there. She's worried about you and that's the first step. You just persuade her that you're in need of a little one-to-one therapy..."

Martin got up quickly, trying to divert Mike to less personal topics. "I've been doing some work over the past few days."

It was true. Part of the time he had been writing furiously, trying to throw up a screen of words between himself and his fear. He spread the manuscript on the table, proudly. "That's one good thing about convalescence, it's given me time to work on my novel."

"Good," said Mike indulgently, allowing himself to be diverted.

Alison came back with the coffee. "Drink this and you'll feel better." She frowned at him prettily. "I don't believe you've been eating at all. You must have been working too hard. You must get out more."

He began to say that he was afraid to go out, but his fears withered before their common sense. When Mike's car roared out of the mews he was sitting in the back with Alison, tasting the smoky sweetness of her hair again. It made him think sickly of the incense they'd burned that night when he realised it wasn't a joke, not a joke at all, when he saw what was on the altar, and the – things – that were done to it, as the smell of blood drowned the scent of the incense…

Strange how smoke clings to the hair. He looked suddenly at Alison in ghastly speculation. No. If he began to suspect her then he really would be mad. She felt his look and turned to him brightly.

"I saw you in the Rising Sun on Thursday," she said, "but you wouldn't even smile at me."

His palms were clammy, his breath coming short again.

"I haven't been out," he said.

"It must have been someone else. What a good thing I didn't try to speak to you," she said lightly.

But the iron bands were tightening round his chest again. Was it walking about London now? Had it come to the mews and waited, lurking every night in the shadows, waiting until he left an empty flat, waiting for it, ashtrays emptied, swept and garnished … he tried to open a window but his hand slid sweatily from the handle. Alison quietly opened the window on her side of the car.

"Don't worry," she said softly, "it will pass."

"Shall I drive to a hospital?" Mike inquired with weary patience, feeling the cold air blast through the car.

"No," said Alison, "he'll be fine as soon as we get there."

Martin lay back, letting them take him where they liked.

~~~

Two or three of the people at the party had seen him about that week. One had spoken to him. He felt like a sleepwalker, like a shadow. He was beyond fear. Every breath was a struggle. He found his way onto the balcony and leaned on the cold railing, looking down into the dark. He wanted to cry.

When he went back to the party Chris and Sue were having a spectacular row. Guests were drifting gently away. Mike was in the kitchen lifting cans of beer, shaking each one hopefully trying to find one with something left inside.

"Alison's gone off," he said reproachfully. "Found herself another man."

"I'll go off myself, I think," Martin said. He couldn't tell them he was afraid to go home and he would have to go sometime.

"See you," said Mike, finding a half-empty can.

Martin went out. He took a taxi but he walked from the corner. He would not even take the taxi-driver for protection.

~~~

He saw, as he came into the mews, that the lights were on in his flat. The curtains had been drawn back.

As he came closer he saw them standing together by the window, Alison with Martin Patterson. It was what he expected.

The iron bands were back, tightening agonisingly around his chest as he turned away, silently, into the dark.

# END OF SEASON

He sat on the hot bright terrace, staring out to sea. The waiter hovered over him, poising the silver coffeepot, murmuring that they also served the English breakfast, asking if he would have more toast, or perhaps a croissant...

Richard looked up at him irritably, wondering if the man had nothing else to do. But it was only too clear that he had not. Everyone else must have had breakfast early for there were no other guests on the terrace, though he did wonder where they might have gone. There were very few sunbathers on the white and glistening beach.

"Where is everyone?" he demanded.

The waiter poured him a third unwanted cup of coffee. "It's the end of the season," he murmured, as if it were something he must apologise for.

The travel agent had said the same thing, balancing his pen between his fingers, as if reluctant to write the instructions that would send his client off at such a time. "It's the end of the season, sir," he had said, but he sounded reproving rather than apologetic, as if his client were making unnecessary trouble.

"But the hotel will still actually be open, won't it?"

"Well ... yes, but they'll be running down, dismissing staff, closing down some of the rooms..."

"But it will be *open*. I mean, I won't have to cook my own breakfast? Or sleep on the beach?"

"Oh no, sir." Again, he sounded put out; clearly there were some things you didn't joke about. "They do keep on some staff for the off-season, of course, but ... but ... most of our clients prefer not to go at the end of the season."

"Do you sell many holidays?" Richard had asked rudely but

the man only looked surprised.

"Most of our clients seem satisfied," he said. The suggestion, unvocalized, but clear, hung between them. Richard could always take his custom elsewhere. He set his jaw aggressively.

"I *prefer* the end of the season," he said.

"Very well." With the air of one who has done his best to save a difficult customer from himself, the clerk began to note flight numbers.

Now, sitting on that bright and desolate terrace, Richard wondered what had made him so obstinate. It was not the petty opposition of a clerk in a travel agency.

No. The phrase itself had appealed to him: "The end of the season – to everything there is a season and time for all things under heaven." He had had his time, his season was at a dead end. An end to Miranda, a nice civilised end. He didn't have to be badgered for maintenance payments, and she let him see the children every month, she consulted him meticulously about their schooling, phoning him in the early evenings:

"I'm so sorry to bother you but…"

"Good heavens, it's no bother at all…"

"But I expect you're going out…"

"Yes but not yet. I've got plenty of time … what about you – do you manage to get out enough? Are you finding the girls a drag?"

"No, no, mother's always ready to babysit for me. And they're so good. No trouble…" The unfinished sentences would hang in the air between them. There was really nothing to say.

It was even worse with the children, two clean and dainty little girls, their clean dainty mother in miniature. They were always too much on their best behaviour, never at ease with him. He was a stranger, after all, his visits always preceded by the same dialogue:

"Come along now, finish up your dinner. You've got to get your clean frocks on. Daddy's coming to take your out!"

"Oh Mummy, do we have to?"

"Yes, you do. Come along now."

So he tried to bribe them. He bought them sweets but he had been away too long, their tastes had changed and he could never remember what they liked. Expensive chocolates, packets of space dust – whatever he offered went uneaten. He took them for elaborate treats, which bored them; paid for riding and dancing lessons, which they took as their due; and when they met they all became more and more nervous. A woman had stopped him in the street once, as he tried to jolly the bored and miserable children along to the next stage of their outing, demanding to know where he was taking the little girls. She had nearly got round to calling the police when a wretchedly embarrassed Kathy had managed to say:

"It's all right. He's our daddy."

Now even Miranda greeted him, when they met at friends' social gatherings (not parties, their party season had ended long ago), as if he were a pleasant stranger she might have met once before and they made light conversation before passing on... Oh, the season of Miranda was certainly over and he was not wholly sorry.

He sipped his cooling coffee. Far, far away along the beach he could see a bright umbrella. At least one other tourist was braving the end of the season. He felt no impulse to make contact. And that was another reason, and a much stronger one than any whimsical liking for a phrase, for coming here at the end of the season. He didn't feel like making contact with anyone. The empty sands pleased him. He could stroll along the shore feeling like a Crusoe, but a Crusoe who would flee from the sight of a human footprint. Even the silent waiter, still hovering at his shoulder, annoyed him. He had the momentary wish to be totally isolated, to live in a space station, served by robots, and then, annoyed by his own unusual fancifulness, he pushed his chair away and stood up.

"The gentleman is going swimming?" the waiter asked.

"Later," Richard brushed him aside and went down into the

still streets. The place had never been a fishing village or a fortress town. It was only a holiday resort built on a barren coast. There were high concrete hotels along the seafront, and behind them shops, cafes. And clubs. Everything for the tourist. Richard walked aimlessly. He had moved only to get away from the waiter. There was nowhere he wanted to go.

The shops were full of souvenirs. He glanced idly at the crowded windows thinking he should buy something for the girls, and get it over with. A pair of tawdry dolls caught his eye; they were absolutely alike apart from the colour of their skirts and shawls. This was important. His two dainty little daughters had inherited Miranda's hard acquisitive streak. They had been known to fight, scratching and tearing at each other's hair over some toy. After all, they were too near in age. That had been Miranda's idea.

"They'll be company for each other," she had said, and laid the basis for a life-long rivalry.

Well, he might as well get the dolls, take them back to the hotel, get a towel and spend the morning on the beach. He pushed at the shop door but it would not open. Impatiently, he looked at his watch; it was ten o'clock, not too early to open, surely, and much too soon for a siesta. He knocked on the glass and shook the door but it was certainly locked. There was no one visible inside either. The dolls were assuming a ridiculous importance. It would have been easy enough to walk on and find similar dolls in another shop – easier still to give up the idea of dolls altogether for the time being, but he stayed there, foolishly, in the broiling sun shaking at the door like an idiot.

A voice called him back to a sense of his own stupidity, a passer-by, trying to explain in gentle halting English that the shop was now closed. "It is the end of the season." He walked away impatiently, hardly thanking the man. Sweat ran down his face and he felt as foolish as no doubt he looked. The sun didn't seem to think it was the end of the season anyway.

He might as well go back to the beach. He turned back to the hotel, noticing for the first time how empty the streets were. Surely the residents didn't evacuate the place too when the season ended. What did happen? Did the weather make a sudden and dramatic change? Mediterranean monsoon rains to make the place uninhabitable? A peculiarly vicious local version of the mistral? Or did some strange madness overtake the locals, making it dangerous to stay? Perhaps there were sinister rites connected with the harvest, or archaic sacrifices to the sea-gods for the fishing. He grinned to himself. If there were such rites anywhere in the world now, they would be made into a tourist attraction:

"Golden Bough Tours, offering a comprehensive tour of the cult sacrifices of the world. See the representative of the Corn God slain in the harvest field, and buy your souvenir hand-crafted gold-look plastic sickle." And this resort, with no crops and no fishing fleet would be the last place for them to linger.

The hotel was cool and very quiet. There was no one at the reception desk but he had kept his key in his pocket while he breakfasted. He went straight up to his room, changed, picked up a towel, and started off for the beach. The complete stillness was beginning to get on his nerves.

The beach was a long strip of white sand. Someone had told him that it had been brought there by lorry, dumped onto a shingle base; it looked so flat and white that it might have been painted, and, but for the red umbrella, it was empty under a hot pale sky. The sand crunched unpleasantly under his feet when he began to walk on it; it might really be artificial, he thought, it felt so coarse and heavy grained, like builders' sand. The sea beat on it with heavy regular surges.

He spread out his towel and lay down, feeling curiously exposed on that white expanse. It was like sunbathing on a parking lot. But that was what he had come for, wasn't it? Sun, sand, sea, and perfect peace?

He lay for a while trying to achieve some sort of peace. When his face began to burn he turned over, so that his shoulders were exposed to the glare, and when that grew uncomfortable he decided to try the sea, though it was not very inviting. He walked out cautiously into the waves.

The water felt odd. He could not define it at first and then, after he had been swimming for a while, he placed it. There was no exhilarating chill, no salty tang – just the thud, thud, thud of the mechanical waves; and the water felt strangely warm. And deoxygenated, as if it had been standing around for a long time in a hot room.

He got out of the water and returned to his towel, the thick gritty sand making a hard coat on his wet feet and legs, like a concrete skin. He sat down and surveyed the scene, occasionally chipping bits of sand off his shins. This was becoming ridiculous. The sea could not have gone off at the end of the season, like all the other tourist facilities. He was imagining things, and he had better face facts. It had been a mistake to come here, end of season or not. What he should really have done was to make a determined effort to get Miranda out of his system once and for all. He should have found another woman. But even as he told himself what he should have done he knew it was out of the question. His season as husband and father, even as casual lover, was ended.

Well, there was no sense sitting there getting burned. He stood up and wandered back to his hotel room, showered to get rid of the sand – which refused to wash down the plug but lay, gritty and unpleasant, in the bottom of the shower – then he threw himself on the bed. The best thing to do would be to cut his losses and fly home but he was reluctant to make the effort he would need to arrange things, explain things… He closed his eyes.

When he woke it was late afternoon. He had missed lunch but he did not much care. He was not hungry, not even especially thirsty in spite of the heat, which seemed to have increased instead of lessened during the afternoon. He had a slight but unpleasant headache.

There seemed little point in lying there, and nothing to do if he got up, but nevertheless he did get up and wandered out onto his balcony. It looked out over the beach and he could see that there had been no new arrivals. Only the red umbrella marked the curve of sand like the last outpost of civilisation. He began to wonder who was lying under it. Surely a woman. Men were never such dedicated sun worshippers.

Perhaps it would be worth wandering down to see what she was like. If she were young, or even not too old, if she were at all passable … it would be worth it to kill this feeling of the end-of-all-things that seemed to have lodged itself in his skull. He didn't go in for pickups as a rule but this was a holiday … they could huddle together, two castaways on a cruel coast. He forgot his earlier picture of himself as a Crusoe who would flee from a footprint.

He gathered up a towel, suntan oil, a paperback, and prepared to stroll casually back to the beach, casually making for the only inhabited spot in all that desert of sand. Well, at least he could still laugh at himself. That was supposed to be a good sign.

The would-be Crusoe, the man who wanted no human contacts, strolled towards the red umbrella, rehearsing some snappy approaches: "I say, are you English?" – but if she were, say, German, she might not like that. "Dr Livingston, I presume?" – no, not if she were a dumb blonde. It might take hours of precious chatting time to persuade her that he wasn't actually looking for a doctor. "Would you like to borrow my suntan oil?" – that might be best. It could lead to all sorts of things.

He reached the red umbrella, his opening line still undecided. Perhaps it was better to leave these things to the inspiration of the moment.

But as it turned out he need not have bothered. There was no one at all lying under the umbrella. It had been left in the sand, as significant as a lifebelt tossing in an empty sea, suggesting that someone had been here once but now was gone for ever. He spread his towel and lay down under it himself. There seemed nothing else to do.

Dinner would be a welcome break in his isolation, he decided. He must find some people in the dining room whatever time he chose to go in. Perhaps the best thing would be to lurk in the foyer, waiting until some likely looking couple went in, follow them, and strike up some sort of conversation. Even if they turned out to be drug addicts, or vampires, or a very boring couple from Penge, it would be better than this.

He hovered in the foyer. It was all very quiet, so quiet that he could hear the thud, thud, thud of the waves. Nothing else… His waiter came up, padding across the wide expanse of marble floor, looking anxious, and still apologetic.

"Would you like to have dinner, now, sir?"

Richard found himself blurting out, much more loudly than he intended, "But where are the other guests?"

"There are no other guests," said the waiter softly. "It's the end of the season."

Richard stared round at the brightly lit room, the set tables he could see beyond the dining room doors…

"You mean all this setup is for one person, just for me?"

"We shall be closing down soon, sir." The waiter did not seem to find the situation ludicrous. "But until we do we try to give good service. However few the guests."

In a daze Richard walked into the dining room. He made his choice from an understandably small menu, and during his unsatisfactory meal the waiter stayed beside his chair.

"What now?" Richard demanded when he had finished. "Will they open the bar just for me? Get the orchestra and the flamenco dancers in?"

"I regret, sir, it is not possible to supply entertainment tonight. But we will certainly open the bar."

"No, that's not necessary. I'll go up to my room."

He felt that he should have warned about this. It was totally ridiculous to keep the whole hotel open for just one man. He had been made to feel foolish and uncomfortable. The only thing to do seemed to be to have an early night, pack and get away first thing in the morning. But first, a hot bath to get rid of the itching soreness that a combination of sun and sand had given him.

The hot tap refused to produce any water at all. The cold one belched out a mouthful of rusty water, and then refused to turn on or off completely, but dripped annoyingly. He lay down on the bed, reflecting that he seemed to have spent most of his time lying down, but at the same time that he had never felt so irritable, so completely unrested. It was the silence, he thought, the utter silence of the empty hotel that was getting on his nerves. There was no sound at all now but the intermittent drip of the tap…

Utter silence… WHERE WAS THE SEA?

Unbelieving, with only the faintest stirring of fear at first, he moved to the balcony. The beach was utterly still. The waves had stopped moving. Even as he watched the stars began to blink out one by one, as the whole place closed down for the end of season.

# FIFTH SENSE

Jos drew in a long breath of summer-scented air, analysing it as he did so. The French windows were open and he could smell the rather dry grass of the lawn, the lusher grass of the field beyond, and beyond that again the faint ammoniac taint of cow. Inside the cottage there was the chemical smell of spray furniture polish, mingled with more wholesome scents from the kitchen: new bread, garlic, and the all-pervading smell of sliced cucumbers. But he knew about the cucumbers. Lucy had made him turn the car round as soon as he arrived that afternoon so he could give Sandra, the daily help, a lift home. Her father had given him a whole armful of salad stuff from the garden, and he could remember loading cucumbers onto the back seat. He couldn't include the cucumbers.

"Dinner won't be long." His wife's voice coming unexpectedly from behind his chair startled him.

"What's that, Lucy?"

"I said that dinner won't be long. You were sniffing the air like an old bloodhound so I assumed you were questing for food."

"No, just indulging in my hobby. I was seeing how many smells I could identify. Have you been cutting up cucumbers?"

"Yes, I thought we'd just have salad tonight. It's been so hot." Lucy perched on the arm of the chair.

"Good." He *could* count the cucumbers then. "And is Sandra still using that lavender polish?"

"Yes, I'm afraid so. I don't like to say too much. I don't think she can actually smell it at all."

"Not over her perfume, no."

Lucy giggled. "I gave her a bottle of very expensive stuff. I pretended you'd bought it for me and I didn't like it. I thought she'd wear that and it would be less off-putting for you. But she's keeping it for best."

Jos laughed. "Never mind. I'll get you some more next time I'm in London, and you can take a bath in the stuff, so I won't be able to smell anything else at all."

"I thought you didn't like perfume."

"I prefer it to chemical lavender, but I think you smell a lot sexier without it."

"Can you really tell the difference between, say, Sandra and me, just by the smell? Even if we're not wearing perfume?"

"Especially if you're not wearing perfume."

I wonder why you've got this sensitive nose..."

"I'm a throw-back," Jos explained earnestly. "Our primitive ancestors used their sense of smell for hunting just as they used their superb hearing. Some people still have muscles that let them move their ears around. I have a hunter's sense of smell. In fact–" he launched himself at her with a low growl "–it shows there's a bit of the beast in me."

Lucy laughed but fended him off. He remembered that the children would be in soon, and allowed her to.

"What about a drink before dinner?" he suggested.

"Yes, why not. There's some sherry in the fridge."

"I need this," he called from the kitchen, juggling ice-cubes. "London was hell. But I made some good contacts today. It should go towards paying Maureen's maintenance for the next few months."

"Oh, Maureen..."

He realised that he had made a mistake mentioning his former wife. He filled two glasses quickly and went back, balancing them and a slippery bottle. "For my next trick," he proclaimed, handing Lucy her glass with a flourish.

"You'll pour rather inferior sherry all over the floor and take the polish off," Lucy said amiably enough, taking her glass. The floors were her particular pride. They had redecorated the cottage themselves, sanding the floors, painting the walls a stark off-white, scouring off, painting out, every sign and remnant of Maureen – though neither would have admitted it. There had been a time when Jos felt he would never smell anything but paint and cleaning fluid again. But it had been worth it. The cottage was really theirs now, clean and fresh and new as their marriage.

Jos leaned back savouring, just for a moment, the pure pride of ownership. He had a real Sunday colour supplement country cottage and a real ... but how to describe Lucy? There was no magazine that came up to her standard. A real Rolls Royce of a wife, he thought, and grinned. She smiled back and there was a moment of complete domestic harmony. And then they heard light footsteps in the garden and the children ran in, bringing with them the smell of rubber beach shoes, clean sweat, and something else that Jos could not quite place. Could it be excitement?

It was. "There's policemen all over the village," said Mark.

"Search parties everywhere, with dogs," Sara, his younger sister, squeaked in confirmation.

"They're asking for civilian volunteers," said Mark.

"Whatever's happened?" Lucy asked them sharply.

"They're looking for daft old Jenny," Mark said with relish. "We saw Sandra's mum and she reckons she's been murdered."

"Says she's been murdered," Jos corrected automatically.

They all knew Jenny. She had vanished some three weeks ago. She must have been in her late teens but she seemed at once younger and very much older. She looked like a little old woman but behaved like a dreamy child. Jos, unkindly enough, called her the village idiot. She was given to wandering the seashore and moors, day and night, in all weathers, so at first her disappearance was hardly noticed. Even her mother – not, in the village opinion, a lot brighter than the girl – had not thought to mention it for several days, but when those days became a week she had become mildly concerned and wandered from house to house "looking for my Jenny". It was a complaint about her activities that had led the police to take an interest, but they had searched and questioned without success.

All they had established was that Jenny had last been seen one evening walking along the cliff path that ran past Jos's cottage at the top of the lane. Most people in the village thought she must have carried on walking down the path to the place where it crumbled away and so over the cliff and into the sea. Someone claimed to remember that there was a full moon that night, and it was well known, they said, that the full moon affected people that way – though Jenny had never before shown any signs of being affected by the moon.

"Why does Sandra's mother think she was murdered?" Lucy asked. "Have they found anything?"

"I don't know," Mark said cheerfully, "but she told us there was a sex maniac killer about and we should run straight home and tell you not to let us stay out so late."

"She said, 'Heaven knows what your own mummy would say'," Sara piped in accents that fell some way short of innocence.

"I'll have something to say to that woman," Jos promised.

"No you won't," said Lucy, trying to speak out of the corner of her mouth, for his ears only. "She's longing for an excuse to stop Sandra coming here. She liked Maureen for some reason, so she can't stand me. But I need Sandra. Now upstairs both of you–" she went on in more normal tones "–and wash your hands for dinner. And pay no attention to the nonsense they're talking in the village. I expect Jenny just forgot her way home. Someone has taken care of her."

The children trailed off up the stairs.

"No, but really," Jos protested as soon as they could be supposed to be out of earshot, "you've been a saint about those kids. I mean, they're mine and I love them and all that, but it's you who's been looking after them so that Maureen could get her holiday in Crete. We really don't have to be put up with malicious comments from Sandra's mum."

"Don't worry darling." Lucy enveloped him briefly in an embrace of warm flesh – and complex and delicious odours. "It doesn't bother me a bit. Have your drink and relax."

But Jos found relaxation difficult. His peaceful evening was already ruined. "I really should join a search party you know," he said uneasily.

Lucy muffled a giggle. "I suppose you could give the tracker dogs some tips."

"No, really I should. I mean, this could be worrying. They wouldn't be mounting a search like this if they didn't think they'd find something. It's not like a normal girl going missing. No boy in his right mind would go off with Jenny."

"She was rather sweet, actually," said Lucy musingly.

"Well, whatever she was, if she has been–" he found himself choking on the word murder and said feebly at last "–made away with, it could mean it's dangerous here. For you and the children. We might have to think about going back to London."

Someone knocked on the door. Jos jumped, spilling sherry, then gulped what was left hastily and went to the door to find, as he had half-expected, a search party on their way to the cliffs. Lucy, who had followed him to the hall, clutched his arm.

"You haven't had your dinner," she protested.

"Keep some for me, will you?" he rummaged for an old jacket. "And Lucy – lock the doors until I get back."

It was lighter outside than he expected. They would have a good couple of hours before it got too dark to see anything. Jos found he did not want to talk to the others and they, beyond a few words of greeting, seemed to feel the same. They paced carefully, strung out across the rough grass, heads down, searching with meticulous care for something no one wanted to find.

Jos was intensely aware of the smells, of trodden grass and the sappy sharpness of crushed bracken, heat sweat, fear sweat and the hot furry smell of the police dogs. And then – something else. The sea, surely. But that would hardly be a new smell, and this was new. Rotting seaweed on the beach below? A dead gull? One of the dogs had caught the scent too. It gave a yowl and pulled back suddenly. Sitting right back on its haunches it howled. Its handler, taken by surprise, stopped abruptly too, and Jos, wishing he had an excuse to do the same, walked on. There was a heavy tangle of blackberry bushes beside the path. Jos parted the branches carefully and saw enough to tell him that Jenny was there. She was little more than a huddle of bones – and worse – wrapped in her red anorak. He let the branches swing back and fainted.

It was only a brief moment of blackness. He came to almost immediately to find the young policeman loosening his collar with dog-scented fingers. The dog itself was crouched some yards away, shivering, hackles raised.

"Sorry about that," Jos muttered. "I feel a fool."

"I'm not surprised you went off," said the policeman. His face was very white in the dusk. "It's an ugly sight."

"Any idea how she – how it happened?"

"I can't say, sir." For a moment he was aloof, professional, and then, abruptly, a very young man in need of reassurance. "The head – seems loose. It *rolled...*"

Jos sat up. The rest of the party was in a huddle, even further off than the dog. It was getting dark.

"Can you get in touch with the other searchers?" he asked.

"Yes." Professionalism reasserted itself. "I've radioed my colleagues. We'd better wait. They'll want to take statements."

It was a long dreary wait on the cliff top. Jos tried to breathe as shallowly as was humanly possible. He told himself that the smell of decay was purely imaginary, there was hardly enough of poor Jenny left to cause it, but still it tormented him. Even after the rest of the police arrived there was no respite. He had to go back to the village police station and make his statement. They did at least give him a cup of strong sweet tea – "for the shock" – but it tasted to him of the disinfectant that seemed to have soaked into the fabric of the place. It was a very long time before he could go home.

Lucy was waiting up. She took one look at his face, hurried him upstairs, and dosed him with whiskey. He fell asleep before he could empty the glass – only to wake what seemed to be five minutes later to hear the telephone ringing. But it was light and a glance at the bedside clock told him it was seven o'clock in the morning. He limped down the stairs expecting a business call from somewhere where the hour was more civilised, and found himself talking to Sandra's mother.

"Sandra will be pleased to come up and help out as usual, but not a step does she take unless she's called for and brought back in the car."

Jos leaned against the wall. The hall smelt of dust. His memory of the previous night was mercifully hazy and he found he was making no sense of the conversation at all. He wondered if he could ring off and start again.

"Is Sandra not well?" he suggested at last.

Lucy appeared at the stair-head, sleep-rumpled and wholly desirable. He felt even more inclined to cut off Sandra's mum and go back to bed, but Lucy had run down to take the receiver from him.

"Oh, I see," he heard her say, "I see. Of course... Yes... Appalling... Oh no. Oh, how dreadful... Do they? Oh God... Yes, yes, of course he will."

She rang off and turned a sick face towards Jos.

"You'll have to collect Sandra in the car. I couldn't follow all that woman was saying, but she's quite right to be worried about her daughter walking up here alone."

"They've decided that Jenny was murdered, then?"

Lucy sat down on the stairs. "I don't really know, Jos. She was saying that Jenny's head was *pulled off.*"

He felt sick for a moment too, remembering the policeman's words: "It *rolled...*" Then common sense, warming as whiskey, came flooding back. "That's impossible. No one's got the strength for that."

"They're not saying it was a human being. Her body had been ... partly eaten. They think it was some kind of animal."

"Now Lucy, look..." He was trying to reassure himself as well as her. "I mean, I found the body, for heaven's sake! It was hidden. Pushed right into the undergrowth. An animal wouldn't do that. I think she wandered about, couldn't find her way back, and died of hunger and exposure. It wouldn't take long. She was a weakly little thing. She hid herself, crawled into those bushes for shelter before she died. And then, well, it's not nice to think about but quite small animals – rats or ferrets – could have made a hell of a mess of her in no time."

Lucy put her hand over her mouth.

"All right, I said it wasn't nice. But it's surely better than imagining that there's some kind of ravening beast prowling the cliffs."

"You'd better go and get Sandra if you want any breakfast," Lucy said, brushing aside his clumsy attempt at comfort. "I'm going upstairs to lie down."

The journey back to the cottage was not easy. Sandra was a fount of unwanted information about the tragedy. Most people, she told Jos, reckoned even Jenny was not daft enough to have laid herself down so close to human habitation. But they did think the body could have been dragged into the bushes. By IT.

"A lot of people reckon IT was a wolf," Sandra continued cheerfully. "They take the heads off, you know."

"I didn't," Jos said faintly, "but where would a wolf have come from?"

"Escaped from one of those safari parks, of course. Or," she added reluctantly, "IT could have been a real big dog. One of those allersations. But it makes you go cold all over, doesn't it? They'd never have found her, you know, if they hadn't had that big search, and they only did that because another girl went missing last week. In Plymouth, that was. She turned up, of course. They found out she'd gone off with a Russian sailor –

well it was two Russians and a Basque – but with two girls missing they thought they had one of those sexual maniacs on the prowl, so they got those old tracker dogs to look for Jenny. My mum says you saw her." She gave her last sentence a slight questioning lift, but Jos did not feel inclined to give her the details she obviously craved.

"Yes," he said repressively.

"My mum got talking to one of the policemen. He said IT had really made a meal of her. They could only recognise her by that old red anorak she always wore. They're getting an expert in from the zoo to identify the tooth marks on her bones."

Jos, remembering those bones, made a great mental effort and avoided running into the hedge.

Later, much of Sandra's information was confirmed by the appearance of the wolf-expert on the local television. He told his horrified audience that the tooth marks were indeed those of a wolf or "similar large carnivore". He insisted, however, that wolves do not make a habit of attacking humans. The story of Little Red Riding Hood he dismissed as an unprincipled libel. Wolves, on the whole, he insisted, only ate humans if they came across their dead bodies. "Unless they're rabid, of course," he added cheerfully as he was faded out, leaving viewers to think about still another horrific possibility over their suppers.

Lucy seemed mercifully unworried by the terrors besieging the village. She had forbidden Mark and Sara to walk alone along the cliffs, and warned them to leave all dogs, however well known to them, severely alone. But she had not put them under house-arrest, a fate inflicted on many of the village children. Mothers were insisting in the teeth, or rather teeth-*marks*, of the evidence, that the killer was human and no child of theirs would leave the house until he had been caught.

Jos discovered, rather unpleasantly, that the police thought they might be right. He was called back to the police station "to clear up a few points" in his statement and found himself being asked where he was on the night that Jenny had vanished.

"I was in London," he said firmly. "I had dinner with friends."

"With friends," the policeman repeated heavily, suggesting, Jos felt, that it was not much of an alibi. Then he added, "Well, London's not all that far on the motorway."

"But you can't mean… I thought the teeth marks…"

"Oh yes, sir. But that could have come afterwards, if you see what I mean."

"So we could have a murderer plus an escaped wolf in the area. Perhaps I should take my family back to London."

"We'd rather you hung on here for a few days. If that's convenient. Sir."

"I see," said Jos, who did see rather too well. He seemed to remember that, after the husband or wife of the victim, the actual finder of the body was the prime suspect. But that was nonsense of course. People like him didn't get accused of murder. Not people with cars and bank accounts and second mortgages. He was beginning to smell his own sweat, even above the harsh disinfectant smell of the room where they were sitting.

"Of course," he said too loudly. "I want to help in any way I can."

"Oh, of course," the policeman agreed.

The interview seemed to be at an end. Jos walked back to his cottage to find Lucy and Mark in the garden drinking lemonade. Mark, who liked the wolf theory, was elaborating it loudly. Jos joined them silently, listening to his son and hoping he was right.

"People buy all sorts of funny pets now," Mark was saying. "I read somewhere that the sewers in New York are full of alligators that people bring back from Florida as pets and flush down the loo when they get too big. Someone could easily have brought a wolf cub abroad and smuggled it through Customs, not realising that it was rabid, and when it got dangerous they just let it go."

"But that would only make sense if it was full-grown when it was brought in," said Jos. He wanted to believe it, and the sheer impossibility of the idea made him irritable. "If a cub had rabies it would just go mad and die and not grow up at all. The virus doesn't lie dormant, you know. And I don't see how anyone could smuggle in a full-grown wolf."

Well, I think it's a perfectly horrible subject," said Lucy, with a rare flash of temper. "And I don't want to hear any more about it."

"I heard an awfully funny story about a wolf," said Mark, ignoring both his elders. "There was a man who kept a pet wolf on his estate in Scotland, and a funny thing happened. It escaped one day..."

"Very funny," said Lucy.

"No, look Lucy, do listen. This wolf thing got away, and not long after they found a wolf dead, killed by a train, I think. Well, they got this man out to identify it and he took one look and said, 'That's not my wolf. Mine was a lot younger.' And they never did find out where it came from."

Lucy shuddered. Jos, interested in spite of himself, said, "Did they ever find the escaped wolf?"

"I don't know. Perhaps it came down here and killed old Jenny."

"That really is enough. Please can we have a change of subject!" Lucy was beginning to sound rather shrill.

Mark, perhaps with the idea of getting off wolves, unwisely moved on to Unusual Pets I Have Read About.

"Wasn't there a man in Birmingham who kept a lion in a council flat?" he asked.

"What about the smell?" said Jos involuntarily.

"The lion didn't mind," said Mark, rolling about on the grass, helpless with laughter at his own joke. Then he sat up again. "Do lions really smell? I mean worse than a cat or a dog?"

"Of course. You get that problem with all meat-eaters, and the bigger they are the worse it is. They have very foul breath too."

Lucy stood up. "If you are really going to give a lecture on the oral hygiene problems of lions, I think I shall have more fun doing the washing-up!" She flounced indoors.

Mark made a face. "What's the matter with her? She's a real bitch today. Is it the wrong time of the month or something?"

"Mark—" Jos, really angry and rather glad to have the chance of bawling someone out, was beginning a rebuke based on the presence of a younger sister when he realised something. "Where is Sara?" he demanded.

"I don't know. I can't take care of her all the time. Since he never, to Jos's knowledge, took care of her at all, this seemed reasonable. "She said something about going to pick blackberries. I told her they weren't ripe yet."

The only blackberry bushes within walking distance for a small girl were on the cliffs. The bushes where he had found Jenny. Jos actually felt his skin go cold.

"I think," he heard himself say in a hideously unnatural voice, "I'd better go and find her. Stay here please, Mark."

He set off down the lane, as slowly as he decently could. He wished, when he had gone a few yards, that he had taken a stick from the hall but he could not go back now, not with his son watching him. Besides what use would a stick be? He needed a shotgun, at least. He was a fool to go alone. No one had been up on the cliffs, except the police, since Jenny had been found.

He sniffed the hot salt hair, trying to detect the reek of dog, or worse than dog, on the breeze. He had read somewhere that wolves can tell if their human prey is unarmed. No doubt the scent of fear was streaming from him, telling any hunter that something helpless was walking in the open. At any moment he dreaded to feel the weight on his back, teeth in his neck, the foul breath... It was almost an anti-climax when he came at last to that terrible tangle of bushes and found Sara quite unharmed, sitting on the short cliff grass happily eating unripe blackberries.

Relief made Jos angry. He actually shook the child. "You're a very naughty girl. You know how dangerous it could be—" But she was gazing up at him unperturbed with an innocent gap-toothed smile.

"Don't be silly, Daddy," she said. "It's quite safe until Saturday. Everyone knows that. The next full moon isn't until Saturday night."

"Sara," said Jos very seriously, "whatever 'everyone' knows, the moon had nothing to do with Jenny's death. She was killed by a very wicked man or perhaps a dangerous animal."

"But it was both," she said, still smiling at him. "It was a werewolf of course."

Jos was so surprised that he let her go and watched helplessly as she skipped ahead of him down the path to the cottage. He could not believe that a child who had had such a modern upbringing could believe something so medieval. It was like discovering that she thought the earth was flat, or Father Christmas was as real as the village policeman... Perhaps she did. He was almost grateful for the episode. Terror had dissolved into farce.

Lucy, to his surprise, found the story less amusing.

"Isn't she a bit old for that sort of fantasy?" she asked. "I don't want to interfere – she's not my child–" (and for the first time Jos thought he could detect an unspoken "Thank God" after that phrase) "–but have you ever thought of taking her to a psychiatrist?"

"There's nothing wrong with Sara," he protested.

"I didn't say there was anything wrong. I just feel that she might need some help. These delusions could become unhealthy. She might start *seeing* werewolves next."

"I think it's time we all went back to London," Jos said longingly. But it was the end of the week before he was told by a polite but, he felt, a rather regretful detective that he was, as far as they knew, in the clear. He supposed they had been checking his London alibi, and wondered fleetingly what it had done for his business contacts. Never mind. He suggested to Lucy that they should all go back and spend the week in London together, but to his surprise she was not enthusiastic.

"The children would hate it. They'd miss the best of the weather. Can't you stay here with us instead?"

He hesitated. And remembered his commitments. "It's no use. I left all sorts of loose ends so I could come down this week. I've got to go back and tie them up. But I don't see how I can leave you here. Not with this trouble…"

She put her arms round him. "You worry too much. I won't let the children out of my sight, I promise. But they'd never forgive us for making them spend a week in gritty old London." And nothing he could say would make her change her mind. So he drove back alone and let himself into their depressing little flat. Even on a hot evening it smelt musty. He sorted his mail, and checked the day's telephone messages. For once, things seemed to have gone rather well in his absence. The loose ends were knitting quite nicely without his intervention. He could really have stayed away until mid-week… Suddenly he made up his mind. He would not spend a lonely night in a chilly bed. He would make a few calls, just to keep things ticking over, and then he would drive back to Lucy and the children. It would be an easy drive down the motorway, under a clear sky. It was full moon, almost as bright as day…

Inevitably the few calls took longer than he had thought. Still, he made good time even with half-an-hour's sleep in a lay-by, and it was still dark when he reached the village. But the street was crowded and the houses lit up. Someone, a policeman, flagged him down and thrust a white and sweating face into his side window.

"Are you on your way home, sir?"

"Yes," said Jos. "What's the trouble?"

"There's been a bit of an accident, sir. A girl's been killed. We're sure it's a wolf. Someone actually came across it, feeding on the body. It got away but we've got the dogs out. Just take care, sir, when you get out of your car. It may be lurking—"

The face went away. Jos drove out of the village. He was not really sure of what he was doing. Nightmare pictures came into his head: the wolf *lurking*... Lucy or one of the children going outside... He arrived at the cottage. In spite of the warning he took no care at all but leaped from the car without thinking of his own danger.

Everything was quiet, so quiet that he found himself creeping up the stairs, almost on hands and knees. No need to frighten anyone. The children's door was half-open. They were both in bed, both asleep. He pushed open his own bedroom door. Lucy was in bed, asleep too. He could see her hair on the pillow. Thank God, Lucy was safe too.

He moved very softly to the bed. The room was tenderly lit by the first flush of dawn. His wife was lying so peacefully, and as he bent over her he could smell the cool scents of her freshly washed hair, the smell of clean bed linen.

And another smell that brought him whimpering to his knees.

Coming so gently and regularly from between her parted lips, the reek of her breath, the foul smell of the newly fed carnivore.

# THE BANKS OF THE ROSES

*Oh when I was a young thing and easy led astray*
*Before that I would work I would sooner sport and play*
*Before that I would work I would sooner sport and play*
*With my Johnny on the banks of the roses.*

It's a blistering hot afternoon in June. The sun's blazing, but great black clouds are piling up on the horizon and the weather will break soon. She can feel the thunder coming – it gives her a strange sick feeling in her stomach, like excitement, but not really, like fear but not quite, like something more than just that a storm is coming…

She sits on the lip of Rosebank Quarry listening to Johnny whistling to her from below. She knows the words to the tune because he sings them to her sometimes. He's got a good voice, she thinks, but he only sings old-fashioned stuff, or songs he's made up for himself. He must have made that one up, and put his own name in it, along with Rosebank Quarry, as near as makes no difference. And still, somehow, it's familiar, as if she's heard it before.

The quarry is where they meet and it's not romantic, like it sounds in the song. It's a gash of red earth and it's got nothing to do with roses. It belonged to a Mr Rosebank years ago, back in history times, but they say he lost his money and went away, and no one wanted it or could be bothered to fill it in. There are stories about it, but they're not romantic either, they're silly. They say someone was murdered there and her blood – it must have been *her* blood, it's always girls who are murdered in stories though really it's the boys who get themselves stabbed in her world – well, whatever, her blood stained the earth deep,

deep red. There must have been an awful lot of it she thinks cynically.

Or, someone else says, a whole bunch of Mr Rosebank's workers were killed when the side of the quarry fell in and it was too dangerous to try to dig them out, so they're all still down there, under a heap of rocks, and the quarry was red for ever after that, and that's why they stopped working it. And her gran had told her that *her* gran's gran had told *her* that there was a pool at the bottom of the quarry that was so deep it could never be measured, and if you went too near something called Jenny Greenteeth would pull you in and drown you. There's a scummy sort of pond down there, all right, but no one could believe it was bottomless. Not with those bits of shopping trolley sticking out of the water like they do. But old people believe in all sorts of rubbish. Her own gran thought you could get appendicitis from swallowing apple pips. And who eats apple pips?

She can't think why anyone would tell stories about apple pips but she knows why they tell them about the quarry. It's because they want people to keep away but no one can be bothered to fence it off. But boys go down there to do whatever stupid things boys do when they're together, and older boys take girls there. Like Johnny takes her. It was Johnny told her about the dead quarrymen, and how their hands could be seen sticking out of the rubble at dusk, trying to get hold of the living, and when he caught hold of her ankle after he'd told her the story she was supposed to jump and squeal. Which she did, of course, but only because he expected her to.

Stories, so many stories. She thinks she's getting tired of them, but she's telling one of her own now, the one about going off with Johnny. Why not? It's not as if her mam would care – glad to be rid of her, more like. The thought of just dropping everything and going away down the road appeals to her. And Johnny's all right. He talks funny sometimes – she wonders if he's bit gone in the head, or maybe he takes drugs although he's never offered her any, but – who cares?

He whistles again, shrill as a bird. Perhaps he's getting impatient. She hopes he is. He needs to know that young she may be, but she's not easy led. Not at all. It's her that does the leading. If she does go with him they'll go where she wants to go, and when she's ready she'll be off by herself. She gives him another nicely judged five minutes then slides down the red bank, letting her skirt, already several inches shorter than school rules require, ride up even further. True, she's wearing knee-socks, which in her opinion look less than seductive but she knows that men don't think the same way about these things. She could have gone home to change when she skipped out of school in the lunch hour – her mam was out but one of the neighbours would be sure to be twitching her curtains, and telling her mam, and mam would feel duty bound to have a screaming row about bunking off school (as if *they* knew or cared how many people stayed after they'd got their names checked on the register) and she's getting bored of rows. She's getting bored of everything except Johnny, and who knows how soon she might get tired of him?

She lands with a squeal and a scuffle amongst the unsavoury rubbish at the foot of the slope, making enough noise to let Johnny know she's here, but he doesn't look round, just sits on that rock beside the pond, whistling, and for a moment she turns cold as if the sun has suddenly gone in – but then he does look at her and smiles that odd smile of his that looks sadder than a frown.

"You got away then?" he says.

"Didn't have to get away. Just walked out."

"Tell anyone where you were going?"

"Why would I? And why would you care?"

He smiles again. "Ashamed of me?"

She doesn't understand that. What's to be ashamed of? She doesn't ask because he's obviously got one of his funny moods on. She could just walk away. She will if it goes on too long. But she doesn't, yet. Instead she sits on the rock beside him and he whistles again, then starts to sing.

*On the banks of the roses my love and I sat down*
*And he got out his violin to give his love a tune.*

She giggles. "Violin. That's one word for it," she says.

"Charming flute," he says. "That's another one."

She laughs again. It's even hotter at the bottom of the quarry than it was on the bank above, as if all the heat has gathered there, running down the sides, filling it like hot treacle. It's hard to move, hard to think. She wants to suggest they find some shade but it's even harder to speak. When Johnny stands up she can barely drag herself up to follow him.

"Where are we going?" she asks, to see if it's worth moving.

"I want to show you something."

She giggles again. "I've seen it."

"Not this, you haven't."

He takes her hand and pulls her to her feet and she gets up unwillingly, but as if it's inevitable. This has got to happen. He drops her hand and walks away and she follows him. She thinks at first he's leading up the bank again but instead he's going towards one of the caves in the sides of the quarry. Normally she would resist. The caves are horrible, smelly, full of rubbish and worse, but now she goes only half-unwillingly. She tells herself that it might at be cooler there at least, but that's not the reason.

"There!" Johnny stands aside from the cave entrance so she can see what's inside. It's hard to focus after the dazzle of the sunlight, but she does and she sees… She sees the floor of the cave and the long deep rectangle dug into the red earth, the pile of soil beside it.

"What…" It's hard to look, hard to see, and she wants to close her eyes now but she can't. She turns away to look at Johnny, to ask him to tell her what it means but it's hard to see him too. He's flickering in and out of focus, and he's dressed differently, sometimes he's wearing a full-sleeved white shirt and breeches like someone in those TV series her gran used to like, sometimes it's something long and white, like a doctor's coat, that she doesn't recognise as a shepherd's smock, and then it's red, the tight red jacket of a soldier, then it's his own T-shirt and jeans. She must have got a touch of the sun, she tells herself, blinking furiously to make her eyes go right. As soon as she can see properly she's off home. Whatever Johnny says.

And then he says something quite mad. "You don't remember the song, do you?"

"The song?" she repeats stupidly. It's so hard to speak, as if her throat is clogged with sand. Should have brought a bottle of water.

And he sings the song. She's never heard that verse before and she wants to say that she can't remember something she's never heard, except that she knows it somehow, she always has known it. That verse that's so often dropped from the song, to turn it into a cheerful song about drink, instead of the eerie story it really is.

*Well, they walked and they talked till they came unto a cave*
*Where Johnny all the day had been digging up a grave,*
*Where Johnny all the day had been digging up a grave*
*For to leave his lassie low among the roses.*

And yes, that is a grave. She remembers the shape and the darkness of it from her gran's funeral. It must have taken a lot of back-breaking work to dig. It isn't a bad joke to scare her. She won't get away with just jumping and squealing. He's quite serious. It really is her grave, or will be, because just now when it is so important to scream and run or plead for her life, she can't do it. She's trapped. She manages to stumble a few steps away from the horror but she can do no more than whisper "Mam!" as if it were a prayer for protection to the only source of protection she knows. But Mam isn't here and Jenny Greenteeth isn't going to erupt from her pond to drag Johnny away into the depths.

He takes out his knife. That too shifts and changes into shapes she doesn't recognise, although one is a bayonet, and one a hedging knife … but all of them are sharp as murder. She takes a step backwards and falls helplessly onto the littered ground of the cave. A ray of sunlight catches the blade and dazzles her as he raises it and it's the last thing she ever sees and her story is ended before it properly began.

Indifferently he rolls her body into the grave he prepared so carefully, but he doesn't fill it. He leaves her tumbled on the red earth where they will find her later, to bring her mother a world of grief, and steps outside. Immediately a flash of lightening sizzles almost in front of him and the clouds spill floods of rain, rain that will blot out his footprints, and hers, and might wash away the blood leaving him as clean as any new-born bairn. If such things matter to Johnny and his like. Probably they don't. He scrambles up the side of the quarry and stands for a while in the rain that hammers down as if it might obliterate the world.

But not a drop touches him.

# THE GODMOTHER

"She's been like this all morning, doctor."

Old Mrs Rothiemay heard her granddaughter's voice, querulous as usual, but now with an undertone of some more positive emotion. Anxiety? Or could it be hope?

"Is she really bad?"

Then the doctor's rumblings, harder to make out because she was less used to his voice, but clearly offering reassurance, suggesting perhaps that there was a lot of it about. Mrs Rothiemay, a gripper all her life, gripped the sheets and wished the voices away.

She was such a very old woman now that she could only manage one thing at a time. Now she did not want to listen, but to think, to remember. Gratefully she let herself sink away from the voices, back through the years... A last shrill exclamation from her granddaughter held her back, but only for a moment,

"She's been like this ever since Den brought her the paper up."

Mrs Rothiemay had started life in the previous century as Susannah Deborah Jewkes, named for her aunt Deborah and her godmother, Susannah Paget. Mrs Paget had proved the better investment. When her namesake was twelve years old she found her a place at Satterthwaite, the big house where she reigned as housekeeper. Aunt Deb had been good for nothing but a plain cross and chain of doubtful metal. The young Susannah, or Sukey as she was called, had even then a well-developed sense for personal property. She wore the cross permanently round her neck, where it left a greenish mark, to keep it away from her sisters. But she was well aware that Mrs Paget was the more glittering prize.

In the weeks before she went away, she drove her family nearly mad with her accounts of the splendours of Satterthwaite and the glorious life she would lead there. It was useless for her mother to point out that she was going as scullery maid and not as an adopted daughter, and that scullery maids do not, as a rule, wear black silk dresses and eat roast chicken every day. Mrs Paget might indeed wear silk but she was the housekeeper. And she would only wear it on Sundays and holidays. And, as for chicken, words failed her! Nevertheless, Sukey went on with her tales. It was unfortunate, perhaps, that Mrs Paget arrived to escort her to Satterthwaite wearing a silk dress so rich that it could have stood alone, without the support of its wearer's ample figure, with silk petticoats *audible* beneath it, and silk stockings. The stockings alone were enough to give a normal child delusions of grandeur, besides giving a prudent mother pause for thought.

Mrs Jewkes studied her old friend carefully as they sat sipping tea and talking over old times, and wondered about those stockings. They certainly were silk. She could hear the rasp as Mrs Paget crossed her ankles. And was that ring on Mrs Paget's large white hand a diamond? Was it possible that such things could be honestly come by, and if they were not was she right to let Sukey go? But after all, Sue had always been a saving woman, and who else had she to spend the money on but herself? Besides both stockings and ring could have been presents. Or bequests. Upper servants *were* sometimes given such things by grateful employers. She did not want to stand in Sukey's way … and she did want the child out of the house. She was undisciplined, lazy and as inquisitive as a monkey.

So Mrs Jewkes contented herself with fervently kissing her daughter, reminding her of her prayers and her duty, and bidding her write a line now and again to let them know how she did.

"You don't want to fret about her," said Mrs Paget comfortably. "Satterthwaite's not China, nor yet Tartary."

And Mrs Jewkes dabbed her eyes with her apron, obscurely comforted by these self-evident truths.

She might have felt some disquiet had she seen her daughter's reception at Satterthwaite. Do even housekeepers, she might have asked, go to the front door? And are they let in quite so respectfully by a liveried manservant?

"Ah, Thomas," said Mrs Paget to the great fine gentleman who opened the door to Sukey and herself, a gentleman so fine that Sukey took him for the master until her godmother spoke. "You can tell the master that I've brought the little girl. I'll take her to my room and give her some dinner for we're both tired after the journey, but when we've had a bite and sup I'll bring her to see him."

And up the great stairs they went, to a room that Sukey thought grand enough for the Queen herself, that Mrs Paget called her sitting-room, and there they sat and had dinner brought to them. They really did eat roast chicken, with bread sauce and vegetables all complete, and after that a sort of creamy pudding. Her godmother drank wine with the meal but Sukey, somewhat to her disappointment, was given milk. The grandeur of her surroundings and her mother's warnings about good behaviour kept her silent, and her godmother seemed pleased with her. After their dinner Sukey, under instructions, washed her face and tidied her hair and then went pattering after her godmother's dark bulk like a pet lamb through the long ill-lit corridors of Satterthwaite to meet her new employer.

It was here that she had her first shock. A little before they reached his room Mrs Paget bent down and murmured that she was not to be afraid, but the master was not quite well and had to sit mainly in the dark for the light hurt his eyes. Sukey was to curtsey as she had been taught, and say yes sir, and no sir, and not ask questions. It had not crossed her mind to question the master but she would dearly have liked to question Mrs Paget. She was given no time but hurried into the dark room, dark not only with the night but muffled from floor to ceiling with great long velvet curtains and lit only by a little fire. There was a sickly sweet smell as if someone had been burning pastilles, and underneath that something rather unpleasant that caught at the throat – and made Sukey think, for no reason that she could imagine, of Farmer Tyson's beast yard.

Mrs Paget stopped just inside the door and pushed Sukey forward.

"I've brought the little girl," she said.

A thin petulant voice form the gloom said, "Well, bring her in, bring her in. Don't hover in the doorway like that!"

Mrs Paget seemed inclined to send Sukey in alone, but she clung to her skirt and in the end she guided the child across the dark room until they came very close to the wing chair by the fire where the master sat. Sukey curtseyed, and then as no one said anything she dared to raise her eyes and look at him. She was almost shocked into an exclamation of surprise. She had been expecting a sick old man huddled up in rugs, wrinkled like grandfather Jewkes. Instead he was young and almost angelically beautiful. True, he was pale, and his brilliant gold head hung back in the chair as if he were too tired to hold it upright, but even his pallor was beautiful, like marble. Sukey, forgetting her manners, stared and stared.

At last he spoke, still in that thin, weak voice, "So. This is Sukey."

"Yes sir, if you please, sir," said Sukey, bobbing another curtsey, to be on the safe side.

The effort of speaking these few words seemed to have exhausted him and there was another long pause. And then he said a rather strange thing, "And you named her?"

"I named her," said Mrs Paget in a queer solemn way, like someone making their response in church.

The master's great blue eyes closed. Sukey half-thought that he was dead, but Mrs Paget shook her gently and whispered, "He's gone to sleep. Quietly now!"

And they both tiptoed away. The dim corridor seemed quite

bright after that dark room and Sukey blinked. She opened her mouth to ask the dozen questions that were buzzing in her head, beginning with "what's wrong with him?" then "is he going to die?" and going on to "what did he mean, asking if you named me?" but Mrs Paget hurried her along so fast that she got no time to ask anything at all.

They went back to Mrs Paget's rooms. Her bedroom led off the sitting-room, and off that again was a little slip of a room which she called the powder-closet, giving Sukey some uneasiness as she took it to mean the place where gunpowder was stored, although she could see none. And here a truckle bed had been set up. Still giving Sukey no time to talk she told her to get herself undressed and into bed as soon as she liked for she must be tired. Once she was in bed Mrs Paget came in, both to take away the candle (for fear of fire, reviving Sukey's fears of gunpowder) and to give her a cup of milk, with honey, to help her sleep. Warm milk and honey must have had a wonderfully soothing power for, in spite of the strangeness of the bed and all those unanswered questions, she fell asleep at once.

The next day came remarkably close to Sukey's dream of life at Satterthwaite. After a breakfast of bread and milk taken in her godmother's room, Mrs Paget told her that although by rights she should now go to the kitchen to start her new duties: "The whole house is quite at sixes and sevens what with the master being took so bad, and Mrs Colleywood, Cook that is, can't be doing with you down there for a while. So, if you'll sit quiet up here and let me see what sort of a hand you are with the needle, like a good girl, maybe you could take a walk in the garden this afternoon. We'll see."

"Is the master going to die?" Sukey inquired cheerfully.

Mrs Paget took a quick shocked breath. "Why no, bless you, he gets these bad turns regular. He'll be right as ninepence in a day or two."

Sukey tried to imagine that strange sick figure "right as ninepence" and failed. Nevertheless she held her tongue and took her godmother's needlework bag when it was offered, with another bag stuffed with scraps of cloth and bits of ribbon, and settled to work. She was very handy with her needle when she cared to be and she set herself the pleasurable task of making a little tablecloth in patchwork, each patch edged with ribbon. Working with such pretty stuffs, at her own pace, gazing out of the window when she cared to, or taking a turn round the room to admire her godmother's handsome china ornaments, hardly seemed like work to Sukey, and she was able to pass the morning very agreeably, though about eleven it came on to rain and she could take no more pleasure in the window.

Mrs Paget brought her a nuncheon of cold bread and meat and admired her sewing. "Why I never saw such fine stitches! You could get to be a lady's maid, Sukey, if you work hard and mind your manners!"

Sukey was flattered but somehow she did not feel that her godmother really had her mind on what she was saying. She broke right through Sukey's discussion of whether a glossy green edging or a dull purple one would look best on a patch of crimson silk, to say, "I'm afraid the weather's changed, Sukey, as you can see, and you can't walk out this afternoon. I must be about my work so you stay here like a good child. There are some journals there with some pretty fashion prints that you can look at if you get tired of sewing."

And she hurried off without waiting for Sukey's answer. Now, Sukey and been unnaturally good for one whole day and a half. She had watched her tongue and minded her manners and studied to please her godmother. But now, left to her own devices for a whole afternoon, it was not surprising that her good behaviour should become somewhat strained.

At first she went back to her sewing, flattered by Mrs Paget's praise of her stitchery. But she still could not make up her mind about the edging and began to think that a rest might do her good. Following the housekeeper's instructions she looked round for the journals she had been given leave to read. They were not immediately visible so she began to hunt for them and found at once a much more absorbing task than either reading or sewing. She began to poke and pry through every drawer and cupboard.

If this was an amusement in Mrs Paget's sitting-room, it was a positive fascination in her bedroom.

Sukey was neat-fingered and knew the penalties of discovery very well. Careful to leave no trace she sorted delicately through drawers of scented under linen, took her godmother's dresses from their hangers to hold them against her own skinny shoulders. And spent a long time over the jewel box admiring the effect of the glittering stones and shiny metal against her own neck and ears. It was at the bottom of the jewel box that she found a small brass key. Now, nothing in either room, not even Mrs Paget's desk, had been locked. Sukey, her curiosity really roused now, determined to find what lock the key fitted.

It was so small that at first she looked for a small box, coming close to disaster when she opened a tiny coffer on the dressing table that proved to be full of face-powder, which nearly spilled all over the floor. When she could not find a box she went back to the desk to search for a locked or, better still, a secret drawer. Again there was no such thing. Back she went to the bedroom. All the cupboards there opened easily.

She drifted to the middle of the room, uncertain, half-willing to give up the search and go back to her sewing. After all, her godmother would very probably soon be back. The afternoon that had been so dark and rainy was ending in a wild golden sunset. It would soon be night … and then, in those last golden rays, she caught sight of a glitter on the dark panelled wall. Idly, she went to see what it might be.

It was, of course, a tiny keyhole. She slipped the key inside, turned it and pulled. The panelling swung open to reveal a hidden cupboard, as tall as a man but very narrow. Hanging inside was what Sukey took to be a nightie of very thin red silk trimmed with gold. There was more silk on the floor, apparently wrapped around something. And there was a picture painted on the inside of the door, a big picture, which Sukey characterised as "mucky". Even as she stooped to investigate the silk wrappings on the floor she heard Mrs Paget's step in the corridor.

She shut and locked the door, put the key back where she had found it, launched herself back into the sitting-room, and was sitting at her sewing with nothing but a slightly heightened colour to betray her when Mrs Paget came in.

Sukey came very close to mentioning her discovery.

If she had not found the key while meddling with the jewel box she might have done so. It never crossed her mind that Mrs Paget knew of the hidden cupboard and its strange contents, and certainly not about the rude picture. She supposed they had all belonged to a previous owner, probably one of the gentry who were well known to admire that sort of thing, and the key had simply been tidied away by Mrs Paget. But one thing that her mother had impressed on her was the meddling was wrong. It could lead to a box on the ears and bed with no supper. Best, she told herself, to keep quiet.

Her godmother seemed even more agitated than she had that morning. She praised Sukey's work again, though anyone but a fool could have seen how little she had done of it, then rustled up and down the room like a large and distracted moth. When at last she settled, it was on a chair a good distance from Sukey, and though she began to talk to her she seemed curiously unwilling to look her in the face.

"You know, Sukey dear," she began, "that gentleman, and ladies too, have all sorts of odd ways…" And then she hesitated for so long that Sukey assumed she had finished and put a few more stitches into her patchwork. But then she started again. "Well, the master has got it into his head that he wants to sit out in the garden. Now, with his eyes being so bad he can only go out at night-time. He'll want things fetched to him, and of course I must wait on him – it's no more than my duty – but I don't care for walking through the grounds alone at night, so I thought that perhaps you, Sukey, could go along with me. You could sleep late tomorrow, you know," she added.

"Yes, I'll walk with you and welcome," said Sukey, as she had been taught. "But won't master take cold?"

"Oh, he'll have a fire," said Mrs Paget briskly.

Now that her message had been delivered she seemed calmer, though she would eat no dinner, and went to lie down for a while when Sukey had eaten hers, promising to call her when it was time to go to the master.

Sukey went back to her sewing. The evening dragged on. It seemed to her that it must be almost morning when her godmother called her, though, in fact, it was not quite midnight, as she saw by the little travelling clock beside the bed. Mrs Paget was already wrapped in a black cloak. She wound Sukey in a shawl, and gave her a covered basket to carry, then led her not down the main staircase but through some narrow passageways and down a steep flight of back stairs, through the empty kitchens and across the stable yard. It was not especially cold, but very dark. The rain clouds had come back and there was neither moon nor star to be seen.

Sukey tried to ask a question or two but she was immediately hushed, and once they were in the park she found she needed all her breath to keep up.

They seemed to walk a very long way, through a shrubbery, across a wide expanse of dark grass, and then downhill, until Sukey smelled stagnant water and saw a lake glimmering ahead. They walked along the lake shore for some way and then at last they glimpsed a fire in the distance. As they got closer Sukey saw that the master had not one fire but four.

They were burning in iron braziers set, though Sukey did not know at the time, at the four points of the compass, in a strange white building that was mostly pillars. He was feeding one of the fires, and he looked worse than Sukey remembered. He was sweating, and he had clearly not even had the strength to dress himself properly for outdoors, for he was wearing what she took to be a long white nightshirt that left his arms bare.

"You're late," he said in his faded voice. "I can hardly hold him."

Mrs Paget briskly shed her cloak and began feeding another brazier from a little basket lying beside it. Sukey was shocked to see that she was wearing nothing but the thin silk robe from the secret cupboard.

Heavy wreaths of smoke, some sweet, some acrid, billowed across their faces. The master stood up, wiping his forehead.

"Take the child into the circle," he said.

Mrs Paget went white. "What!" she hissed. "I know a trick worth two of that. Take her yourself. I've done my part."

Sukey looked round for the circle they were talking about, and saw it, drawn in what looked like brownish chalk on the white marble floor. There seemed no reason why anyone should be as frightened by it as Mrs Paget and the master so obviously were. Sukey yielded to her curiosity and stepped in of her own accord to see what all the fuss was about.

And at once she knew. The floor seemed to open in a sickening downward spiral and at the same time it could not be opening because she did not fall, although she felt all the horrible sensations of falling.

Yet it must be opening for something was coming through it.

Sukey felt physical sensations that might be compared to being drowned in freezing sewage that burned like acid while it froze. The mental sensations were indescribable, but included a sort of sickness of the mind that she was sure would have sent her mad if it had gone on a moment longer. For it stopped quite suddenly.

The Thing rejected her, literally hurling her outside the circle beyond the light of the braziers.

She landed on her face in the grass. For a moment she lay still until the sound of her godmother's screams spurred her into action. She stood up, some instinct warning her not to look behind, and ran for the house. But however fast she ran, however often she fell, and stumbled up again, and ran on, she did not lose her grip on that christening gift from her Aunt Deborah, that cross of dubious metal, but undoubted power, that she found herself clutching so tightly in her hand.

The scandal, when it broke next morning, was only concerned with the master, who had been found beside the lake, half-naked and wholly dead, and Mrs Paget who was still just alive but "quite silly like" and wearing what appeared to be a red silk nightdress of the most indecent sort. Amongst her fellow servants that nightdress was the most fruitful topic of interest and speculation, throwing the master's death quite into the shade. And the later discovery in the lake of a collection of bones that seemed to have belonged to quite a number of young girls was hushed up.

Sukey never talked.

She never told anyone, either, of what she found in her godmother's secret cupboard. In fact, she burned it before anyone could see it, which was a pity perhaps. A contract with the devil's own signature might have interested a number of people. But Sukey felt she was justified. No one likes to make public the fact that she has been sold to Satan by her own godmother. And that there appeared to be no escape clause.

The master's will was made public and caused a lot more gossip. He gave instructions that he should be buried in a room built on to the family mausoleum especially for him. He was to be sitting in a chair, fully dressed in his everyday clothes with a bottle in his hand. The floor was to be sprinkled with certain herbs and a quantity of broken glass. The gossips said that all this was to prevent the devil collecting his body. His soul had already been lost that night by the lake when he failed to deliver – whatever he had agreed to deliver, every seven years in return for long life, riches and beauty.

It was all a lot of nonsense, of course. Sukey had been sent to a less glamorous but safer place, and eventually she grew up, married, and tried to forget. Over the years she had managed to persuade herself that everything had indeed been some sort of nightmare, the product of an overactive imagination.

But now she had been forced to reconsider. It had been the half-forgotten name of Satterthwaite that had drawn her eye to the newspaper item with its unpromising headline: *So much for tradition*. It told reasonably accurately what it described as the legend of how the master of Satterthwaite had been buried, and described how that little room had been opened recently by a curious historian wishing to check the accuracy of what he called "folk memory".

Of course, he had found that the story had been all nonsense. The room was quite empty.

The devil, Mrs Rothiemay, nee Sukey Jewkes, could see, was not so easily cheated.

# THE LADY WHO RODE
# THE CENTRAL LINE

"I saw Lenin on the Underground today," said Mrs Paggledon casually.

Her daughter-in-law Helen, who was sprinkling oregano onto a saucepan of bolognaise sauce, let her hand slip. ("Very savoury–" her husband was to say later, picking dry greenery from between his teeth "–but a bit – Italian.") Then she collected herself and remembered what the psychiatrist had said about not arguing

"You see, once you argue you accept her fantasies. You give them a basis in reality. You know, and I know, that she can't have met – who was it?"

"Well, it's quite a lot of people," Helen said apologetically, though she did not know what she had to apologise for, really. "It's usually Russians. Dead Russians, like Tolstoy or Trotsky and sometimes Stalin, but they can be English. She saw William Morris once in a launderette."

Helen did not add that it was William Morris who had really rung the alarm bells for her husband Herbert. No expert on foreign affairs – for all he knew Trotsky was alive and well and still taking his vodka with ice – but even he realised that the famous manufacturer of Victorian wallpaper must be dead.

"Is, er, socialism a common factor?" the psychiatrist asked.

"It could be," Helen agreed doubtfully.

"And, er, death?"

"Death?"

"I mean, all the personalities your mother-in-law claims to encounter are in fact dead? She never sees current leaders of the few remaining communist states? Or, for instance, the Queen?

Many of my patients see members of the Royal family."

But Helen had to admit, regretfully, that her mother-in-law never did see members of the Royal family in the Underground. Of if she did she had not found them worthy of mention.

"So…" He tapped his front teeth with his pen. It was a very cheap plastic biro and Helen wondered why a professional man like that did not buy himself a nice gold-mounted fountain pen. "So. We have two common factors. Socialism and death. Interesting. I should like to meet your mother-in-law. It is, of course, easier to treat a patient one has actually met."

"I'm afraid that's out of the question," said Helen firmly. "We really hoped you'd be able to suggest some way of dealing with it…" What she had really hoped was that he would say these things were quite normal at Mrs Paggledon's age, and easily cured. Some sort of capsule, three times a day, that could have been administered secretly in a cup of tea, was what she would have liked.

"I see. Well, it all comes down to the point I made earlier. To argue is to accept. You know – if she said, for the sake of example, that she met a neighbour in the street, you might say, "Oh no, she's gone to her sister's, you couldn't have seen Mrs Brown today." But that accepts the possibility of her at some time and in some place *actually* meeting Mrs Brown."

"But what should I say?" Helen demanded, coming as close to snapping as her nature would allow. "If I say, 'Oh really, and was he looking well?' every time she says she's met a dead Russian on the Central Line, it's surely encouraging her even more."

"Well, do as you would when your daughter tells you about her imaginary friends, or pets—"

"Do you mean it's hereditary?" Helen said, horrified. "Do you mean Anthea will start seeing things?"

"Good heavens, no. In a child of that age it's perfectly normal. Most of them have an invisible friend or pet. My own daughter had one called Bunnikins. She used to get most upset in supermarkets if shoppers trod on him without realising. And of course, as they couldn't see him, it happened quite often. My wife had to stop taking her shopping in the end – which might, of course, have been the idea…"

Helen cut through this cosy reminiscence. "Anthea hasn't got anything like that." She spoke bravely but she felt uneasy. Perhaps this wasn't normal. After all, if a psychiatrist's daughter went about with invisible rabbits it must be normal.

"Oh well, if she had you might say, when she talked about them, 'that's nice, dear' or an equivalent and just go on with what you were doing. Not make a big *thing* of it."

"That's nice, dear," Helen repeated with all the false conviction of a television commercial.

"Yes," the psychiatrist agreed doubtfully, "or the equivalent. But whatever you do don't argue with her."

"That's nice," said Helen to her mother-in-law and went on trying to fish bits of oregano out of the sauce with a teaspoon.

"There's no need to take that tone," said Mrs Paggledon bridling. "I know you don't believe me…"

"I didn't say that," Helen said hopelessly.

"You implied it. Your tone implied it. Oh, it was Lenin all right. Vladimir Ilyich, I called, and he turned round without thinking."

"Did anyone else in the carriage turn round?" Helen asked before she realised she had been trapped into arguing again, and so accepting the fantasy.

"Oh everyone turned round. But he looked startled. Guilty. He got off at the next stop so he knew I'd recognised him," she finished triumphantly.

Helen gave up on the oregano and tried to change the subject.

"Shall we have a cup of tea before Herbert comes in?" she suggested cosily.

"I'll have some tea if you're making it. But I shall take mine in my glass with the special holder, and no milk if you please." She left the kitchen.

Helen sighed. The Russian influence was getting stronger. Very probably her mother-in-law wouldn't want spaghetti bolognaise for dinner at all. What did they eat in Russia? Goulash? Or was that Hungary? Wearily she loaded the tea tray and took it into the lounge where her daughter sat stolidly watching the television. Mrs Paggledon had taken up her knitting and everything looked reassuringly domestic.

But— "I have a theory," said Mrs Paggledon.

"What about, dear?" Helen said, hoping it was about knitting patterns. "Not so close to the screen, Anthea, please."

"She needs glasses," said Mrs Paggledon, momentarily distracted.

"The optician says she doesn't," said Helen, unwilling to go over very old ground again but grateful for any distraction from the subject of Russian ghosts.

"Nonsense," said Mrs Paggledon, "if you don't wear glasses when you need them your eyes get worse and worse. It's well known. I had very weak eyes as a child and I wore glasses until I was seventeen. Then my eyes were completely cured and I have had exceptionally good sight ever since."

Helen only replied to this piece of manifest nonsense with a sigh.

Mrs Paggledon started another row of knitting. "Now, as I was saying, my theory is that the Underground's Central Line is a sort of Purgatory for Communists. It could even be Hell. They're doomed to ride on and on, enduring all the horrors of a nationalised transport system."

Helen had not read Dante so she did not suggest that the Circle Line might be more suitable. Instead, she said foolishly, "But where do they go at night?"

How cross the psychiatrist would have been! And so would Herbert, who had not paid his exorbitant fees to have the advice ignored so wantonly.

"You don't understand. They're not like you and me, they won't need breakfast, or a wash and brush up. I expect they just dematerialise when the Tube shuts. Or they could sit on the embankment with all those poor homeless people."

Helen began to feel this conversation was unsuitable for tender ears. "Why don't you go out and play in the garden, dear?" she asked her daughter.

"What with?" said Anthea, who was watching an Open University broadcast on social engineering. Helen wondered if she should suggest an invisible friend. Or pet?

"Just run along, dear," she said firmly.

Anthea, a stolid and obedient child, stumped rather than ran into the garden. Her square little figure could be seen passing and re-passing the French windows as if pacing a prison exercise yard. Helen sighed again.

"There's no need to send the child outside just because I start talking to you about my revenants," said her mother-in-law.

"About what? I thought you said they were Russians, dear."

"They are not always Russians. But they are always revenants. Meaning, dear–" she added kindly "–people who have come back. From the dead."

"Ghosts?" Helen gasped.

"Not ghosts in any vulgar sense. Not you're Gothic raw-head-and-bloody-bones. But certainly discarnate entities."

Helen wondered where her mother-in-law found words like that. She herself had enough trouble with crosswords if the clues went above seven letters. "But why don't they haunt their own countries? Or their own homes? I mean, why should William Morris go into a launderette?"

"I don't know, I'm sure. He had a big bag of washing with him, that I can tell you. One of those blue plastic things that make all the clothes sweat so that they're wringing wet again by the time you get them home."

Helen took a long gulp of tea. Mrs Paggledon continued cheerfully: "I mean, there are so many people in the streets, and the tubes, and the launderettes, these days. And some of them look so strange. It stands to reason that they can't be ordinary people. I reckon there are a whole lot of revenants about that we don't even recognise. I mean, it's obvious."

"But…" said Helen and was silent. There certainly were a lot of strange-looking people about: those young people who dressed in black and put black lines round their eyes. And only the other day she had seen a girl with orange hair, who had been wearing footless leopard-skin tights and orange socks (they matched her hair), gold plastic sandals, a very short leather skirt and a purple satin waistcoat. It was mid-morning too, so she could hardly have come from a fancy-dress party. And you never saw clothes like that in the shops. So where did they come from? No doubt there was a sensible explanation but she couldn't immediately think of one.

"I expect they send you back to a different country once you're dead so you won't be recognised. After all, you wouldn't want to keep bumping into relatives, would you, even if there hadn't been any kind of unpleasantness over the will. They slipped up with those Russians. Of course, there's not many people on the Central Line actually taking a course in Russian history and who have the time to look round. I don't suppose they bargained for me," Mrs Paggledon concluded smugly.

Helen scoured her brain for some kind of theological counter to this. "What about heaven? And – the other place?"

"I think Heaven is where you find it. Just like Hell being other people, like that Frenchman said. I suppose you might be sent to the South of France if you'd led a good life, and that was what you fancied. I'd like to travel myself. India. Nepal. Tibet. No worry about frontiers, I suppose…" She looked dreamy for a moment. "I mean, Helen, have you seen all those young people about now? The ones with spiky hair in funny colours and the really odd clothes?"

Helen, remembering those leopard-skin tights, could only nod.

"Well, I think that they are from another planet. They're still revenants, still dead, in their own world, but they've never really lived in this world at all. I think there's a war going on where they come from because they all look so young and they look sort of glazed, as if they'd been through a lot. And you mostly see them in the Underground too, very rarely in the streets. It's probably something to do with the light. Revenants have always been sensitive to light."

"How would they get on in the South of France then?" said Helen.

"Dark glasses," returned Mrs Paggledon promptly. "And there's another thing. Think of all those people you see wearing dark glasses, even in the rain, and on the Tube. I wonder if they're all revenants too."

Anthea stumped into the lounge. "Daddy's home," she announced without rapture.

Helen rose gratefully to her feet to greet her husband with the time-worn phrase: "Herbert, I'm very worried about your mother."

"Now, you know what the psychiatrist said," Herbert muttered, looking over her shoulder to see if his daughter and mother were within ear-shot. He wished to guard them from that word as carefully as any Victorian paterfamilias protected his women folk from smuttier terms.

"I can't help it, Herbert. I'm starting to believe her."

Herbert took a deep breath. He shuddered at what that man might charge for treating two women. "We'll talk it over later," he told his wife soothingly.

Their talk came to no very happy conclusion. Herbert was not going to have any blood relative of his pronounced insane, or "mental" as he put it to himself, unless and until she committed multiple murder or was caught shoplifting. They had consulted the psychiatrist under the strictest confidence and Herbert would not even dream of letting the patient in on the secret. "You know how mother talks," he had said plaintively. "She'll be telling strangers on the Tube."

"She shouted 'Vladimir Ilyich' on the Tube today," Helen

told him. "Herbert, is that normal?"

"I expect they thought she was swearing," he said hopefully. "You hear a lot of elderly ladies swearing on the Tube these days. Look, mother's just getting a bit eccentric in her old age. You can put up with it, surely. It won't be forever. You know about her heart…"

"I don't mind her being eccentric. But she makes it sound so real."

"Now Helen, you know that's nonsense. If Lenin and Trotsky were riding round on the Underground you don't suppose the only person to have noticed it would be one daft – er – silly old woman. There'd be a panic."

Helen began to agree with him. She had a receptive personality. The bolognaise sauce was the result of a radio programme on brighter cooking. She agreed but she was not happy about it.

Next day she felt even less happy. Mrs Paggledon came home in the middle of the afternoon looking much shaken.

She sat down and drank her tea with milk in it without complaint. Then she said, "Helen, they're on to me."

"What?"

"I was sitting in a half-empty carriage and a young man in a fur hat sat down beside me. He leaned towards me and said, very softly, 'you know'."

"You know what?"

"Just that at first. Those two words. But of course he meant that I know about the revenants. He was wearing dark glasses as well as the hat, by the way. It was my calling out to Lenin yesterday that put them on their guard. I should have realised."

"Now mother, this young man, did he do anything *strange*? I mean, was he *familiar* in any way?" Helen asked nervously. Mrs Paggledon was by no means a glamorous old lady, but you did get all sorts of odd people on the Underground.

"Oh, no," said Mrs Paggledon innocently. "I'd certainly never seen him before. I think he's one of the executive, not a true revenant. I suspect he is a psychopomp."

This sounded like psychopath to Helen and she said so.

"No dear. A psychopomp is a conductor of the dead." Helen visualised an undertaker with a peaked cap and a ticket machine. Mrs Paggledon went on talking. It seemed to sooth her.

"Mercury was a psychopomp. And Anubis, the Egyptian jackal god. Of course the young man could have been Anubis himself. The fur hat could have been jackal fur. It might have been hiding his ears."

Helen sat down.

"They would definitely need someone like that to tell people where to go and to explain the rules, you see."

"Did he say anything else?"

"Yes dear, after a while he did. And that is what I found so disturbing. He said, 'Have you told anyone else?' and his tone were quite blood-chilling."

"And what did you say?"

"I lied of course, my dear," said Mrs Paggledon stoutly. "I was thinking of you and Anthea. I said no."

"Thank God for that," said Helen without thinking.

Then she pulled herself together. She remembered what Herbert and that very expensive psychiatrist had said. She forced herself to smile and say, "Really, mother, you shouldn't talk to strange men in the Tube, you know. Whatever would Herbert say?"

Mrs Paggledon shook her head. "It's all right, my dear. It was wrong of me to try to involve you. It's more dangerous than I realised. If anyone ever does ask you about me, tell them I was a silly old woman who got a bit strange in her old age."

"Mother, do you feel quite well?" Helen demanded, disturbed by this excursion into the past tense.

"I feel perfectly well. But I'm going to die."

"We're all going to die at some time, mother—"

"But I am going to die at eight o'clock on Wednesday the fourteenth. He told me. I've been given three days to arrange my affairs, and on the fourteenth he will come to lead me away. I know too much, you see."

"Now look, mother, you've – you've not been yourself recently. You may have met someone on Tube who was a bit eccentric, a foreigner, or something like that, and you ... well you got a bit muddled by what he said. That's all."

Mrs Paggledon smiled briefly. "All right dear, if it comforts you to think so we'll say that's what happened. Now I've got a lot to sort out. I think I'll go to my room."

Everyone had told her that it would be a mistake to have her mother-in-law live with them. Helen had laughed. She got on very well with Mrs Paggledon, she would protest. She was such a lively old lady, always out and about. She loved to be on the move. She was out almost every day of the week, doing that mature students' course in Russian history. Why, she'd even travel round on the Tube rather than sit at home and do nothing. She'll keep herself amused, she'll be no trouble, she'll be company for me, especially with Herbert away such a lot on business.

And now this.

It was all Herbert's fault of course. It was all due to his greed, to him making his own mother take advantage of the property boom to sell her house (much too big for her now) and come and live with them as a paying guest (we must let her keep her independence).

And now Herbert's mother had gone quite spectacularly mad, and Herbert was away on one of his business trips that Helen had always suspected were mixed with more than a little pleasure, and he wouldn't be back until Thursday.

Helen summoned up all her courage and phoned Herbert's hotel. He was not there but she left a message that he was to come home at once, without even waiting to phone her to ask what was wrong. Then she did what she should perhaps have done first, and phoned the doctor.

"I'm sorry to bother you," she said, her voice sounding silly and artificial in her own ears, "but my mother-in-law says she's going to die."

"For heaven's sake," said the receptionist, "it's after six o'clock, you know."

"That's all right," she heard herself say in the same silly voice, "it's actually scheduled for the day after tomorrow at eight, but perhaps I could get her to change it. What are your surgery hours, by the way?"

She dropped the receiver then and began to laugh and cry at once. When the doctor did arrive he found a hysterical young woman being competently looked after by a calm old lady. Explanations, which were involved without being lucid, made no reference to Mrs Paggledon's imminent death. Later that evening Herbert phoned. He said he could not get home even if he wanted to. There was a rail-strike and both the motorway and the airport had been put out of action by freezing fog. Besides, he felt that whatever the emergency was, Helen was able to cope.

So she settled down to watch her mother-in-law prepare for death. She parcelled out her clothes into bundles, marked Charity Shop, Jumble Sale and Dressing-Up-Box; she tied labels, mostly marked "Anthea" and "Helen" to her few small pieces of jewellery; she burned all her letters; tidied her photograph album; and finally she called her solicitor, insisted on a home visit, and made a very workmanlike will, leaving most of her capital in trust for Anthea apart from a substantial bequest to the Tibetan refugees. (Herbert was to fight this tooth and nail later, but it could not be faulted.) Then she had her hair done, and a manicure – and took a last trip on the Central Line.

She came back at around six o clock, seeming mildly excited.

"You're looking very well, mother," said Helen firmly.

"I'm feeling much better, dear. I've seen that young man again. I'm sure he *is* Anubis, by the way. He told me that he thinks they can arrange travel for me, in India and Tibet, isn't that lovely! And even other planets later, if I want. I've led a rather selfish useless sort of life, he said. I had a good brain and a capacity for study that I never really started to use until it was very late, and I was unfaithful to poor Herbert's father several times although, apparently, that's less important than the laziness, but that bequest stood in my favour. I'm sorry I had to deprive Anthea of that money but I was so afraid they'd send me to the Paris Metro. Or New York of course. And he assures me that the – passing – will be quite painless."

"Please don't talk like that, mother."

Mrs Paggledon leaned forward and patted her hand with a surprisingly tender gesture. "Don't worry, my dear. I'm going to have a bath, and then we'll have a nice cup of tea. He should be here soon after that."

Helen whimpered.

"You won't see him, my dear. Not this time. And when he does come for you, he'll be very welcome. You'll see."

Helen heard her running her bath upstairs. She began to cry, then she pulled herself together and filled the kettle. By the time Mrs Paggledon was ready Helen had laid a tray with the best china and taken it into the lounge. They drank their tea, making awkward conversation about the weather, like strangers in a station waiting room. When they had finished, Mrs Paggledon dabbed her mouth with her handkerchief and said, "That was very nice, my dear. Now, if you don't mind I'll go upstairs by myself. It's nearly eight o'clock."

Helen watched her go out of the room and then sat back in her chair, hands pressed against her eyes, in case she should see … in case she should see – what? A man with a jackal's head? An undertaker in a peaked cap? A young man in a Russian-style hat made of grey fur?

It was a long time before she could make herself leave the chair. When she did it was ten past eight. She went upstairs. Mrs Paggledon was lying on her neat bed in a clean nightdress. She might have fallen peacefully asleep but she was in fact dead. It had apparently been quite painless.

Helen spent quite a long time under the care of the

psychiatrist. After all, he had only her word for what her mother-in-law had told her. Even Herbert had heard most of it at second-hand. It took her some time to realise that they both thought that she had been hallucinating; and when she did, she agreed with them at once. That would be so lovely. She'd had a nervous breakdown, brought on by her mother-in-law dying so suddenly while she was all alone in the house, Anthea having been providentially sent to stay with a puzzled friend for the night. And everything that led up to that death had been a delusion. Of course. Of course.

She had finished her treatment. She was sitting at home one night, quite cured, quite happy, when BBC television showed a documentary on the forbidden city of Lhasa. There was a quick rather blurred shot of a street in Lhasa, a house in Lhasa, and an old Tibetan woman living in Lhasa. An old Tibetan woman who wore large sunglasses. And Mrs Paggledon's crisp old-fashioned perm.

Helen is such a nice girl, such a lovely girl, so unselfish, she'll do anything for you. And she's always so busy. She took her degree, as a mature student, and now she does part-time teaching as well as studying for a post-graduate qualification. But she never neglects her family, and as for her friends – well you've only got to ask. That's what everyone says. Well, perhaps there is one thing she won't do. You must never ask her to travel on the Underground.

# CHOSEN GIRL

The woman called Sweet Grass stopped her work for a moment to look uneasily at the mob of children playing in front of the huts. They had suddenly gone quiet, always a sign of mischief, but for a few heartbeats she could not see any particular reason for the hush. Then the group parted in a curiously formal movement and she saw her own daughter led forward, a lop-sided wreath of flowers on her tangled golden hair. Shouting incoherently she darted forward to catch the child by that hair with one hand, and snatch off the flowers with the other, flinging them down to grind them to pieces under her hard bare heel, at the same time slapping at her own daughter, and any other child within range, until the girl twisted round and sank her small white teeth into her mother's wrist. Sweet Grass let her go and the child darted away with the others, shrieking. The woman stood dully watching the blood ooze through the ring of teeth marks.

"They were playing at Brides," said one of the other women mildly.

Sweet Grass returned to her sewing. "I – did not know that. The flower crown – it is bad luck I think."

Her neighbour nodded, understanding. Brides wore crowns of flowers, of course, but so did the Chosen Girl, the one who could never be a bride, and the time of choosing was coming very close. Trying to be helpful she said, "She is very pretty. Surely there is some boy who might…"

Sweet Grass shook her head and added another bead to the design growing under her fingers, without looking much at what she was doing. There was such a thing as being too pretty. Too pretty and too poor. She would bring nothing to a husband but that beautiful mass of golden curls. Her mother had not even managed to teach the child her skill with the needle. Who would take a useless beauty into their household? Besides she was a summer child, her father some stranger her mother had danced with at the festival, and such children were not lucky... Sweet Grass realised that the other woman was staring at her work, and looked down wondering if she had made some stupid mistake. And saw the scatter of shiny red beads she had sewn, like drops of blood...

Later, lying awake in the chill darkness, listening to her daughter's breathing, she thought of running away. It was spring. The weather would be kind. If they could get safely through the forest they would surely, some time, come to another village, where they could settle. Her own skills would make them welcome anywhere ... but the forest was dangerous. In her mind she saw green eyes shining through the thickets, eyes too bright for men, too knowing for beasts ... and could she persuade the child to come with her? She should have gone long ago when the child was small enough to carry. She tossed and whimpered but her daughter, still too young to have a name, slept sweetly.

The Old Women came at dawn, as if her fears had brought them. One of them carried a jar of honey drink for Sweet Grass and sat with her until she had drained it. The other two gave leaves to her daughter to chew, leaves that would give her strength to dance through the day and take away her fear. They washed her, and combed out her golden curls, while her mother sobbed and drank. They put a green robe on the child, who would never have any other name but Chosen Girl now, and crowned her with a wreath of hawthorn-blossom, and led her out to the place of stones where the village people waited.

And there she danced, at first leaping and whirling alone, dancing as the leaves she had eaten taught her. Then she lead the dances of the village, first the children's singing games, next the languorous dances of the girls, where they swirled in wide slow circles to display their hair and their richly embroidered skirts, while she spun in the centre of their circle, then the wild leaping sword dances of the boys, where she darted between them as they clashed their blades and slashed at each other's flesh until their blood ran down, then the hunting dances of the young men where she became both hunter and quarry, arrow and spear, and at last the secret dances of the Old Women, that on this one day could be shown to all eyes though many of the men hid their faces and would not look for fear, but the Chosen Girl looked, and danced step for step with them, her swift feet mocking their stiff steps.

The air grew chill towards sunset and even the children grew weary of the dance, but the Chosen Girl danced on alone again. The Old Women brought Sweet Grass from her hut, sick and staggering, to see the end. She watched, helplessly, as the child danced herself at last to a stand-still, and the Old Women gathered round her. They took away the green dress and over her white nakedness they wrapped a red cloak, stiff and blotched with stains of darker red. Then they turned the girl towards the forest and gently urged her down the path that led towards the trees. Everyone watched breathlessly as she skipped away, under a bloody sky, towards the Oldest Women of all who waited for her in the green darkness. They were, after all, expecting her. The scent of blood on her red cloak would draw them too.

Mother Bear, Grandmother Wolf. Waiting for the Chosen Girl.

# MR MANPFERDIT

An ill-matched couple are walking down the Strand on a bright Spring morning. One is big clumsy, slovenly even, in his ill-fitting scratch wig, curiously scorched on one side where he often holds a candle too close to his head to help his short-sighted eyes when he reads; cat hairs all over his waistcoat; and linen that could do with the attentions of a good laundress. Or even a bad one. The application of hot water and a scrubbing-board, however carelessly done, could bring nothing but improvement. (It might easily do some good if applied to the wearer of that linen, too.) He has been mistaken for an idiot when in company, albeit an idiot miraculously inspired to speak out against the Whig government, but he is the great Dr Samuel Johnson, Dictionary Johnson, a giant of learning and a giant in body too. He once lifted a man off his feet (someone who had been causing trouble in a theatre) and pitched him over the balcony rail into the pit below. (A full-grown man – think about it but, under no circumstances, try it. Manners are different today and a brawl in a theatre involving a literary man can include, at the most, a few clumsy punches, or the throwing of the contents of a glass of wine, never the hurling of an opponent.)

The other – but you will have guessed. It is the dapper Scotsman James Boswell, a man with oddly romantic yearnings, and, occasionally, an inconveniently Gothic turn of mind. (He once managed to terrify a whore in Edinburgh by innocently asking her, at a most inopportune moment, if she had ever given any thought to life after death…)

But at this moment the couple are in search of neither whores nor brawls. They are going to see a centaur.

There are many strange creatures which can be viewed, for a

due exchange of coin, in Johnson's London. Tired of London means tired of life, as Johnson has so famously pronounced, for London offers everything the heart can desire, which currently includes hairy boys, calculating pigs, men with scales, and girls as small as fairies, mermaids, a giant crocodile, a porcupine (and, the unkind might suggest, Dr Johnson himself, the celebrated talking bear…).

If they have to go a-monster hunting, Boswell, perhaps, might prefer to peep at a bare-breasted mermaid, or run a connoisseur's eye, perhaps even a jeweller's glass, over the tiny perfections of the smallest woman ever seen in London. But the good Doctor has insisted on the centaur. Boswell wonders why. Does the idea of a centaur suggest to him the possibility of rational conversation? Wasn't Cheiron a schoolmaster, a teacher of the young, as the Doctor himself had once been? (Better not think too much of Nessus, or those drunken centaurs, starting a fight at a wedding, where fights do so often start, judging by today's tabloid headlines. "Bride Spends Wedding Night in Casualty. Groom in Jail: 'It was meant to be the happiest day of my life,' sobbed pretty Kylie-Lee." And so it might have been but for those centaurs.)

This centaur has been advertised in the April number of *The Gentleman's Magazine* (April, eh? That wouldn't be April the First, would it?). His name is given as Mr Manpferdit, and he offers himself for show between the civilised hours of ten in the morning and four in the afternoon "the rest of the time being necessary to comb and curry himself, to stir up his litter and study English history". The Doctor, who might usefully devote a little of his own time to combing and currying but, as we can see, does not, has suggested an early visit, and Boswell can do no other than agree. He himself is combed, even curried, but a little frayed at the edges, as if he has not been to bed at all, although here his looks belie him. He certainly has been to bed but the experience was energetic and enjoyable, as he believes, to both parties, rather than restful, and he could do with a snooze. He blinks at the crowds pushing or drifting their way along the Strand, keeps an eye on his pockets, and shakes his head ruefully at certain friendly ladies who seem inclined to greet him all too familiarly, but all, as it were, at one remove. The Doctor is talking, but his words too seem to come from a distance, hollowly, as if from the depths of a cave where, perhaps, a centaur is couched on his bed of dried grasses.

"...the combat between the Lapithae and the Centaurs, you will remember is one of the items offered to Duke Theseus as part of his wedding festivities in the Bard of Avon's fairy comedy..."

But the Duke chooses Pyramus and Thisbe instead, Boswell remembers, wondering if a mischievous Theseus has ever confounded the other actors by making the wrong choice, and wondering loses the thread of the Doctor's discourse again because when he returns to it, it seems that the Doctor has found a more modern example.

"Dean Swift and his rational horses, the Houyhnhnms..." The Doctor makes this word a surprisingly successful imitation of a horse's snorting whuffle. Several people turn round to look. A carriage horse seems inclined to reply. By the time his companion has recovered from his embarrassment the Doctor has, apparently, moved to Cornwall (almost as wild as the Highlands of Boswell's native land, and like them, with its own language and custom...).

"...the hobbyhorse which can, in primitive communities, form a central part of their celebrations could be the *fons et origo* of the legends of the centaurs..."

"Then you do not believe that there can be such a thing?" Boswell exclaims. So why the devil are we walking half across London to interview a hobbyhorse? He adds, but only to himself.

"But sir, I did not believe in the Cock Lane Ghost," the Doctor protests. "Nonetheless I felt myself bound to investigate it."

Boswell is glad he was not in London for this particular episode. He has no wish to spend long hot evenings crowded into a tiny room with half literary London, waiting to see if the ghost of a young woman who seems to have died of smallpox will manifest herself through a sleepy scared little girl. Little Elizabeth Parsons... The ghost had returned to accuse her – husband? – no he wasn't her husband, he'd been married to her sister which meant they couldn't get married even when the sister was dead, something to do with the Anglican prayer book and forbidden degrees of kindred – a Man may Not Marry his Great Uncle's Cousin, or some such thing, but they'd been living as man and wife ... to accuse her common-law husband, then, except that they don't have them in England, to accuse him of murder. Arsenic in the purl... She'd never actually spoken but she'd made her feelings known by making scratching noises. Hence the popular nickname of Scratching Fanny, an unfortunate soubriquet perhaps, suggesting as it does, to Boswell at least, one of the more exotic entries in Harris's List of Covent Garden Ladies along with Mrs Golightly's Scolding Daughter and Long-Haired Mrs Wilmington. And it had all been a fraud after all, he reminds the Doctor.

"Perhaps," Dr Johnson rumbles, "perhaps."

"But the child was found secreting a board in her stays so that she could make the knocking and scratching noises that had so impressed the *mobile*—" The *mobile vulgus* he had been going to say, now fashionably truncated to "mob" but the Doctor cuts him off heavily.

"The child had been told that her father would be sent to Newgate if the manifestations stopped," the Doctor says judicially. "At the last there was, perhaps, fraud, but who can say how it began? There have been other cases."

The Demon Drummer of somewhere or other, Boswell thinks. That seemed to like bedrooms too. And weren't young girls involved in that? Young girls, and beds, lifted bedcovers, and a restless spirit... Boswell decides not to pursue this train of thought. Instead he thinks of something sensible to say about centaurs.

"The life of a man far exceeds that of a horse. How can it be that such a hybrid could exist? Would not the human part find himself, all too soon, tied to a dying animal?"

"Ah," the Doctor sighs gustily, "and which of us is not? You are a young man but do you not already fear the failure of your – more animal parts?"

Boswell bridles. His animal parts haven't let him down yet, thank you very much! Indeed, it was to distract those very animal parts (young girls … beds…) that he raised the question of the possible lifespan of centaurs in the first place.

"And what would such a creature eat? With a human mouth and an equine – an equine digestive economy?" How much grass could he himself chew his way through, he wonders? He tries to remember the conventional representation of a centaur. Could there be a human stomach in there as well? His mental eye moves over those shining flanks, those glossy sides … and … of course there are other attributes … those animal parts … perhaps he has more in common with a centaur than he first thought. Perhaps that is why the Doctor has chosen him as his companion on this bright Spring morning.

A young woman, unsuitably clad for this time of day, powdered and patched, her hair dressed with gaudy but drooping feathers, whisks up her skirts unnecessarily high to avoid the filth of the kennel (and to give the gentlemen a good view of her ankles, encased in dirty white stockings) and calls a friendly greeting. The Doctor shakes his head.

"No, no, my girl, it won't do," he says benignly enough.

But his companion feels that it might do very nicely. As well as those stockings, the young woman has revealed down-at-heel satin shoes, one ornamented with a paste buckle, one not. For some reason he finds this rather piquant and for a moment he toys with the idea of leaving his companion for a few minutes (and it will certainly take no longer) to escort this gutter-nymph into a side alley… But no. He sternly brings his mind back to the topic of the day. More or less.

"Female centaurs," he blurts. "Centaur – ah – mares. Are there any classical representations of the female of the species? Or any mention of them in classical myth?"

"Female centaurs," the Doctor rumbles thoughtfully, "centauresses…" He tries the word, plural, feminine, on his tongue and shakes his head. "I do not think so. No, I do not think so. Nor female satyrs either…"

And there's a pity, Boswell thinks. He'd walk quite some distance to see a female satyr (satyress?). Mentally, he brushes out the lingering image of thread stockings and satin shoes replacing them with dainty little hooves, ankles and shins covered in glossy fur – but his satyr lady persists in wearing a puce satin sacque (although she is holding it above her knees) and a fashionable little hat perched between her horns… For a moment he is chasing this charming vision through the avenues of a formal garden but before he can catch up with her he brings himself sternly back to the subject under discussion.

"There are indeed pictorial representations of infant satyrs," he remembers, "but I do not recall one of a centaur foal."

The Doctor pauses, then pronounces: "The Emperor Claudius was presented with the corpse of a baby centaur preserved in honey. It had been born to a mare belonging to a landowner in his dominions and it was considered to be ill-omened. We may suppose it to have been some deformed birth, some sport of nature which was taken to resemble the classic centaur."

So. No centaur babies then – well, unlikely with no centaur ladies. But someone in Ancient Rome had believed there could be. And when he found one he sent it to the Emperor. He, Boswell, would have wanted to be very sure of his ground before he troubled that gentleman.

"The classic centaurs are frequently represented as ravishers of human women," the Doctor murmurs. "Perhaps it was generally supposed that they were forced to do so because they had no females of their own. According to his own advertisement, this centaur is proposing to offer rides to ladies who wish to take the air. Perhaps they should look to themselves..."

Boswell coughs. "Surely the ancients did not contemplate the – ah – congress of a woman with a horse?" Even a horse with a man's head and chest. But then, what is the story of Hercules and Nessus about if not such an attempted – congress? But the Doctor is ponderously shaking his head.

"The centaur here is but a figure or metaphor for savage plains-dwelling people – wanderers perhaps, riders and herdsmen like the Hunnish people. Just as the satyr is a figure of the ethnic forest dweller."

The satyress peeps out at Boswell again, this time from behind a tree. She is wearing a wreath of oakleaves, and a necklace of rowan berries – with very little else as far as he can see. But the Doctor's voice saves him from further shocking revelations.

"Or not of men at all, but of apes," he pronounces. "A glimpse of a furred ape amongst the branches might suggest the notion of a faun or a satyr..."

"Apes," Boswell protests, "are not native to Greece." But too late. The face of his satyr lady is already furring and flattening, her arms lengthen, and only the breasts, still tantalising cream and roses under the spreading pelt, retain their human outlines, perversely enough as if they were still buoyed up by a pair of stays.

"But the Greeks were great traders and voyagers," the Doctor points out, "besides their military expeditions. They may easily have seen apes upon their travels. Did not Alexander conquer India? From whence, we are told, came Dionysus and his band of satyrs."

"And his maenads," Boswell protests. A vine-crowned maenad, worn out by the Bacchic revel, reclines under the tree abandoned by his satyr lady. She is wearing a white chiton, ornamented with artificial ivy leaves, and little gilt sandals. Her hair, under the ivy crown, is puffed and powdered. The whole effect is perhaps more suggestive of a masquerade ball than an antique grove, and not necessarily the worse for that.

"But we are told the maenads tore both men and cattle to pieces in their frenzy. Is this not more suggestive of the depredations of great apes than of delicate human females?"

Through the trees Boswell glimpses a shaggy figure waving a thighbone. He retreats briskly before he has seen enough to speculate as to what kind of creature that bone might have been torn from. He is now thoroughly puzzled. They have risen early and embarked upon a goodish walk to meet, not the hobbyhorse as he first thought, but a metaphor, or perhaps a Hun (he sees this last as a Highland cateran, perched on a rough little pony). Or, and this is far more likely, a Hoax, like the Cock Lane Ghost or the Bottle Conjuror.

"We are told that the hero Hercules was driven to madness when he put on a shirt poisoned with the blood of the centaur Nessus," the Doctor states, "and is a shirt a natural attribute of the classic centaur? Does it not rather suggest—"

"A Highland cateran," Boswell responds promptly, although would the blood of a Highlander prove poisonous? It wouldn't surprise Boswell, who has his own prejudices. The Highlands are not yet Romantic.

The Doctor nods, perhaps a little puzzled by his young disciple's thought processes, but then he often is. They have reached the end of the Strand now and they are about to plunge into that narrow and perilous maze of alleyways that make up Seven Dials, where Mr Manpferdit has chosen to take up residence. In some places the streets are too narrow and crowded for the two to walk abreast, and the Doctor walks ahead, forging his way through the crowds by ignoring them. Boswell, bobbing in his wake like a small but jaunty craft, tucks his elbows over his pockets and fends off the more overt attempts on his watch with the odd jab of his cane.

And so they come to Horsethimble Lane, which leads into Horsethimble Mews where, perhaps attracted by the curious name, Mr Manpferdit has his lodgings. It is reached through a brick archway, but the archway is closed off with a great wooden door which looks most inhospitable. But there is a small human-sized portal, and the Doctor pushes it gently so that they can pass through – into a different world.

The Mews is quite empty. It is very quiet after the bustle of Seven Dials. The cobbles are thick with straw and even the sound of their footsteps is lost. The air itself is softened by a kind of golden haze, though this, as Boswell tells himself firmly, will come from the masses of hay and straw that must, necessarily, be kept there.

Most of the stables seem to be empty and the rooms above them are shuttered and still.

The buildings, Boswell notices, seem particularly ramshackle as if Horsethimble Mews is about to fall softly into ruin, to retreat to a country lane set, incongruously, in the middle of Seven Dials. Some of the walls seem to be only kept upright by the green blanket of creeper that covers them; some seem to be actually turning into hedges. But there are signs of human occupation: strangely enough there are tubs of brightly coloured flowers in one corner of the mews, as if someone had ambitions to make a garden, and a spade leans against the wall. Boswell blinks and tries looking at that spade again. But no, he still sees it: the handle seems to be carved from some kind of dense white bone (could it be ivory?) into the shape of a serpent's head, a serpent's head with eyes of angry ruby. He wonders if he should draw the Doctor's attention to it but remembers his short-sight and refrains. And could some of that greenery twining about the stable door be vine leaves?

For the first time since they set out he begins to feel a real unease. He realises that he does not want the centaur to be real. He wants a trick, a joke, something that will be congruous with this modern Age of Reason. Failing that, he would like to leave at once, expend a shilling on that girl in white stockings, or another like her if that one is not to be found, and then sit in a coffee house talking politics or bawdy, or... But the Doctor is forging ahead. He knocks on the vine-wreathed door and calls cheerfully, "Mr Manpferdit? Are you ready to receive visitors?"

There is a stirring inside. A rustle of straw, and the unmistakeable clop of an unshod hoof on a stone floor. And the door opens.

The first thing that Boswell thinks is that he did not realise that a centaur would be so big. But the head and chest, although human, are in proportion to the equine parts and he finds himself looking up into the face of something very like a giant. But there is nothing in the least coarse about the features. On the contrary, the face is flawlessly beautiful. The chestnut hair is thick and glossy, tied at the back of the neck with a simple black ribbon. The centaur wears neither beard nor, Boswell notices, shirt. His splendid chest, which might prove an excellent model for a sculptor, is bare. He bows gravely to his visitors and for a moment Boswell wonders if he will address them in Attic Greek. And if they will understand him if he does. But then he smiles and says, with an admirable English accent: "Good day, Doctor – and Mr Boswell."

"You know us?" Boswell blurts.

Mr Manpferdit smiles again. "But who does not know Doctor Johnson? And his amiable companion." A bow, this time just for Boswell. "Pray – come in."

He backs carefully into the stable, followed by the Doctor and his undoubtedly amiable, but completely stunned companion. They find the stable a curious amalgam of the human-domestic and the equine – a mixture only to be expected in the lodgings of a centaur, Boswell tells himself. There is a heap of clean and golden straw (Mr Manpferdit's bed?), a manger (empty – has Mr Manpferdit breakfasted all ready?), two shabby but well-upholstered chairs (for visitors?), and a heavy wooden table which is just not quite the right height for a man. And on the table a collection of wooden bowls, cups, plates and a jug. Against the wall is a kind of stand with an array of curry combs, brushes, and implements whose nature Boswell cannot even guess at (perhaps for the care of the hooves), which is, presumably, Mr Manpferdit's dressing-table. And there is, rather incongruously, a clean piece of curtain, checked blue and white cloth, which can be drawn across the stable door.

But everything is very clean. The golden haze which still hangs in the air has not descended as dust anywhere in the stable. The floor beneath the table and the chairs has been most scrupulously swept... And the place smells pleasantly of clean horseflesh and fresh straw – really, he has been in human habitations which have been a great deal more offensive to the sight and the nostrils.

"Pray, gentlemen," the centaur brings them further inside with a fluid movement of his bare arms, "pray, be seated. May I offer you some refreshment?"

Boswell, momentarily terrified that his patron will be offered a truss of hay or a peck of oats, and offend their host by his refusal ("a fool would have swallowed it..."} is about to say no, but the Doctor, dry after his walk, has already accepted. The centaur fills three cups from the tall jug and, still gracefully, he hands two of them to his guests. They all sip. Boswell cannot tell what the liquor is; it has the sharp flavour of soured milk, but there is sweetness too, honey perhaps and the taste of herbs and barley. It is oddly reminiscent of his native land, offering, as it does, the flavours of Atholl brose and cold Scotch broth. And it is damnably strong stuff. Boswell can take his drink (he'd better, in this century and in his profession) but a few swallows of this stuff, he can tell, will overset him entirely. But he drinks a little more. Odd how the taste grows on one... The Doctor is sipping politely enough, although he would probably prefer a dish of tea. Boswell puts his half-full cup down carefully and looks round the stable again. There is a shelf of books which he missed on his first survey – perhaps volumes of English history which Mr Manpferdit, according to his advertisement, has set himself to study. As to the other part of his programme – offering rides to ladies – Boswell has no doubt that he will have more takers than he will know what to do with. Particularly as they (the ladies) will no doubt find it necessary to keep their seats on that glossy back by wrapping their arms around Mr Manpferdit's splendid chest… Boswell dabs at his upper lip, which has become unaccountably damp, and hopes the centaur will put a shirt on before embarking on this part of his programme.

He sits down and the Doctor follows his example. Mr Manpferdit folds his strong legs and disposes himself on the heap of straw.

"This is very pleasant," he says in his deep voice. "I hardly dared hope that the great Doctor and the famous Mr Boswell would seek me out in my humble abode. But it was in that very hope that I travelled to England."

"From Greece?" the Doctor enquires.

"From the mountains of Macedonia," Mr Manpferdit replies.

"And you came to England to meet me?"

"In the hope of meeting you and people like you. The climate – that is, the intellectual climate, of my native land is most uncongenial to such as I."

"Indeed?" the Doctor takes a swig of his drink. "In what way? How has the very cradle of classic civilisation become uncongenial to its children? Ah – I suppose that even there the people no longer believe…"

The centaur smiles, showing what Boswell must admit are a most magnificent set of teeth. "On the contrary. They believe, but they believe in too much, in blood-sucking demons with hooves and horses' tails. I have no desire to be degraded to a mere peasant bogy. And as for sucking blood…" He waves such an unpleasant notion aside.

"So you made what must have been a difficult–" he thinks about the logistics and emends this to "–an almost impossible journey – for the sake of rational society?" the Doctor asks. He sounds distinctly dubious.

Mr Manpferdit smiles again. "And, of course, for women."

"Ah, women," the Doctor rumbles. "On questions of women you must apply to my – er – amiable companion here."

Boswell almost protests. It was not he who had to tell Davy Garrick that he wouldn't visit him backstage anymore because the sight of half-dressed actresses "excited his amorous propensities" (or "caused his genitals to quiver" in the first and unauthorised version). That was the Doctor. And he is – was – a married man. But he refrains from saying so. Instead he murmurs "women…" in what he hopes is a neutral encouraging tone, but instead, he realises too late, makes him sound like Captain MacHeath. He tries again.

"You came to seek the – er – society of ladies?" Now he sounds like a clergyman.

The centaur raises that magnificent head. "I came," he declares, "to find a mate."

Now they are both looking at him with astonishment.

"I am," he spreads those graceful hands again, "for lack of a better, something of a leader amongst the poor remnant of my people. I mediate between them and those human creatures who penetrate our mountain home. And from them I have heard stories, carried by travellers, and among those stories I heard the name of a great City."

"London," the Doctor murmurs.

"London," Mr Manpferdit agrees earnestly. "They told me it is surely the capital of the world. The spoils of the most distant countries are brought here for the delight of its inhabitants. Here, of all places, I might expect to find a companion and a helper–" he pauses "–a wife."

"And can you not find such a one in your native mountains?" the Doctor enquires.

"Alas, I cannot. I have seen my companions fall away, some to become all horse, degraded to mere brute, some to turn to the daemonic creatures of peasant belief, or lie down and die for sheer lack of a reason to live… Only I have retained the hope brought to us from beyond the horizon by travellers, the hope that in London I might really find all that the heart can desire."

Ah. So that's it. A casual phrase by the good Doctor has achieved resonance in the Macedonian mountains which, perhaps, he never intended. And here is this simple magnificent creature, drawn by strange hope... Boswell takes another long drink of that mysterious liquor and wonders what they can do. He supposes he could find a lady who would – well – offer her services to the centaur. But he feels that that is not really what Mr Manpferdit is looking for. Not if he wants a companion – a helper – a wife. They have come back to the question he raised during their walk: where might they find a lady centaur? Perhaps, he thinks weakly, they should advertise? But the Doctor is leaning forward and speaking earnestly.

"You will find many good and strange things in London, but I fear, Mr Manpferdit, you will not find what you are seeking. A thing of such beauty and wonder cannot exist in this mundane world. The light of reason which has risen upon this age has driven such visions away. All my life I have longed for ghosts and spirits, but when I sought for them all I have found is trickery and deceit. You, a creature of legend, seeking for legendary beauty will also find, I fear, nothing but disappointment."

Mr Manpferdit stands up, not in the scrambling way of ordinary horses, Boswell notices, but managing those long legs with the same grace he has shown in his upper body. His tail swishes and for a moment Boswell half-fears an angry rush, great hooves battering at their heads, and wonders what he will do. Heroism suggests that he – at the very least – should throw himself between the Doctor and danger; common-sense tells him to drop under the table, but before he can do either he realises that the centaur is still smiling.

"Oh great Sage of the City of Heart's Desire – shall I prove you wrong?" he says.

And now the Doctor has heaved himself to his feet. "Ah, Mr Manpferdit – if only you could."

And the centaur gives a strange high cry, a sound as if his horse-nature is calling through his man's throat. Outside in the city streets the horse-drudges of London, toiling with carriages and carts, riding-horses parading in the park, and pampered cavalry mounts, all hear. They rear and dance, remembering that their ancestors, at least, once ran free on the great grassy plains, and reply, trumpeting their allegiance so that the air is filled with their weird music of drumming hooves and wild cries, and to this strange fanfare the door of Mr Manpferdit's stable opens (or perhaps it falls away with the crumbling walls) and into the golden mews steps – ah – a vision of such beauty that both the Doctor and his young friend see her through a mist of tears.

It is a centaur-lady (never, never would you call such a creature a mare). She is a little smaller than Mr Manpferdit, although both men must still look up into her face. And that face is exquisite: high wide cheekbones, large and long-lashed eyes of a wonderful golden brown, a short straight nose, and a generous scarlet mouth … although it must be confessed that Boswell's eyes have already skimmed that marvellous face and fastened on the splendid breasts, creamy white, with delicate roseate nipples, ample but firm… He longs to weigh them in his hands (they would surely spill deliciously over his palms) to bury his face between them… Or he could drown in that wonderful hair, white-gold like her tail, hair that springs back from her broad brow and flows over her bare shoulders to where her slender waist springs from her golden flanks… He makes a determined effort to pull himself together and removes his hat to make a formal bow and manages, through dry lips, to offer a proper greeting.

"Good day to you – er – Mistress Manpferdit," he says.

But Doctor Johnson is kneeling on the straw-scattered cobbles of Horsethimble Mews, his shoulders shaking with sobs, his face buried in his hands.

Mr Manpferdit comes forward and takes his lady's hand and they stand before the kneeling Doctor. "Look up," Mr

Manpferdit says. "Look up. See what I have found in your City of Heart's Desire."

"Do not be afraid," his lady says in a beautiful bell-like voice (rather deep for a woman, Boswell thinks, but still – wonderful). "You are part of us. We are one with you."

The Doctor raises his head. The tears shine on his cheeks in the golden light. Somehow Horsethimble Mews has become very much larger, indeed, somewhere quite different, and they are standing on a shining hillside with an over-arching sky of burning blue. Above them, on the crown of the hill, stands a white building consisting largely of slender white pillars, perhaps a temple, perhaps a house for centaurs, for there are other centaurs now, centaur men as handsome as Mr Manpferdit, centaur ladies, with flowers in their hair, and little gangling centaur foals. They stretch out their hands to the two humans and Boswell finds himself filled with the desire to tear off his foolish coverings of coat and shirt and breeches and run up that flower slope as naked as the centaurs (except that even now he fears he would make a less than classic figure – rather he would resemble one of Dean Swift's Yahoos scuttling amongst his beautiful rational horses). But the centaurs are coming to them, sweeping down the hillside in a golden thunder of hooves, and gleaming flanks, tails as splendid as banners and beautiful, bountiful breasts...

He glances at the Doctor. He has risen to his feet and he too is gazing yearningly at the centaur herd who are bearing down on them. He spreads out his arms as if to gather them all in ... and suddenly the centaurs, the shining hillside, the white temple – all are gone and they are standing on the dirty cobbles of Horsethimble Mews.

For the cobbles are dirty. The golden straw which seemed to cover them when they first entered it is merely filthy. The tumbledown buildings are soot-stained and ugly. The place smells of damp and cats and – worse. There are no vine leaves, not even any common creeper, no tubs of bright flowers. A spade leans against a wall in one dirty corner. The handle is splintered and broken. Perhaps it might be mistaken, by sun-dazzled eyes, for a serpent's head. The golden haze which lay over the Mews has gone. Indeed it has begun to rain.

And in the stable … the place is empty but for a heap of dirty straw, an unspeakable mattress, a pile of empty gin bottles in the corner – and the rear portion of a stuffed horse. It too is dirty and it has an indefinably *nibbled* look.

The Doctor, who does not seem in the least put out by the extremely strange events of the last (how long? – half an hour – it could hardly be more), raps on the half-door with his cane and calls, "Mr Manpferdit? Mr Manpferdit?"

Something emerges from the shadows at the far end of the Mews. It is old and, as it draws closer, it becomes evident that it is deeply unsavoury. Closer still it reveals itself to be a woman wrapped in an assortment of rags. A grimy bandage is twisted round her forehead, covering her eyes, but she seems to see well enough.

"'E's gorn," she says hoarsely.

"The centaur?" the Doctor enquires hopefully.

"Don't know about no sentry," the creature replies. "'E wasn't no sojer that I knew of. 'E said 'e was a seaman. 'E's been gorn a week or more. I reckon the pressgang gottim. And good riddance, 'cept for the rent 'e owed me," she adds on the off-chance, as it were.

"A sailor?" the Doctor says musingly. "A sea-horse perhaps."

And Boswell sees a kind of marine-centaur, fins instead of fetlocks, tail and beard flowing into foam, blowing some kind of shell. But it is white and cold. Mortal hands have carved it from marble, and it riots with mermaids and dolphins around a fountain in some Italian square.

"'E leaned over the stable-door," the woman is becoming quite eloquent, perhaps under the influence of the coin the Doctor has pressed into her hand, "so you couldn't see 'is front legs, with that 'orse thing propped up behind 'im, letting on as 'e was some kind of raree show. Which, in the mornings when 'e was sober was orl right. But – lor' bless you for a kind gennleman – in the afternoons when 'e'd a drop taken they couldn't take 'im serious and by the evening 'e couldn't stand up."

Boswell feels an enormous and totally unreasonable disappointment. He'd known the centaur couldn't be real. He hadn't even wanted it to be. He should be worried by that curiously vivid waking dream instead of regretting that he has now come back to reality. He doesn't want to find himself in Bedlam entertaining visiting ladies and gentlemen by mistaking them for centaurs…

The Doctor raises his disreputable hat to the old woman and prepares to lead the way out of the Mews. She follows them to the gate muttering blessings – perhaps – and stands there to watch them go. As Boswell negotiates the heaps of filthy straw he glances back for some reason, no reason: the dark ragged figure is outlined sharply against the rainy light and he notices, he who notices the details of all women, that she has unusually thick coils of hair slipping from the ragged shawl pulled over her head. And then … he sees one of the coils dart a flat head and flick a forked tongue…

He is about to say something when he sees that she is raising a hand to the bandage … not wanting to spend his life as an unappreciated statue in Seven Dials he grasps the Doctor's arm and urges him forward. He mutters something about coffee and they hurry back towards civilisation.

# STORY NOTES

## Tina Rath

"The Fetch", one of the stories in this collection was first published by Ronald Chetwynd-Hayes in *The 19th Fontana Book of Great Ghost Stories*. Last year I contributed a story to the collection *Shadmocks and Shivers* produced by Shadow Publishing to celebrate his centenary. Which tells you quite as much as you need to know about how old I am, and how long I have been writing. I am probably best known for my short stories, due to the fact that none of my novels have been published, but I also write and perform verse. I am hoping to bring out a collection – *A Garland of Wolfsbane* – based on my time as Resident Poet with the Dracula Society this year. I live in London with my husband, a singer and musician, and also a writer. He co-wrote "Casualties of the System" which is also included in this collection – and should write more. I have a PhD, and wrote my doctoral thesis on *The Vampire in Popular Fiction*. My finest hour was an interview with Anthony Head (Giles from *Buffy*); my least happy appearance was in a newspaper which published headshots of two doctors, one the young and heartbreakingly handsome Dr John William Polidori and the other – me. Otherwise I am an elderly actress, beginning to specialise in Alzheimer's patients, but still with most of my teeth and all of my faculties, who can still sing a top C.

I was very grateful and flattered when Peter asked if I would be interested in having a collection published (definitely a hand-off-at-the-wrist moment) and I do hope you have enjoyed or will enjoy it. So thank you, Mr Coleborn.

**Talking to Strangers in Finsbury Park** — I really did hear an expert explaining that communication with aliens would be impossible because we had no concepts in common. And I wondered if sentient beings might have more in common than you – or he – might think, particularly when it came to packets of biscuits. And jars.

**This is How it Happened** — I write my own versions of fairy tales. Someday I will publish a collection of these. This one came to me as if it were being dictated when I was playing a resident in a home for the elderly, and incompetent, in a short indie film. I couldn't write it down then but as I was going straight on to my story-telling group from the filming I told it there just as it had come to me (*and* I sang the start of *Vissi d'arte* for them), and wrote it down later.

**A Visit to Blastings Manor** — I wrote this for a Christmas Ghost Story competition for the local paper. I put every haunting I had ever heard of into it, and then made some more up.

**Barefoot Withouten Shoon** — Many years ago the *Daily Mirror* used to publish a poem every day. This verse, by John Lydgate, was one of them, and it stayed with me, not because I pitied the horse but because the phrase "barefoot without shoon" resonated with me, sounding not like poverty but freedom (I have a long mutually hostile history with shoes). I want to go barefoot withouten shoon too.

**Ilona** — This story grew from the image of a woman using a domestic implement – in this case a mop – to wreak summary justice. I still like it.

**Beautiful Boy** — I wrote this after a seminar on writing vampire stories run by Nancy Kilpatrick at a convention. Thank you, Nancy.

**The Man Who Love his Luscious Ladies** — I heard the term "Feeder" – someone who enables and encourages his/her partner to overeat – in a soap opera, I think, and thought immediately that it might work two ways … the feeder *to* might also feed *on*…

**Christmas with the Family** — A touch of folk-horror, possibly brought on by that moment when you have got up very early to catch the bus, and arrive at your destination to realise that the day's work hasn't even started, and you're not absolutely sure if you aren't still in bed – or dead...

**Scruffy the Vampire Slayer** — A tribute to two of my favourite characters, Buffy and Giles – from, of course, *Buffy the Vampire Slayer*.

**Sitting Tenant** — I read – or possibly heard – about the state of some houses which have to be cleared after their owners had died, and wondered if any influence might linger...

**The Chest** — There can be problems when partners split up. Especially with the furniture. I simply took it to extremes.

**A Straightforward Procedure** — Another story which came from that seminar, where someone suggested that vampirism and plastic surgery had something in common (there are even "vampire injections").

**Night Out** — The first story I had published in the more mainstream press – the woman's magazine *Woman's Realm*. And it had an *illustration*!

**Diversion** — This was a story that came to me during the hot days of summer when I was travelling on the W12 bus. It was sparked by the sight of a very small child wearing silver shoes. She looked from hers to mine and gave a small grave smile of approval. I like to think that someday she might read this story, and remember...

**A Trick of the Dark** — This came from a random thought about park keepers. Do they always go home at sunset (when parks usually close)? Or might there be another reason for a young man's regular appearance in the twilight?

**Casualties of the System** — I wrote this with my husband Tony. An item in the news about sending youthful criminals on safari inspired him with the idea of time safaris. And no, we are not *recommending* cruel and unusual punishments for the young.

**"It's White and It Follows Me"** — This was inspired by a description of the joke called "Selling a Bargain" in Francis Grose' "classical *Dictionary of the Vulgar Tongue,* outlined in the first paragraph. Apart from that, none of the historical detail is accurate, or intended to be. It's a fantasy version of the reign of Queen Anne (except for the detail about the orangery – no one realised it should have a glass roof and from an orange point of view it was rather a failure).

**Tea Dance** — I wondered why old ladies shouldn't have demon lovers? So this one has.

**Extended Family** — I was looking for an exotic legend and a friend who was currently living in Thailand suggested this one. The same theme of the extended arm turns up in a short story by William Sanson, "A Woman Seldom Found", set in Italy, and Laurence Hope's poem, "The Guru's Tale", set in India. I took it back to Thailand and domesticated it.

**The Fetch** — I got the last line of this before the rest of the story – a variation on the theme of the doppelgänger. Sometimes, as in "Barefoot Withouten Shoon" I get the title first – and there can be some years between the line or the title and the arrival of the rest.

**The Bus** — Who hasn't – at the end of a long wait in the cold for a bus – hasn't wished to drop their heavy shopping bag or briefcase and just get on the next bus to somewhere else? Mrs Fortescue makes the final leap, and who can blame her?

**The Co-Walker** — The passage that the unfortunate Martin reads in the story is from Robert Kirk's *The Secret Commonwealth,* a seventeenth century collection of folklore – the phrase "it returns to its own herd" haunted me and the story grew out of it.

**End of Season** — When I was in Bali I went, rather late one evening, to eat in a small café. They apologised that very little food was left but I was quite happy with noodles and whatever the sauce was … later I wondered what I would do if, perhaps, next time I went, there was no food at all and the island began to close down...

**Fifth Sense** — Another piece of casual reading mentioned that carnivores typically had foul breath. "What a good way to recognise a werewolf!" I thought and the last line of "Fifth Sense" came to me. All I had to do was write the rest.

**The Banks of the Roses** — More folk-horror. There are various versions of the song. Usually the girl is pregnant and her lover murders her to rid himself of an encumbrance, but in the one that haunted him there is no reason – "and he left her lying there amongst the Roses" – presumably the other verses dropped off at some point. When I read this at a BFS convention I sang the verses – I was suffering from a very longstanding cough and my voice was probably not at its best. My small but startled audience did not recognise what is a rather familiar folksong from my rendition, and asked me if I had written it myself...

**The Godmother** — An item in a newspaper was the inspiration for this story. Just a small reference to a piece of local folklore about a man who was said to have had left instructions for his corpse to be disposed of in the way the Master of Satterthwait had done – but recent investigations had proved the room was empty. So much for "folk memory" – but perhaps it hadn't been empty, to start with, and the devil was not so easily tricked...

**The Lady Who Rode the Central Line** — I was travelling on the Underground one day, although I cannot guarantee it was the Central Line, and I saw someone who was the image of Lenin... The rest of the story came from that.

**Chosen Girl** — My version of two fairy stories – "Little Red Riding Hood" and "Goldilocks".

**Mr Manpferdit** — I found Mr Manpferdit in Lisa Picard's *Dr Johnson's London*. She quoted a genuine advertisement in the *Gentleman's Magazine*, April 1751, for a centaur (who turned out to be "an enterprising sailor"). I thought Dr Johnson should certainly meet him, and Boswell, who wasn't actually introduced to him until 1763 had to accompany him. So he did. Writers can do things like that.

~~~

I do often find the title of a story before I find the story. Some which have come to me but are still unwritten include: "The Roaring Kitten and the Tiny Messiah" (and no, I have no idea what that would be); "Lady Mary, When She Danced"; and "You Have Lain All Wrong, Lassie" (which will somehow involve a water-horse. Perhaps.

# ACKNOWLEDGEMENTS

"A Trick of the Dark" was originally published in *The Mammoth Book of Vampires*, 2004

"A Straightforward Procedure" was originally published in *Dark Bits*, 2013

"A Visit to Blastings Manor" was originally published in *All Hallows 1*, 1989 (winner of the ghost story competition in the Walthamstow *Yellow Advertiser*, 1985)

"Barefoot Withouten Shoon" was originally published in *Midwinter's Entertainment*, 2016

"Beautiful Boy" was originally published in *Full Fathom Forty*, 2011

"Casualties of the System" (with Tony Rath) was originally published in *The 8th Black Book of Horror*, 2011

"Christmas With the Family" was originally published as "Family Christmas" in *Silent Companion*, 2015

"Chosen Girl" was originally published in *Visionary Tongue*, 1998

"End of Season" was originally published in *The Magazine of Fantasy & Science Fiction*, 1984

"Extended Family" was originally published in *Exotic Gothic 3: Strange Visitations*, 2009

"Fifth Sense" was originally published in *The 17th Fontana Book of Great Horror Stories*, 1984

"Ilona" was originally published in *Supernatural Tales 23*, 2013

"It's White and It Follows Me" was originally published in *Strange Tales III*, 2009

"Mr Manpferdit" was originally published in *Strange Tales*, 2003

"Night Out" was originally published in *Woman's Realm*, 1985

"Scruffy the Vampire Slayer" was originally published in *His Red-Eyes Again*, 2013

"Talking to Strangers in Finsbury Park" was originally published in *Dark Horizons 43*, 2002.

"Tea Dance" was originally published in *The Silent Companion 2*, 2007

"The Banks of the Roses" was originally published in *The Ghastling 7*, 2019

"The Chest" was originally published in *Hearts and Other Dead Things*, 2016

"The Co-Walker" was originally published in *Hideous Dreams*, 2001

"The Fetch" was originally published in *The 19th Fontana Book of Great Ghost Stories*, 1983

"The Godmother" was originally published in *Ghosts & Scholars*, 1986

"The Lady Who Rode the Central Line" was originally published in *Amazing Science Fiction*, 1985

"The Man Who Loved His Luscious Ladies" was originally published in *Cellar Door: Words of Beauty, Tales of Terror*, 2013

The following stories are original to this collection. All © Tina Rath 2020

"Diversion"
"The Bus"
"This is How It Happened"
"Sitting Tenant"